THE VEGAN COOKBOOK

THE
VEGAN
COOKBOOK

Over 200 recipes
all completely free from animal produce

Alan Wakeman
and
Gordon Baskerville

faber and faber
LONDON · BOSTON

First published in 1986 by
Faber and Faber Limited
3 Queen Square London WC1N 3AU
Reprinted 1988, 1990 and 1991

Printed in Great Britain by
Clays Ltd, St Ives plc

A CIP record for this book
is available from the British Library

ISBN 0–571–13820–9

For the many friends
who field-tested these recipes for us.
No more prohibitions on making changes,
no more tiresome questionnaires to fill out –
just good food to enjoy.

Contents

Introduction

These are gratifying times for vegans. Hardly a day goes by without the publication of yet another scientific report confirming what we have always known – that our diet is far healthier than that eaten by the majority of the population. In particular, the McGovern Report in the USA and the NACNE report in the UK both advocate a substantial *increase* in the amount of vegetables, whole grains, pulses and fresh fruit eaten, and a corresponding *reduction* in the consumption of animal produce. Indeed, some doctors now believe veganism to be the most effective treatment for a range of 'Western' diseases from asthma to obesity. (In a remarkable clinical trial in Sweden, reported in the *British Journal of Nutrition* (Vol 52, pages 11–20, 1984), twenty-nine patients suffering from chronic hypertension were put on a vegan diet for a year. All showed marked improvement, and some recovered completely. Most were able to stop taking the drugs they had expected to need for the rest of their lives.)

'But what on earth do vegans eat?' people ask. All the while veganism is defined in terms of what we do *not* eat, this is understandable; but when you stop to consider that over 6000 plants have been identified as edible, you realize that it is also simply idiotic. Furthermore, perfectly ordinary people unwittingly eat vegan meals every day of their lives – salads, bread and jam, fresh fruit, baked beans on toast and so on.

So our chief objective in writing this book was to provide a wide spectrum of recipes, from the everyday to the celebratory, for people who enjoy good food, have no desire to eat anything that isn't delicious as well as healthy and who have decided to become vegan – perhaps because of the very real health risks now known to be associated with the consumption of animal produce, perhaps for other reasons. (See Appendix 2, Seven Reasons to be Vegan, page 274.)

Becoming vegetarian is easy. You simply stop eating carrion. Becoming vegan is harder – because excluding dairy produce from the diet makes some conventional cooking techniques difficult or impossible. (In cookery, eggs and milk are chiefly used for their properties of thickening, setting and binding, not for their taste.) As a result, we've had to invent a lot of *new* techniques. It has been a fascinating and rewarding challenge and writing this book has been a most enjoyable experience. But we do hope that people will think of our techniques as a springboard for their own ideas and not as the basis of a new orthodoxy.

Important Notes

If you are new to veganism, please read the *Notes on Vegan Nutrition* on page 269 before converting to an exclusively vegan diet.

We've used a few unusual ingredients so if you come across any you're not familiar with, please refer to the *Glossary* on page 287 for more information.

Please note that the word 'margarine' in the recipes should be taken to mean *'vegan* margarine' throughout. For more information and notes on where to buy vegan margarine, see page 234.

The nutritional analysis values are based on *McCance and Widdowson's The Composition of Foods* by A. A. Paul and D. A. T. Southgate (4th revised edition), Her Majesty's Stationery Office, London, 1978 and on *Food Composition Table for Use in East Asia*, FAO, Rome/US Dept. of Health, Education & Welfare, Bethesda, Maryland, USA, 1972. But please note that the figures given should be treated as an *approximate* guide only. The exact nutritional content of foods varies widely with the season, the prevailing weather conditions, the soil, the fertilizers used and so on. Note also that the nutritional values given for salads include the full value of the dressings in the calculations; bearing in mind that some people leave most of the dressings on their plates while others mop up every last drop with bread, the critical factor is not how much of the dressing you put on the salad, but how much of it you put in your mouth!

The recipes shown on the cover photograph are (from left to right):

(Back row) *Cauliflower Catalan Style* (page 66), *A Simple Table Wine* (page 266), *Savoury Carrot Jelly* (page 39), *Creamed Spinach* (page 114).
(Third row) *Mushroom Pie* (page 88), *Spiced Biscuits* (page 214), *Fresh Fruit Tart* (page 156).
(Second row) *Tofu Stir-Fry* (page 63), *Caramel Cream Pudding* (page 153), *Savoury Tomato Jelly* (page 38).
(Front row) *Three Seed Bread* (page 210), *Wheatberry and Bean Salad* (page 133).

Soups

Soups

A good soup can be the basis of a simple, nourishing lunch, a light evening meal, a quick snack at any time, or it can be the starter for something big. But please don't be tempted to use *tinned* soup, even if you're short of time. The simple recipes from early in this section take hardly a moment or two longer than it takes to open a tin, pour the contents into a saucepan, heat them up and transfer the mixture to a bowl (time yourself if you don't believe us!) and a home-made soup is, of course, from a different dimension. Besides, tinned soups are full of chemicals – preservatives to increase their shelf-life, artificial flavourings and colouring agents and sugar, and are seldom vegan, even the vegetarian ones. (Close scrutiny of the list of ingredients usually reveals the presence of animal products of the factory farming industry.)

An electric blender makes a soup-maker's life easier and we have assumed that you have one. (If you haven't, you can still make most of the soups using a hand-mouli or by simple sieving – indeed, some dedicated cooks insist that the resultant purées are superior and claim not to mind the extra work and washing up.)

We've given you lots of recipes to start you off but why not try *inventing* your own? You can start by dicing any root vegetables you happen to have and sautéing them in oil or margarine with herbs and a bay leaf, or you can work from the basis of almost any leftovers, including the final stages of a stockpot.

To provide the basic liquid, or for thinning, use vegetable water or stock, liquidized tomatoes or tomato juice, soya milk, red or white wine, stout, beer, or grapefruit, apple or orange juice.

To thicken, use flour or arrowroot (dissolve it in a little cold water before adding it to the saucepan), rolled oats or oatmeal, pulses (lentils are particularly good because they cook so quickly), potatoes, agar flakes or carrageen.

To season or flavour, use herbs, spices, yeast extract, Vecon vegetable stock, miso, tomato paste, salt and pepper.

To make a soup more nourishing and attractive, add any of the following just before serving: fresh chopped herbs, *croûtons* (see below), spoonfuls of *Vegan Sour Cream* (page 240), *Vegan Yoghurt* (page 245) or try adding diced or blended tofu.

To make *croûtons*, dice a slice of wholewheat bread (or toast) and fry the pieces in oil with a clove of crushed garlic added to the pan. Drop them into the soup straight from the pan just before serving and they will make the most appetizing sizzling sound, look gorgeous and taste wonderful.

To turn a simple soup into a complete meal, serve it with slices of whole-wheat bread or toast spread with nut-butters, tahini, yeast extract, or one of the many spreads from the *Spreads* section or dips from the *Starters* section, or with *croûtons* as described above; follow it with a salad and round it off with fresh fruit and coffee and you have a nutritionally-sound, delicious and healthy meal. Add a bottle of wine and you have a spread that can be set without shame before your favourite friends, vegan, vegetarian or omnivore.

Although a hot soup is a perfect way to start a winter meal, don't forget about *cold* soups in summer. There's no more appetizing way to start a summer dinner-party than with a home-made, chilled soup. Again we have given a number of recipes to get you started.

TOMATO SOUP
allow 5–10 minutes to prepare

To Serve 3–4

Imperial (Metric)		American
1 lb (½ kg)	fresh or tinned tomatoes	1 lb
½ pint (¼ litre)	soya milk	1¼ cups
1 tsp	mixed spice	1 tsp
1 tsp	salt	1 tsp
1 tsp	freshly-ground black pepper	1 tsp

1 Skin the tomatoes (page 259).
2 Put all the ingredients in a blender and blend to a smooth frothy cream.
3 Transfer the blended mixture to a saucepan and warm through over a medium heat, stirring continuously. Serve very hot.

Each serving (of 4) provides: 38 kcal, 3 g protein, 1 g fat, 5 g carbohydrate, 2 g fibre.

If you use tinned tomatoes this recipe is so quick, cheap and delicious that you may well wonder why anyone would ever bother to buy tinned tomato soup with all its chemical additives but perfectionists, of course, will prefer to use fresh tomatoes and this takes a little bit longer.

For extra bezaz, add *croûtons* (page 15) or stir in a tablespoonful of *Vegan Sour Cream* (page 240) or *Vegan Yoghurt* (page 245) just before serving.

MUSHROOM SOUP
allow about ¼ hour to prepare

To Serve 4

Imperial (Metric)		American
½ lb (¼ kg)	mushrooms	½ lb
1½ pints (¾ litre)	soya milk	3½ cups
1	clove garlic	1
1 tsp	salt	1 tsp
1 tsp	freshly-ground black pepper	1 tsp

1 Wash and coarsely chop the mushrooms and put them in a large saucepan with the soya milk. Bring quickly to the boil, then reduce heat and leave to simmer, uncovered, for 10 minutes, stirring often.
2 Meanwhile, skin and crush the garlic, add it to the pan and stir well in.
3 Remove pan from heat, transfer the mixture to a blender, add the salt and pepper and blend to a smooth, frothy liquid. Return to pan, reheat gently and serve.

Each serving (of 4) provides: 102 kcal, 8 g protein, 3 g fat, 7 g carbohydrate, 3 g fibre.

We've put this recipe early in this section because it is so quick and simple to make – but this doesn't mean that it wouldn't do as the starter to a special-occasion dinner-party. Indeed, one of our circle of friends who sampled it during our field trials rated it 'Triple A', asked for second and third helpings and claimed that it was the best recipe we'd come up with. While we couldn't agree with that, it was a useful reminder that making things more complicated doesn't necessarily make them taste better.

Adding wholewheat *croûtons* (page 15) at the last moment before serving gives the soup extra dash and verve.

CAULIFLOWER SOUP
allow 20 minutes to prepare

To Serve 6

Imperial (Metric)		American
1	large cauliflower	1
1 tsp	salt	1 tsp
1½ pints (¾ litre)	soya milk	3½ cups
4 tbs (60 ml)	sunflower oil	4 tbs
1 tsp	ground nutmeg	1 tsp
	salt and pepper to taste	

1   Cut the cauliflower into the smallest possible florets and dice the stems and outer leaves. Plunge into fiercely-boiling salted water until tender (about 5 minutes). Remove from heat and drain.
2   Put the cooked cauliflower into a blender together with the soya milk, sunflower oil and nutmeg and blend to a creamy (though still granular) texture.
3   Transfer the mixture to a saucepan, add salt and pepper to taste, reheat gently and serve. (If it seems too thick, add more soya milk till you get the consistency you prefer.)

**Each serving (of 6) provides: 54 kcal, 5 g protein, 12 g fat,
4 g carbohydrate, 3 g fibre.**

Cauliflower has a subtle, delicate flavour which is easily smothered if you use too many herbs and spices but nutmeg complements it perfectly. Although we have put this recipe in the everyday section because it is so easy to make, it is a perfect way to start a dinner-party because you can prepare the soup hours in advance and simply reheat it just before your guests arrive, or you can leave making it till the last moment.

ONION SOUP
allow 40 minutes to prepare

To Serve 4–6

Imperial (Metric)		**American**
4½ tbs (65 ml)	olive oil	4½ tbs (65 ml)
1 lb (½ kg)	onions	2 large
1½ pints (¾ litre)	water	3½ cups
3 tbs (45 ml)	soya sauce	3 tbs
1 tsp	freshly-ground black pepper	1 tsp

1 While the oil is heating in a large saucepan, peel and slice the onions into thin rings.
2 Add them to the pan and cook gently, stirring occasionally, till they are completely soft (about 15–20 minutes).
3 Add the water, soya sauce and pepper and simmer for a further 10 minutes and serve.

Each serving (of 6) provides: 139 kcal, 1 g protein, 13 g fat, 6 g carbohydrate, 1 g fibre.

This simple clear soup is a perfect starter for a substantial meal. Try adding *croûtons* (page 15) to it just before serving. Delicious!

LENTIL AND TOMATO SOUP

allow 50 minutes to prepare

To Serve 4–6

Imperial (Metric)		American
1 oz (30 g)	margarine	2 tbs
1	clove garlic	1
1 lb (½ kg)	onions	2 large
2 lb (1 kg)	fresh or tinned tomatoes	2 lb
6 oz (180 g)	red lentils	1 cup
	salt and pepper to taste	

1 Put the margarine in a large saucepan over a low heat.
2 While it is melting, skin and crush the garlic, skin and chop the onions, add them to the pan and sauté till transparent.
3 Skin the tomatoes (page 259) and liquidize them.
4 Add them to the pan together with the lentils and stir continuously over a medium heat till the mixture boils, then reduce heat and simmer, partially covered, for 30–40 minutes. Stir from time to time and add a little water if necessary to prevent the mixture from becoming too thick. When the lentils are soft, add salt and pepper to taste and serve.

Each serving (of 6) provides: 180 kcal, 10 g protein, 4 g fat, 27 g carbohydrate, 7 g fibre.

This nourishing soup makes a good starter to any winter meal and as it will keep well for several days, provided it is brought to the boil at least once a day, it makes sense to prepare a lot and use it for a range of meals.

GREEN PEA SOUP
allow 1¼ hours to prepare

To Serve 6

Imperial (Metric)		American
½ lb (¼ kg)	green split peas	1 cup
2 oz (60 g)	margarine	4 tbs
2	cloves garlic	2
1 lb (½ kg)	leeks	1 lb
1½ pints (¾ litre)	water	3½ cups
1	lemon	1
3 tbs (45 ml)	soya sauce	3 tbs
1½ tbs (25 ml)	wine vinegar	1½ tbs
½ pint (¼ litre)	soya milk	1¼ cups

1   It's preferable to pre-soak the split peas (see page 261) but, if you haven't, put them in a saucepan, cover with boiling water and set aside.
2   Melt the margarine in a large saucepan over a low heat. Skin and crush the garlic and add it to the pan. Carefully wash, trim and chop the leeks, add to the pan and sauté till tender, increasing the heat as necessary (about 10–15 minutes).
3   Drain the split peas, stir them into the pan, add the water, bring to the boil then reduce heat and simmer, partially covered, till soft (about 40–50 minutes).
4   Meanwhile, squeeze the lemon, set the juice aside and get all the other ingredients ready.
5   As soon as the peas are soft, remove the pan from heat, add the lemon juice, soya sauce, vinegar and soya milk, then transfer to a blender and blend to a smooth, thickish liquid. (You'll probably have to do it in two stages.)
6   Return the blended soup to the saucepan, warm through and serve.

Each serving (of 6) provides: 260 kcal, 13 g protein, 9 g fat, 32 g carbohydrate, 8 g fibre.

This provides an almost perfect balance of essential nutrients so you can feel virtuous as you tuck in!

It's also excellent chilled – though you'll probably need to thin it down with a little extra cold soya milk just before serving.

CREAM OF PARSLEY SOUP
allow ½ hour to prepare

To Serve 4–6

Imperial (Metric)		American
2 oz (60 g)	margarine	4 tbs
1	medium onion	1
1	clove garlic	1
½ lb (¼ kg)	potatoes	½ lb
1½ pints (¾ litre)	water	3½ cups
½ lb (¼ kg)	tofu	1 cup
1	large bunch parsley	1
	salt and pepper to taste	

1 Put the margarine in a large saucepan over a low heat.
2 While it is melting, skin and chop the onion, add to the pan and leave to cook gently. Skin and crush the garlic, add it to the pan and sauté until the onion is transparent. Don't let the mixture brown.
3 Wash and dice the potatoes (peel them if you wish), add them to the pan and stir continuously for a few moments before adding *half* the water. Bring quickly to the boil then reduce heat, cover and leave to simmer.
4 Put the rest of the water into a blender and crumble in the tofu. Now coarsely chop the parsley, set a few sprigs aside to use as a garnish and add the rest to the blender with the salt and pepper. Blend to a smooth, pale green cream.
5 As soon as the potatoes are completely cooked and beginning to break down, remove pan from heat, combine the two mixtures and blend again thoroughly.
6 Return the blended soup to the saucepan and reheat gently for a few minutes. Check the seasoning and adjust if necessary, garnish with the sprigs of parsley and serve.

Each serving (of 6) provides: 145 kcal, 5 g protein, 10 g fat, 10 g carbohydrate, 4 g fibre.

Parsley is much too good to use only as a garnish for other things. This flavoursome soup is full of vitamins and nutrients as well as being a delight to the eye. The perfect way to start a special dinner.

APPLE AND PARSNIP SOUP
allow ½ hour to prepare

To Serve 6–8

Imperial (Metric)		American
2 oz (60 g)	margarine	4 tbs
1 lb (½ kg)	parsnips	1 lb
1½ tbs	mustard powder	1½ tbs
1 lb (½ kg)	cooking apples	2 large
2 pints (1 litre)	water	5 cups
1½ tbs (25 ml)	soya sauce	1½ tbs
1 tsp	caraway seeds	1 tsp
	salt and pepper to taste	

1 Put the margarine to melt in a large saucepan over a low heat.
2 Peel and chop the parsnips.
3 Stir the mustard powder into the melted margarine and when it has completely dissolved add the chopped parsnips and stir till they are all well coated. Cover and leave to cook gently.
4 Meanwhile, core and chop the apples (peel them if you wish) and add them to the saucepan together with the water. Bring quickly to the boil then reduce heat and simmer, partially covered, till the apples begin to break down (about 5–7 minutes).
5 Remove from heat and transfer the mixture to a blender. Add the soya sauce and blend to a smooth, rich, thick texture.
6 Put the mixture back into the saucepan, add the caraway seeds and salt and pepper to taste, reheat gently and serve.

Each serving (of 8) provides: 125 kcal, 2 g protein, 7 g fat, 14 g carbohydrate, 4 g fibre.

Do try this satisfying, fruity, winter soup even if you don't usually like parsnips. You may be pleasantly surprised.

It keeps well, provided it is brought to the boil at least once a day.

For variety, try fennel seeds instead of caraway, or try adding ¼ tsp chilli powder.

CELERY AND COCONUT SOUP

allow ½ hour to prepare

To Serve 4–6

Imperial (Metric)		American
1	large head of celery	1
1½ pints (¾ litre)	water	3½ cups
1 tsp	salt	1 tsp
3 oz (90 g)	creamed coconut	⅓ cup
½ tsp	freshly-ground black pepper	½ tsp

1. Break the celery head up into individual stalks and wash thoroughly.
2. Chop the stalks into bite-sized lengths, including the green leaf tips, unless these are badly discoloured, and put them into a large saucepan together with the water and salt. Bring quickly to the boil then reduce heat and simmer, partially covered, till tender (about 15 minutes).
3. Meanwhile, dissolve the creamed coconut in a little hot water taken from the saucepan.
4. As soon as the celery is tender, take some more water from the saucepan and add it to the dissolved coconut until it is fairly thin, then pour the mixture back into the saucepan and stir well in. Add the pepper, check the seasoning and adjust if necessary.
5. The soup may be served immediately, just as it is, or you may wish to liquidize it first.

Each serving (of 6) provides: 100 kcal, 2 g protein, 9 g fat, 2 g carbohydrate, 6 g fibre.

The soup is attractive enough, with its pale green celery pieces floating in creamy white coconut milk, to serve without liquidizing; it's a matter of taste. But in the unlikely event that your guests leave you any, liquidize it, store it in the fridge and serve it chilled. It's so good like this that you may prefer it this way in the first place, especially in summer.

As an added feature, try sprinkling celery seeds over the soup just before you serve it.

CHICK PEA AND ROSEMARY SOUP

allow 2 hours to prepare
(if you have pre-soaked the chick peas)

To Serve 6

Imperial (Metric)		American
½ lb (¼ kg)	chick peas (dry weight)	1½ cups
½ lb (¼ kg)	onions	2 medium
3 tbs	rosemary (preferably fresh, chopped)	3 tbs
3 pints (1½ litres)	water	7½ cups
1½ tbs (25 ml)	soya sauce	1½ tbs
1½ tbs	miso	1½ tbs
1	lemon	1
	salt and pepper to taste	

1 Drain the chick peas of their soaking water and put them in a large saucepan.
2 Skin and chop the onions and add them to the saucepan together with the rosemary and water. Bring quickly to the boil, then reduce heat and simmer, partially covered, till they are quite tender (about 1–2 hours).
3 Transfer the cooked chick peas and any remaining water to a blender and add the soya sauce.
4 Finely grate the lemon rind and add it to the mixture, then squeeze the lemon and add the juice. Blend to a rich, smooth, thick consistency.
5 Return the blended soup to the saucepan, warm through, add salt and pepper to taste and serve.

Each serving (of 6) provides: 156 kcal, 10 g protein, 9 g fat, 6 g carbohydrate, 22 g fibre.

This is substantial enough to make a simple meal in itself, served with lots of wholewheat bread or a salad. Add a glass of wine each and round it off with fresh fruit and coffee and you have a satisfying and delicious everyday meal.

LENTIL AND APRICOT SOUP
allow ½ hour to prepare

To Serve 4–6

Imperial (Metric)		American
½ lb (¼ kg)	onion	2 medium
3 tbs (45 ml)	oil	3 tbs
½ lb (¼ kg)	red lentils	1¼ cups
½ lb (¼ kg)	cooking apple	1 large
¼ lb (125 g)	dried apricots	1 cup
2 pints (1 litre)	water	5 cups
¼ tsp	chilli powder	¼ tsp
	salt to taste	

1 Skin and chop the onion, put in a large saucepan and sauté in the oil until transparent.
2 Add the lentils and fry gently for a few minutes, turning continuously.
3 Peel, core and chop the apple and add it to the saucepan with the apricots and water and bring the mixture quickly to the boil, then reduce heat and simmer, partially covered, until the lentils soften (about 20 minutes). Stir the mixture from time to time to prevent sticking.
4 Remove from heat and add the chilli powder and salt to taste. Be careful not to overdo the chilli powder – a quarter of a teaspoonful should suffice!
5 Transfer the mixture to a blender, liquidize and serve.

Each serving (of 6) provides: 261 kcal, 11 g protein, 9 g fat, 37 g carbohydrate, 11 g fibre.

This fruity soup is guaranteed to cheer you up on a freezing cold and wet winter day but it is also good in summer with the chilli omitted.

WATERCRESS SOUP
allow ½ hour to prepare

To Serve 6–8

Imperial (Metric)		American
2 oz (60 g)	margarine	4 tbs
1	medium onion	1
½ lb (¼ kg)	potatoes	½ lb
2 pints (1 litre)	water	5 cups
2 bunches	watercress	2 bunches
1	lemon	1
2 tsp	soya sauce	2 tsp
½ pint (¼ litre)	soya milk	1¼ cups
	salt and pepper to taste	

1 Put the margarine in a large saucepan over a low heat.
2 While it is melting, skin and chop the onion, add to the pan and sauté until transparent. Don't let it brown.
3 Wash and dice the potatoes (and peel them if you wish), add to the pan and stir continuously for 2–3 minutes.
4 Now add the water and bring quickly to the boil, then reduce heat and simmer, uncovered, for 5 minutes.
5 Finely chop the watercress and set about a quarter of it aside to use as a garnish. Add the rest of the chopped cress to the pan and simmer for a further 5 minutes.
6 Meanwhile, grate the lemon rind and stir the grated peel into the mixture.
7 Squeeze the lemon and add the juice to the mixture.
8 Remove pan from heat and stir in the soya sauce. Transfer the mixture to a blender and liquidize thoroughly.
9 Return the blended soup to the saucepan, stir in the soya milk and reheat gently for a few minutes.
10 Add salt and pepper to taste and serve garnished with the rest of the chopped cress.

Each serving (of 8) provides: 103 kcal, 3 g protein, 7 g fat, 9 g carbohydrate, 4 g fibre.

This delicate soup has a subtle flavour that is the perfect way to start a dinner-party, but don't try serving it after something with a strong taste. The recipe provides enough for 6 generous servings or 8 if it is to be followed by a substantial meal.

CARROT AND ORANGE SOUP
allow 40 minutes to prepare

To Serve 6–8

Imperial (Metric)		American
2 lb (1 kg)	carrots	2 lb
1 pint (½ litre)	orange juice	2½ cups
1 tsp	salt	1 tsp
1	large orange	1
1	lemon	1
5 tbs (75 ml)	oil	5 tbs
½ pint (¼ litre)	soya milk	1¼ cups
	pepper to taste	

1 Wash, top and tail the carrots (or peel, as necessary) and slice them very thinly. Put them into a large saucepan with the orange juice and salt, bring quickly to the boil, then reduce heat and simmer, covered, till very tender (about 15–20 minutes).
2 Meanwhile, coarsely grate the orange peel and set aside.
3 Squeeze the orange and the lemon and set the juice aside.
4 Remove the carrots from heat as soon as they are soft, add the oil, orange peel, juices and soya milk, transfer to a blender and blend to a smooth, creamy (though still granular) mixture. Transfer back to the saucepan and reheat gently. Add pepper to taste and serve.

Each serving (of 8) provides: 154 kcal, 2 g protein, 10 g fat, 15 g carbohydrate, 5 g fibre.

This soup has a gorgeous colour and is equally good hot or chilled.

Serve it hot as a starter to a winter meal, with curry and rice to follow, or chilled, in summer, followed by a cold flan and salad.

PEAR AND GINGER SOUP
allow 40 minutes to prepare

To Serve 6–8

Imperial (Metric)		American
2 oz (60 g)	margarine	4 tbs
1½ tbs	freshly grated ginger	1½ tbs
	(or ¾ tbs dried ground ginger)	
2 lb (1 kg)	pears	2 lb
1	lemon	1
1 pint (½ litre)	water	2½ cups
	salt and pepper to taste	

1 Put the margarine to melt in a large saucepan.
2 Grate the ginger into the melting margarine and leave to cook gently over a low heat.
3 Slice the pears in half and remove the pips and stalks then chop them up and add them to the saucepan, stirring each time you add more till they're all done.
4 Squeeze the lemon and add the juice to the pan.
5 Now add the water, bring quickly to the boil, reduce heat and simmer, covered, till the pears are cooked right through (about 20–30 minutes depending on how ripe they are).
6 Transfer the mixture to a blender and blend to a rich, smooth, creamy liquid.
7 Return the blended soup to the saucepan, add salt and pepper to taste, reheat gently and serve. (If the soup seems too thick, add a little water to get the consistency you prefer.)

Each serving (of 8) provides: 108 kcal, negligible protein, 6 g fat, 14 g carbohydrate, 3 g fibre.

Although we have given a quantity for dried ginger, the soup is only really worth making if you can get fresh.

It's also good chilled.

GAZPACHO
(Spanish Chilled Cucumber and Tomato Soup)
allow 2 hours to prepare
(including 1½ hours to chill)

To Serve 6

Imperial (Metric)		American
1 lb (½ kg)	fresh or tinned tomatoes	1 lb
1	large cucumber	1
1	medium green pepper	1
1	small onion	1
2	cloves garlic	2
5 tbs (75 ml)	olive oil	5 tbs
5 tbs (75 ml)	wine vinegar	5 tbs
1½ tbs (25 ml)	lemon juice	1½ tbs
1 tsp	dill	1 tsp
½ lb (¼ kg)	whole tomatoes	3 large
	salt and pepper to taste	

1 Put the skinned tomatoes (page 259) in a blender.
2 Wash the cucumber and pepper, cut off a quarter of each and set aside, and remove the seeds and pith from the pepper. Coarsely chop the remainder and add to the blender. (It isn't necessary to peel the cucumber.)
3 Skin and coarsely chop the onion, skin and crush the garlic and add to the blender.
4 Add the oil, vinegar, lemon juice and dill and blend to a thick, smooth liquid. Transfer to a tureen or suitable serving-bowl.
5 Chop the remaining cucumber, pepper and the whole tomatoes as finely as possible, stir them into the soup and season with salt and pepper (only if you think it needs them!). Chill for at least 1½ hours before serving.

Each serving (of 6) provides: 150 kcal, 2 g protein, 13 g fat, 7 g carbohydrate, 3 g fibre.

This is a wonderful soup to serve outdoors on a hot summer's day: add some ice cubes from time to time to keep it chilled and follow it up with a salad and *Savoury Summer Tart* (page 87) and you have the perfect alfresco meal.

BEETROOT SOUP
allow 1 hour to prepare

To Serve 4

Imperial (Metric)		American
1 lb (½ kg)	raw beetroot	1 lb
1 pint (½ litre)	water	2½ cups
½ pint (¼ litre)	orange juice	1¼ cups
½ tsp	salt	½ tsp
2 tsp	dill	2 tsp

1 Wash, peel and dice the beetroot and put them in a large saucepan with the water. Bring quickly to the boil, then reduce heat and simmer, partially covered, till soft (about 45 minutes).
2 When the beetroot are soft, put them in a blender with the cooking water and all the remaining ingredients and blend till smooth.
3 The soup can now either be returned to the saucepan and warmed through – if you wish to serve it hot – or chilled in the refrigerator till needed if you wish to serve it cold.

Each serving (of 4) provides: 76 kcal, 2 g protein, 0 g fat, 18 g carbohydrate, 4 g fibre.

Serve this spectacular, vivid soup as a starter and follow it up with *Cashew Loaf* (page 89), *Mushroom Pie* (page 88) or *Savoury Festive Loaf* (page 90).
  If you can only get pre-cooked beetroot, you can still make the soup, but in this case use orange juice for the full amount of the recipe liquid (1½ pints/¾ litre/3½ cups) and proceed directly from step 2.

VICHYSSOISE
(French Leek and Potato Soup)
allow ¾ hour to prepare

To Serve 6

Imperial (Metric)		American
2 oz (60 g)	margarine	4 tbs
1 lb (½ kg)	leeks	1 lb
½ lb (¼ kg)	potatoes	½ lb
¾ pint (400 ml)	water	2 cups
3 tbs (45 ml)	soya sauce	3 tbs
1 pint (½ litre)	soya milk	2½ cups
	salt and pepper to taste	

1 Melt the margarine in a large saucepan over a low heat. Meanwhile, trim, carefully wash and chop the leeks. Now sauté them in the saucepan till tender (about 15 minutes).
2 Wash and chop the potatoes (peel them if you wish) and add them to the pan with the water. Bring quickly to the boil, then reduce heat and simmer, partially covered, till the potatoes are soft (about another 15 minutes). Remove from heat.
3 Transfer the mixture to a blender, add the soya sauce and soya milk and blend to a smooth consistency.
4 The blended soup can now either be returned to the saucepan and warmed through if you wish to serve it hot, or chilled in the refrigerator till needed if you wish to serve it cold (the traditional French way). Season with salt and pepper to taste just before serving.

Each serving (of 6) provides: 184 kcal, 6 g protein, 10 g fat, 18 g carbohydrate, 5 g fibre.

This is good for a special occasion supper-party as it can be made well in advance, is equally good hot or cold and, although it's so easy to make, always seems to impress people.

Try serving it as a substantial starter, followed by *Bulgur Bake* (page 59) or *Ratatouille* (page 65), or use it as the centre-piece of a light lunch with lots of wholewheat bread and served with a light, dry wine.

WINE AND WALNUT SOUP
allow ½ hour to prepare

To Serve 4

Imperial (Metric)		American
6 oz (180 g)	walnuts	1½ cups
½ pint (¼ litre)	water	1¼ cups
2 oz (60 g)	margarine	4 tbs
2	cloves garlic	2
1½ tbs	wholewheat flour	1½ tbs
6 fl oz (175 ml)	sweet white wine	¾ cup
½ pint (¼ litre)	soya milk	1¼ cups
1½ tbs (25 ml)	soya sauce	1½ tbs
1½ tbs (25 ml)	lemon juice	1½ tbs
1 tsp	mixed spice	1 tsp

1 Bring a pan of water to the boil, plunge in the walnuts and boil for 2–3 minutes. Remove from heat and drain.
2 Put the blanched walnuts in a blender with ½ pint (¼ litre/1¼ cups) fresh cold water and blend to a thick, smooth consistency. Set aside.
3 Put the margarine to melt in a large saucepan. Skin and crush the garlic, add it to the pan and cook gently for a few minutes.
4 Stir in the flour and cook for a couple of minutes before adding the walnut purée. Mix thoroughly.
5 Now add the remaining ingredients a little at a time, stirring continuously till well heated.

Each serving (of 4) provides: 441 kcal, 8 g protein, 36 g fat, 12 g carbohydrate, 3 g fibre.

This spectacular and substantial soup is best followed by a light main course such as *Savoury Summer Tart* (page 87) or *Carrot Flan* (page 72).

Starters

Starters

The starter is the prologue to the meal, setting the scene, giving a sense of occasion. It should *look* good enough to arouse a general glow of pleasurable anticipation at the prospect of the meal ahead, *taste* good enough to stimulate the taste buds and so whet the appetite but be *small* enough not to fill you up before the play begins.

Dips are particularly good for breaking the ice at a meal where some of the guests don't know one another so we've put them in this section too, but we've also included a number of other recipes that have the right attributes for perfect starters: they can be prepared well in advance (leaving you free to concentrate your energies on the main course) and they are visually attractive enough to be conversation-pieces. But don't forget that *soups* also make excellent starters so if you're planning a meal it's always worth having a look in the soup section first.

Although many of our starter recipes take quite a lot of time and care to prepare remember that it is precisely this that signals to your guests that you hold them in esteem and that the meal is going to be a worthwhile and pleasurable experience. Everyone knows that sinking feeling in an unknown restaurant when you realize that the starters on the menu are all of the slice-of-melon, half-a-grapefruit variety. Don't make this mistake! To continue the theatrical analogy – if your starter is the curtain-raiser *grab your audience in the first act!*

SAVOURY TOMATO JELLY

allow 1½ hours to prepare
(including cooling and setting time)

To Serve 6

Imperial (Metric)		American
2	lemons	2
2 lb (1 kg)	fresh or tinned tomatoes	2 lb
3 tbs (45 ml)	soya sauce	3 tbs
1 tsp	freshly-ground black pepper	1 tsp
4 tbs	agar flakes	4 tbs
12	stoned black olives	12

1 Cut one of the lemons in half and set aside 6 very thin slices to use as a decoration.
2 Squeeze the lemons and put the juice in a blender. Add the skinned tomatoes (page 259), soya sauce and pepper and blend till smooth.
3 Transfer the blended mixture to a saucepan, bring quickly to the boil, then reduce heat, stir in the agar flakes and simmer, uncovered, for 5 minutes, stirring continuously.
4 Remove from heat and pour into individual serving-dishes.
5 Refrigerate when cool.
6 Decorate the individual jellies with the slices of lemon and the halved black olives. Serve chilled.

Each serving (of 6) provides: 42 kcal, 2 g protein, 1 g fat, 6 g carbohydrate, 4 g fibre.

If you really want to impress your friends, set the jelly in a ring mould and make a *Pepper Salad* (page 123) to put in the centre. If you have trouble getting the jelly out of the ring mould, proceed as follows: first tip and rotate the mould to loosen the jelly then place the serving-dish on top of the mould, invert the whole thing and, bringing it sharply downwards, stop suddenly. Be sure to position the mould carefully because once the jelly has dropped you won't be able to move it again.

SAVOURY CARROT JELLY

allow 1½ hours to prepare
(including cooling and setting time)

To Serve 4–6

Imperial (Metric)		American
1	lemon	1
3 tbs	agar flakes	3 tbs
1¼ pints (650 ml)	carrot juice	3 cups
1½ tbs (25 ml)	soya sauce	1½ tbs
	freshly-ground pepper to taste	

1 Cut thin slices of lemon (to use as a decoration), then squeeze the rest and set the juice and slices aside.
2 Put the agar flakes in a small saucepan together with about a quarter of the carrot juice and bring quickly to the boil, then reduce heat and simmer for 5 minutes, stirring continuously.
3 Remove from heat, stir in the rest of the carrot juice, the lemon juice, soya sauce and freshly-ground black pepper to taste, and pour into individual serving-dishes.
4 Refrigerate when cool.
5 Decorate the individual jellies with the slices of lemon or halved black olives. Serve chilled.

Each serving (of 6) provides: 29 kcal, 1 g protein, negligible fat, 7 g carbohydrate, 3 g fibre.

This delicious jelly also makes a good tart filling: simply make a pre-baked pastry shell (see page 207) and pour the jelly into it instead of into individual dishes. The result is good enough to serve as a main course.

For variety, try using a combination of carrot and mixed vegetable juices.

PEPPER JELLY
allow 1½ hours to prepare
(including cooling and setting time)

To Serve 4–6

Imperial (Metric)		American
1 lb (½ kg)	red, yellow or green peppers	2 large
1	lemon	1
3 tbs (45 ml)	soya sauce	3 tbs
½ tsp	freshly-ground black pepper	½ tsp
2 tbs	agar flakes	2 tbs
¼ pint (125 ml)	water	½ cup

1 Wash and chop the peppers, taking care to remove all the seeds, and put them in a blender.
2 Squeeze the lemon and add the juice to the blender.
3 Add the soya sauce and ground pepper and blend to a smooth (though granular) paste.
4 Put the agar flakes and water into a small saucepan, bring quickly to the boil, then reduce heat and simmer for 5 minutes. Remove from heat.
5 Add the blended peppers to the saucepan and mix thoroughly before pouring into individual serving-dishes. Refrigerate when cool.
6 Decorate the individual jellies with slices of lemon or halved black olives. Serve chilled.

Each serving (of 6) provides: 46 kcal, 2 g protein, 1 g fat, 8 g carbohydrate, 2 g fibre.

Note that if you *peel* the peppers (see page 260) you'll get a richer, deeper colour and a smoother texture but you'll lose some of the crispness and taste.

If you are cooking for a really special occasion, make this recipe three times over using a different coloured pepper each time and set each separately in a ring mould. You could substitute *Savoury Tomato Jelly* (page 38) for the red layer and pile *Asparagus Salad* (page 137) in the middle.

CURRIED LEMON DIP

allow 40 minutes to prepare
(including ½ hour to chill)

To Serve 6–8

Imperial (Metric)		American
½ lb (¼ kg)	tofu	1 cup
1	clove garlic	1
1	lemon	1
5 tbs (75 ml)	soya milk	5 tbs
1½ tbs (25 ml)	soya sauce	1½ tbs
2 tsp	*Garam Masala* (page 257)	2 tsp

1 Chop the tofu up and put it in a blender.
2 Skin and crush the garlic and add it to the tofu.
3 Squeeze the lemon and add the juice.
4 Now add the other ingredients and blend to a smooth cream.
5 Chill for at least ½ hour before serving.

Each serving (of 8) provides: 26 kcal, 3 g protein, 1 g fat, 1 g carbohydrate, negligible fibre.

Serve this simple, but delicious, dip as a starter with sticks of fennel, celery or raw carrot in summer, or with *Plain Oatcakes* (page 220) in winter.

SAVOURY PEANUT DIP
allow 40 minutes to prepare
(including ½ hour to chill)

To Serve 6–8

Imperial (Metric)		American
1 lb (½ kg)	tofu	2 cups
2	lemons	2
5 tbs (75 ml)	olive oil	5 tbs
5 tbs	peanut butter	5 tbs
5 tbs (75 ml)	soya milk	5 tbs
3 tbs (45 ml)	soya sauce	3 tbs
1 tsp	mustard powder	1 tsp
2 tsp	freshly-grated ginger (or 1½ tsp dried ginger)	2 tsp
1 tsp	freshly-ground black pepper	1 tsp
½ tsp	cayenne pepper	½ tsp

1 Dice the tofu and put it into a blender.
2 Squeeze the lemons and add the juice.
3 Now add all the other ingredients and blend to a smooth cream. (Add a little water if it seems too thick.)
4 Chill for at least ½ hour before serving.

Each serving (of 8) provides: 213 kcal, 9 g protein, 19 g fat, 3 g carbohydrate, 2 g fibre.

This can be served with sticks of celery, fennel or carrot as a starter to a summer meal, with *Plain Oatcakes* (page 220) for a winter meal, or any time as a snack. It is also good for buffet parties and as a sandwich filling.

GUACAMOLE
(Mexican Avocado Dip)
allow 20 minutes to prepare

To Serve 6–8

Imperial (Metric)		American
3	large ripe avocados	3
2	lemons	2
4	cloves garlic	4
1 tsp	salt	1 tsp
¼ tsp	chilli powder (more or less to taste)	¼ tsp
¼ tsp	paprika (optional)	¼ tsp

1 Scoop out the flesh of the avocados and put it in a blender.
2 Squeeze the lemons and add the juice.
3 Skin and crush the garlic and add it to the blender together with the salt and chilli powder and blend to a smooth cream.
4 Transfer the mixture to a suitable serving-bowl, sprinkle the top with paprika and serve.

Each serving (of 8) provides: 130 kcal, 3 g protein, 12 g fat, 2 g carbohydrate, 2 g fibre.

For variety, try stirring in very finely chopped raw vegetables such as celery, fennel, radishes, red or green peppers or tomatoes.

CARROT DIP
allow 50 minutes to prepare
(including ½ hour to chill)

To Serve 6

2 lb (1 kg)	carrots	2 lb
4	cloves garlic	4
¼ pint (125 ml)	sunflower oil	½ cup
3 tbs (45 ml)	olive oil	3 tbs
¼ pint (125 ml)	wine vinegar	½ cup
1½ tsp	salt	1½ tsp
2 tsp	freshly grated ginger (or 1 tsp dried ginger)	2 tsp
½ tsp	paprika	½ tsp
	pinch cayenne pepper	
2 tsp	cumin seeds	2 tsp
	chopped chives or parsley to garnish	

1 Peel and chop the carrots and plunge them in a large pan of fiercely boiling water. Reduce heat and continue cooking till tender (about 8–10 minutes).
2 Skin and crush the garlic and put it in a blender with all the other ingredients.
3 Drain the carrots, add them to the blender and reduce to a smooth cream.
4 Transfer to a suitable serving-dish and chill for at least ½ hour before serving, garnished with chopped chives or parsley.

Each serving (of 6) provides: 342 kcal, 1 g protein, 33 g fat, 10 g carbohydrate, 5 g fibre.

Serve this dip as a starter with thin slivers of raw carrot, fennel or celery or with *Plain Oatcakes* (page 220). It is also good for buffet parties and has such an attractive colour that if you set it out among other dishes, your guests will make a beeline for it.

HUMMUS
allow 1–2 hours to prepare
(if you have pre-soaked the chick-peas – see page 261)

To Serve 6

Imperial (Metric)		American
½ lb (¼ kg)	chick peas (dry weight)	1½ cups
2	lemons	2
2	cloves garlic (or more to taste)	2
5 tbs (75 ml)	olive oil	5 tbs
3 tbs	tahini	3 tbs
	salt to taste	
	parsley or paprika as garnish	

1 Rinse and drain the pre-soaked chick peas, return them to their saucepan, cover with clean water and bring quickly to the boil, then reduce heat and simmer, partially covered, till tender (about 1–2 hours).
2 Grate the lemons and put the grated peel in a blender, then squeeze the lemons and add the juice.
3 Skin and crush the garlic and add to the blender together with the olive oil and tahini.
4 As soon as the chick peas are tender enough, add them to the blender together with enough recipe water to blend all the ingredients to a smooth paste. Add salt to taste and blend again.
5 Decorate with a little chopped parsley or sprinkle with paprika. Refrigerate till needed.

Each serving (of 6) provides: 298 kcal, 10 g protein, 25 g fat, 4 g carbohydrate, 22 g fibre.

Hummus is an ideal starter to a meal. Serve it as they do in the Middle East on individual plates, decorated with black olives, or as a dip with fennel or celery. It will keep for several days in a fridge so if you have any left over you can use it as the basis for snacks for days after your dinner guests have departed.

FALAFELS

allow 1–2 hours to prepare
(if you have pre-soaked the chick peas – see page 261)

To Serve 4–6

Imperial (Metric)		American
½ lb (¼ kg)	chick peas (dry weight)	1½ cups
2	medium onions	2
2	cloves garlic	2
1	bunch parsley	1
1 tsp	ground coriander	1 tsp
1 tsp	ground cumin	1 tsp
½ tsp	turmeric	½ tsp
¼ tsp	chilli powder	¼ tsp
1 tsp	baking powder	1 tsp
3 tbs	wholewheat flour	3 tbs
4 tbs	wheatgerm	4 tbs
	oil for frying	

1 Put the soaked chick peas into a large saucepan with enough water to cover, bring quickly to the boil, reduce heat and simmer till tender (about 1–2 hours).

2 Meanwhile, prepare the other ingredients in a large mixing-bowl: skin and finely dice the onions, skin and crush the garlic, finely chop the parsley and add everything to the bowl together with all the remaining ingredients except the wheatgerm and the oil. Mix together thoroughly.

3 As soon as the chick peas are tender transfer them to a blender together with enough recipe water to blend to a thick, crunchy paste. Transfer the paste to the mixing-bowl and combine with the other ingredients. Set aside for an hour.

4 Put the wheatgerm in a shallow dish, drop spoonfuls of the falafel mixture into it and shape into small, coated balls – if you're going to deep-fry or bake them – or into shallow cakes if you're going to fry them in a pan.

5 The falafels can be deep-fried in vegetable oil till golden brown, baked in a moderate oven (20 minutes at 350°F/177°C/gas mark 4) or fried in olive oil in a frying-pan till browned on both sides. (If you deep-fry them, lay them on kitchen paper to remove any surplus oil before serving.)

Each serving (of 6) provides: 175 kcal, 11 g protein, 9 g fat, 9 g carbohydrate, 23 g fibre.

Serve these nutty, savoury cakes in the authentic Middle Eastern manner, a few each on a dish of *Hummus* (page 45). They also make good snacks, served with a salad. They are good both hot and cold.

SAVOURY CRUNCHIES

allow 1 hour to prepare
(if you have the cooked soya beans)

To Make About Two Dozen

Imperial (Metric)		American
1 lb (½ kg)	soya beans (dry weight)	2½ cups
(cooked according to the method on page 261)		
3 tbs (45 ml)	soya sauce	3 tbs
1	large onion	1
3 tbs (45 ml)	oil	3 tbs
2	cloves garlic	2
1 tsp	rosemary	1 tsp
1 tsp	thyme	1 tsp
1 tsp	mixed herbs	1 tsp
3 oz (90 g)	wheatgerm	1 cup
2 oz (60 g)	wholewheat flour	½ cup
2 oz (60 g)	buckwheat flour	½ cup
1 tsp	baking powder	1 tsp

1 Put the cooked soya beans and any remaining water in a blender, add the soya sauce and reduce to a crunchy paste (add more water if necessary to assist with the blending). Transfer to a bowl and set aside.

2 Skin and finely chop the onion and sauté in a frying-pan with the oil until transparent.

3 Skin and crush the garlic, stir it in with the onion and continue heating for a few more minutes.

4 Put the herbs, flours, baking powder and half of the wheatgerm into a bowl and mix together thoroughly.

5 Now add the onion and garlic and the blended flours to the soya bean paste and mix thoroughly. Set aside for half an hour.

6 Put the rest of the wheatgerm on to a large plate and drop spoonfuls of the mixture on to it and, using your fingers, form into small, coated balls.

7 Arrange the balls on a greased baking-tray and bake in a hot oven (425°F/218°C/gas mark 7) for 20 minutes.

Each Savoury Crunchy provides: 138 kcal, 9 g protein, 6 g fat, 12 g carbohydrate, 1 g fibre.

These are splendid served straight from the oven, but they're also good cold. They can be served as a main dish – try *Creamed Mushrooms* (page 107) or *Grated Courgettes with Garlic* (page 98) or *Baked Parsnips* (page 110) as side dishes – or they make delicious snacks. Try putting two or three in pitta bread with some salad, hot or cold.

PEPPER MOUSSE
allow 1½ hours to prepare
(including cooling and setting time)

To Serve 6

Imperial (Metric)		American
1	lemon	1
1 lb (½ kg)	skinned or tinned red peppers	2 large
½ lb (¼ kg)	tofu	1 cup
¼ pint (125 ml)	soya milk	½ cup
1 tsp	salt	1 tsp
1 tsp	ground white pepper	1 tsp
2½ tbs	agar flakes	2½ tbs
¼ pint (125 ml)	water	½ cup

1 Squeeze the lemon and put the juice into a blender.
2 Skin the peppers (see page 260) and add them to the blender together with the tofu, soya milk, salt and pepper and blend to a smooth foamy cream.
3 Put the agar flakes and water into a large saucepan, bring quickly to the boil then reduce heat and simmer for 5 minutes. Remove from heat.
4 Now add the blended pepper foam to the saucepan and mix well in. Pour into individual moulds or serving-dishes. Refrigerate till set and chilled.
5 Decorate the individual mousses with thin slices of lemon, halved black olives or chopped parsley.

Each serving (of 6) provides: 73 kcal, 6 g protein, 3 g fat, 7 g carbohydrate, 2 g fibre.

If you can't be bothered with skinning the peppers yourself – and it is a bit of a performance – tinned ones are perfectly acceptable and in this case you can use the liquid from the tin to boil the agar flakes in.

For really special occasions, set the whole mixture in a ring mould and make a *Pepper Salad* (page 123) to pile in the centre.

CUCUMBER MOUSSE

allow 1½ hours to prepare
(including cooling and setting time)

To Serve 6–8

Imperial (Metric)		American
1	large cucumber	1
1 pint (½ litre)	soya milk	2½ cups
1½ tbs	freshly-grated ginger (or ¾ tbs ground ginger)	1½ tbs
½ tsp	salt	½ tsp
½ tsp	white pepper (preferably freshly ground)	½ tsp
4 tbs	agar flakes	4 tbs

1 Peel and chop the cucumber and put it in a blender.
2 Add ¾ of the milk, the grated ginger, salt and pepper and blend to a smooth foamy liquid.
3 Put the rest of the milk in a small saucepan, add the agar flakes, bring quickly to the boil then reduce heat and simmer for 5 minutes, stirring continuously.
4 Now thoroughly combine the two mixtures and pour into individual moulds or serving-dishes.
5 Refrigerate till set and chilled.
6 Decorate with thin slices of cucumber or lemon, halved black olives or fresh chopped herbs. Serve chilled.

Each serving (of 8) provides: 27 kcal, 2 g protein, 1 g fat, 2 g carbohydrate, 1 g fibre.

For really special occasions, set the whole mixture in a ring mould and make a *Cucumber, Yogurt & Ginger Salad* (page 139) to pile in the middle.

Although we generally prefer to leave all vegetables whole, note that for this recipe the cucumber must be peeled or you may have trouble getting your mousse to set.

CELERY AND COCONUT MOUSSE
allow 1½ hours to prepare
(including cooling and setting time)

To Serve 6–8

Imperial (Metric)		American
1	large head of celery	1
1½ pints (¾ litre)	water	3½ cups
3 oz (90 g)	creamed coconut	⅓ cup
2½ tbs	agar flakes	2½ tbs
	salt and freshly-ground white pepper to taste	

1 Wash and finely chop the celery (including the green leaf tips unless they are badly discoloured) and put it into a large saucepan with the water. Bring quickly to the boil, then reduce heat and simmer, partially covered, till tender right through (about 15 minutes).
2 Meanwhile, dissolve the creamed coconut in a little hot water taken from the saucepan until it is thin enough to mix in with the cooked celery. Before mixing it in, however, spoon out enough water from the saucepan to dissolve the agar. Transfer the celery and coconut to a blender and blend till smooth and creamy.
3 Put the agar flakes and the reserved water in a small saucepan, bring quickly to the boil then reduce heat and simmer for 5 minutes.
4 Pour the dissolved agar into the celery and coconut mixture and stir well in. Season with salt and pepper to taste and transfer to individual serving-dishes.
5 Refrigerate when cool.
6 Decorate the individual mousses with halved green olives or thin slices of lemon. Serve chilled.

Each serving (of 8) provides: 75 kcal, 1 g protein, 7 g fat, 2 g carbohydrate, 4 g fibre.

Serve this exotic mousse as a starter to *Savoury Avocado Tart* (page 84) or *Mushroom Pie* (page 88).

BEETROOT MOUSSE

allow 2 hours to prepare
(including 1 hour to set and chill)

To Serve 6

Imperial (Metric)		American
1 lb (½ kg)	raw or cooked beetroot	1 lb
1½ pints (¾ litre)	soya milk	3½ cups
2 tbs (30 ml)	soya sauce	2 tbs
2½ tbs	agar flakes	2½ tbs
¼ pint (125 ml)	water	½ cup

(Note: if the beetroot are already cooked, peel and chop them and proceed from step 2.)

1 Wash, peel and dice the beetroot and put them in a large saucepan with the soya milk. Bring quickly to the boil then reduce heat and simmer, partially covered, till tender (about 45 minutes).
2 Put the cooked beetroot and the soya milk and soya sauce in a blender and blend to a smooth, foamy cream.
3 Put the agar flakes and water in a small saucepan, bring quickly to the boil then reduce heat and simmer for 5 minutes, stirring continuously.
4 Combine the agar solution with the beetroot mixture, mix thoroughly, pour into individual serving-dishes and leave to set. Refrigerate till needed. Serve chilled.

**Each serving (of 6) provides: 96 kcal, 6 g protein, 2 g fat,
12 g carbohydrate, 4 g fibre.**

This looks spectacular – especially if you set it in a ring mould – tastes wonderful and has the added bonus of providing an almost perfect balance of essential nutrients. What more could you ask of any dish?

It makes the perfect starter for really special occasions. Individual mousses can be decorated with slices of lemon, stuffed green olives or juniper berries. A mousse set in a ring mould can have a *Pepper Salad* (page 123) piled in the middle.

BABA GANUSH
(Aubergine and Yoghurt Dip)
allow 2¼ hours to prepare
(including baking and chilling time)

To Serve 6

Imperial (Metric)		American
1	large aubergine	1
1 tsp	oil	1 tsp
¼ pint (125 ml)	*Vegan Yoghurt (page 244)*	½ cup
1	lemon	1
1	clove garlic	1
1 tsp	soya sauce	1 tsp
1 tsp	freshly-ground black pepper	1 tsp
2 tbs	chopped parsley	2 tbs

1 Thinly coat the whole aubergine with oil and bake for 1 hour in a moderate oven (350°F/177°C/gas mark 4). Don't remove the stalk, it will help you with the next stage.
2 Remove the baked aubergine from the oven and peel it under running cold water. The simplest way is to pick it up by the stalk using an oven glove, make a nick near the stalk using a sharp knife and simply tear off long strips of skin.
3 Chop the peeled aubergine and put it in a blender.
4 Squeeze the lemon and add the juice to the blender.
5 Skin and crush the garlic and add it to the blender.
6 Now add all the other ingredients and blend to a smooth, creamy consistency.
7 Check the seasoning and adjust if necessary, then transfer to a suitable serving-bowl, garnish with sprigs of parsley and chill for at least an hour before serving.

Each serving (of 6) provides: 31 kcal, 1 g protein, 1 g fat, 3 g carbohydrate, 4 g fibre.

This is another dish from the Middle East. Serve it as a starter to a meal with a bowl of black olives, or at buffet parties with sticks of fennel or celery. For variety, try substituting 4 tablespoonfuls of tahini for the yogurt.

LEMON GALANTINE

allow 1½ hours to prepare
(including 1 hour to cool and set)

To Serve 6–8

Imperial (Metric)		American
½ lb (¼ kg)	broccoli	½ lb
½ lb (¼ kg)	tomatoes	½ lb
1	small cucumber	1
1	small yellow pepper	1
12	stoned black olives	12
1½ pints (¾ litre)	water	3½ cups
2	lemons	2
1½ tbs (25 ml)	soya sauce	1½ tbs
½ tsp	salt	½ tsp
1 tsp	freshly-ground black pepper	1 tsp
4 tbs	agar flakes	4 tbs

1   Wash the broccoli, cut off the florets and thinly slice the stems. Cook, either by steaming, or plunging into boiling, unsalted water till tender (about 5 minutes). Remove from heat, rinse in cold water and drain in a colander.

2   Skin the tomatoes (page 259) and cut them into halves or quarters (ornamentally shaped if you wish). Set aside. Peel and slice the cucumber. Wash the pepper and cut into thin rings, removing pith and seeds as you go. Set aside.

3   Carefully arrange all the vegetables in decorative layers in a suitable mould (a large bread tin will do if you have nothing else). Put the peppers and olives in first, followed by the tomatoes and broccoli, and the cucumber slices last. Follow this order and the vegetables won't attempt to float and ruin your arrangement when you pour in the jelly.

4   Boil the water in a large saucepan.

5   Meanwhile, squeeze the lemons and add the juice to the saucepan. Add all the remaining ingredients and simmer for 5 minutes or until the agar has completely dissolved.

6   Carefully pour the jelly over the vegetables in the mould, taking care not to disturb them. Refrigerate when set.

7   Turn out on to a suitable serving-dish, garnish with more slices of cucumber, olives or parsley. Serve chilled.

Each serving (of 8) provides: 37 kcal, 2 g protein, 1 g fat, 6 g carbohydrate, 3 g fibre.

This looks stunning and tastes wonderful. Serve it either by slicing with a thin sharp knife or by scooping with a spoon.

Main Dishes

Main Dishes

It may be a hangover from pre-vegetarian consciousness that even vegans tend to expect a meal to consist of the vegetarian equivalent of 'meat and two veg', but meals don't have to be constructed in this way – in fact in most parts of the world they aren't: in most of the Middle East and all the Far East, China and Japan, meals usually consist of lots of tiny, appetizing dishes, each of which provides the individual guest with only two or three mouthfuls at the most – but what a delicious way to eat! In the West few of us are willing to spend the hours and hours needed to prepare such complicated spreads (we're all so busy rushing about) but they are a useful reminder to us to be flexible in our approach to planning what we eat and how we present and serve it.

Thus, most of our soups, starters, salads and even side dish recipes could be the main course of a nourishing and satisfying meal. Indeed, some of the meals which have been best received by our friends during the testing of the recipes in this book have consisted of nothing else!

Nevertheless, the dishes we have gathered together in this section have a number of features in common that make them particularly useful as a centre-piece to build a meal around: they all provide adequate servings for at least four people; they are all visually attractive; they are all substantial and nourishing enough to leave guests feeling satisfied; and the 'special' ones are spectacular enough to give a meal a sense of occasion.

A word or two about flans and tarts. When we were trying out our creations we were struck by the different reactions we observed, depending on what we *called* our recipes. Thus when we first tried out 'Savoury Avocado Tart', we called it 'Avocado Flan'. Unfortunately it seems that people have expectations dependent on names and therefore 'a flan should be like an *egg* quiche', i.e. with a filling that has set firm. So, alas, our guests at this first tasting turned up their noses because the filling remained soft and creamy. Well, we learned our lesson. The next time we tried it out we called it 'Savoury Avocado Tart' and our guests were ecstatic. 'Delicious!' they cried. 'Wonderful! How do you do it?' The sad fact is that a rose by any other name would not smell as sweet.

So, we have called pastry shells with fillings 'flans' if the filling sets firmly enough to cut out a wedge that will retain its shape even when served hot, straight from the oven, and 'tarts' when the filling remains soft and creamy but slightly runny.

Remember that if you're too pressed for time to make a flan shell, any of the flan (and tart!) fillings can be made up, put in a shallow ovenproof dish and baked without the pastry. Serve them with wholewheat bread to compensate for the lost 'protein complementarity'.

Finally, a word or two to vegans who live alone: don't assume that these main course dishes aren't for you. Remember that, unlike their meat-based equivalents, they all keep well and even those that don't reheat well are good cold. So if you don't have the time or inclination to spend more than one afternoon a week cooking, why not spend it making a savoury flan (or tart!) that you can conveniently serve cold or put in a packed lunch, or making a large casserole or stew that can form the basis of many meals during the week that follows?

BULGUR BAKE
allow 50 minutes to prepare

To Serve 4–6

Imperial (Metric)		American
6 oz (180 g)	bulgur	1 cup
scant pint (½ litre)	boiling water	2 cups
1 tsp	salt	1 tsp
½ lb (¼ kg)	courgettes	2 medium
½ lb (¼ kg)	carrots	½ lb
1	large cooking apple	1
6 oz (180 g)	tofu	¾ cup
½ pint (¼ litre)	water	1¼ cups
3 tbs (45 ml)	soya sauce	3 tbs
2 tsp	mustard powder	2 tsp
2 tsp	vinegar	2 tsp

1 Put the bulgur in a saucepan and pour the boiling water over it. Stir in the salt, cover and set aside for 10–15 minutes until all the water has been absorbed.
2 Wash, top and tail the courgettes, quarter them lengthwise and chop them into bite-sized chunks. Wash, top and tail the carrots (peel them if necessary). Wash and core the apple. Now coarsely grate the carrots and apple into a large mixing-bowl, add the chopped courgettes and the soaked bulgur and mix well. Transfer the mixture to an ovenproof dish.
3 Put all the remaining ingredients in a blender and blend till smooth. Pour over the bulgur mixture and leave to soak in for a few minutes.
4 Bake in the middle of a moderate oven (350°F/177°C/gas mark 4) for half an hour. Serve immediately.

Each serving (of 6) provides: 156 kcal, 7 g protein, 2 g fat, 30 g carbohydrate, 6 g fibre.

The vegetables lend a crunchy texture to this light dish. Try serving it with *Fried Cucumbers* (page 100) or *Creamed Mushrooms* (page 107) and follow it up with *Baked Bananas* (page 148) or *Vanilla Dessert* (page 147).

CASHEW AND MUSHROOM ROAST

allow 50 minutes to prepare

To Serve 4

Imperial (Metric)		American
½ lb (¼ kg)	bulgur	1 cup
1 pint (½ litre)	boiling water	2 cups
1 tsp	salt	1 tsp
1 oz (30 g)	margarine	2 tbs
2	medium onions	2
½ lb (¼ kg)	mushrooms	½ lb
¼ lb (125 g)	cashew nuts	1 cup
1½	lemons	1½
	salt to taste	
	parsley for decoration	

1 Put the bulgur in a saucepan and pour the boiling water over it. Stir in the salt, cover and set aside for 10–15 minutes until all the water has been absorbed.
2 Meanwhile, put the margarine in a large saucepan over a low heat.
3 While it is melting, skin and finely chop the onions, add them to the pan and sauté until transparent.
4 Finely chop the mushrooms, add them to the pan and continue to sauté for a few more minutes.
5 As soon as the bulgur is ready, stir it into the pan together with the cashew nuts and continue heating gently.
6 Grate the lemon rinds and stir the grated peel into the mixture.
7 Squeeze the lemons and add the juice to the mixture, stirring continuously.
8 Remove pan from heat, check the seasoning and add a little salt if necessary, transfer the mixture to a shallow baking dish and heat through in a moderate oven (350°F/177°C/gas mark 4) for 20 minutes.
9 Garnish with sprigs of parsley and serve.

Each serving (of 4) provides: 404 kcal, 13 g protein, 20 g fat, 47 g carbohydrate, 11 g fibre.

Serve with a plain salad to make a light meal or with another main dish, such as *Mexican Beans with Chilli* (page 79), *Broccoli and Lasagne* (page 67) or a savoury flan or tart, to make a more substantial meal.

COURGETTE AND TOMATO CRUMBLE

allow 1 hour to prepare

To Serve 4–6

Imperial (Metric)		American
½ lb (¼ kg)	courgettes	½ lb
½ lb (¼ kg)	mushrooms	½ lb
1	medium green pepper	1
1 lb (½ kg)	fresh or tinned tomatoes	1 lb
1 tsp	freshly-ground black pepper	1 tsp
1 tsp	salt	1 tsp
6 oz (180 g)	wholewheat flour	1½ cups
2 oz (60 g)	rolled oats	¾ cup
¼ lb (125 g)	margarine	½ cup

1 Wash, top and tail the courgettes, quarter them lengthwise and chop them into bite-sized chunks. Wash and slice the mushrooms. Wash the pepper, remove the seeds, coarsely chop and mix with the courgettes and mushrooms. Place the mixture in a shallow baking-dish.

2 Put the skinned (page 259) tomatoes, pepper and salt into a blender and blend till smooth. Pour over the vegetables in the baking-dish.

3 Now combine the flour and oats in a bowl and cut and rub in the margarine.

4 Sprinkle the crumble mixture to cover the whole surface of the vegetables in the baking-dish and bake in a moderate oven (350°F/177°C/gas mark 4) for 40 minutes. Serve hot, straight from the oven.

Each serving (of 6) provides: 318 kcal, 7 g protein, 18 g fat, 32 g carbohydrate, 7 g fibre.

This is light to the palate but substantial in nourishment. It could be served with a simple salad to make a light meal, or with another main dish, such as a savoury flan or tart. It's also good cold.

For variety try sprinkling sunflower or sesame seeds over the top before baking.

MIXED VEGETABLE STEW
allow 40 minutes to prepare

To Serve 4–6

Imperial (Metric)		American
3 tbs (45 ml)	oil	3 tbs
2 tsp	whole cumin seeds	2 tsp
½ lb (¼ kg)	onions	2 medium
2	cloves garlic	2
¼ lb (125 g)	mushrooms	¼ lb
1½ lb (¾ kg)	fresh or tinned tomatoes	1½ lb
½ lb (¼ kg)	red lentils	1¼ cups
3 tbs (45 ml)	soya sauce	3 tbs
½ lb (¼ kg)	courgettes	2 medium
	salt and pepper to taste	

1 Put the oil and cumin seeds in a large saucepan over a low heat.
2 Skin and chop the onions and add them to the pan.
3 Skin and crush the garlic, add it to the pan and sauté the onions and garlic till transparent.
4 Wash and chop the mushrooms and add them to the pan. Leave to cook gently for about 5 minutes, turning occasionally.
5 Add the skinned (page 259) tomatoes, lentils and soya sauce, bring quickly to the boil then reduce heat and leave to simmer, partially covered.
6 Wash, top and tail the courgettes and chop them up into bite-sized pieces. Add them to the pan and stir well in.
7 Leave to simmer, still partially covered, till the lentils are completely soft (about 15–20 minutes).
8 Check the seasoning, add salt (if you wish) and pepper to taste, and serve.

Each serving (of 6) provides: 245 kcal, 13 g protein, 9 g fat, 31 g carbohydrate, 9 g fibre.

Ring the changes on this stew by adding other vegetables, or use fewer tomatoes and add a glass of dry red wine, or stir in a tablespoonful of peanut butter just before you serve it.

It's filling and substantial enough to make a complete meal served with green vegetables or a salad, or serve it with one of the many side dish recipes.

TOFU STIR-FRY
allow 50 minutes to prepare

To Serve 4

Imperial (Metric)		American
½ lb (¼ kg)	tofu	1 cup
3 tbs (45 ml)	soya sauce	3 tbs
3 tbs (45 ml)	oil	3 tbs
1	medium onion	1
½ lb (¼ kg)	carrots	½ lb
6	sticks celery	6
1	medium green pepper	1
½ lb (¼ kg)	mushrooms	½ lb
½ lb (¼ kg)	bean sprouts	½ lb

1 Cut the tofu into ¾ in (2 cm) cubes, place in a small bowl and pour the soya sauce over. Set aside to marinate.
2 Put the oil in a wok (or large frying-pan) over a medium heat. Skin and chop the onion and add it to the wok. Wash, top and tail the carrots then cut them into long thin strips and add them to the pan. Stir thoroughly. Reduce heat to low, partially cover the vegetables (a saucepan lid will serve) and leave to fry gently for about 10 minutes, lifting the lid occasionally to stir.
3 Wash and chop the celery and stir it in with the other vegetables. Leave to cook for 5 minutes.
4 Wash the pepper, remove the seeds and pith and cut it lengthwise into thin strips. Stir into the wok and leave to cook for 10 minutes.
5 Wash and drain the mushrooms. (Leave them whole if they are small, or cut them in halves or quarters if they are large.) Stir them into the wok, add the tofu cubes and soya sauce and leave to cook for 5 minutes.
6 Wash and drain the bean sprouts, add them to the wok and stir-fry them for 2–3 minutes. Serve immediately.

Each serving (of 4) provides: 216 kcal, 10 g protein, 15 g fat, 11 g carbohydrate, 8 g fibre.

This can be served just as it is, with rice, to make a simple meal. Or it can be turned into a more elaborate (and authentically Chinese) dish by serving it with *Sweet & Sour Sauce* (page 171) or given an Indonesian flavour with *Spicy Peanut Sauce* (page 172). If you're going to add a sauce, be careful to drain away any excess liquid from the vegetables as you remove them from the wok.

WINTER VEGETABLE STOCKPOT
allow 1 hour to prepare

To Serve 6–8

Imperial (Metric)		American
¼ lb (125 g)	margarine	½ cup
4	cloves garlic	4
½ lb (¼ kg)	onions	2 medium
1	head of celery	1
3 lb (1½ kg)	mixed winter vegetables (see note)	3 lb
	dried herbs to taste (see note)	
3 tbs	miso (or 1½ tbs yeast extract)	3 tbs

(Note: suggested vegetables to use in the order in which they should be added to the pan, after step 1: *carrots, potatoes, turnips, swedes, parsnips, Jerusalem artichokes, leeks, peppers, cabbage, cauliflower, mushrooms, tomatoes, etc.* Suggested dried herbs to try (in no particular order): *sage, tarragon, basil, parsley, thyme, marjoram, oregano, dill, etc.;* or try a few spices: *coriander, cardamom, turmeric, paprika, cumin, etc.*)

1   Melt the margarine in a large saucepan. Skin and crush the garlic, skin and chop the onions, wash and chop the celery. Sauté the garlic, onions and celery for 5 minutes, then leave to cook gently, turning every now and again, while you prepare the other vegetables.
2   Clean, trim and chop the remaining vegetables into bite-sized pieces, adding them to the pan as you do them.
3   Stir in the herbs and spices you've chosen and continue to cook gently for a further 5 minutes.
4   Now add enough water (or vegetable stock, left-over soup, tomato juice or other vegetable juice, wine, stout, or soya milk) to cover, and mix well in. Bring quickly to the boil, then reduce heat, cover and simmer till the root vegetables are just tender. Stir in the miso and serve.

Each serving (of 8) provides: 223 kcal, 4 g protein, 13 g fat, 23 g carbohydrate, 9 g fibre.

The stockpot keeps well provided it is brought to the boil at least once a day. When it starts to get low, simply add extra vegetables. To make it thicker, add lentils or pre-cooked split peas, or dissolve 3 tbs wholewheat flour in a little of the stock and stir it back in. To make it thinner, add a little dry red wine, or liquidized tomatoes, or any vegetable stock you happen to have to hand, or water. Try also adding pre-cooked wholewheat berries, rice or any pulse.

In colloquial French, to shut up house is: *fermer la marmite*, which literally means 'shut down the stockpot' because a stockpot like this really can be kept going all winter.

RATATOUILLE
(Traditional Vegetable Stew from Provence)
allow 40 minutes to prepare

To Serve 4–6

Imperial (Metric)		American
¼ pint (125 ml)	olive oil	½ cup
1 lb (½ kg)	onions	2 large
2	cloves garlic	2
1 lb (½ kg)	green peppers	2 large
1 lb (½ kg)	red peppers	2 large
½ lb (¼ kg)	aubergine	1 medium
1 lb (½ kg)	courgettes	2 large
1 lb (½ kg)	fresh or tinned tomatoes	1 lb
	salt and pepper to taste	

1 Put just over half the oil in a large saucepan over a low heat.
2 Skin and chop the onions, add them to the pan and sauté for 5 minutes. Don't let them brown.
3 Skin and crush the garlic and add it to the pan.
4 Wash the green peppers, remove the seeds and pith, and cut them into strips. Add them to the pan and sauté for a few minutes, increasing the heat slightly if necessary.
5 Repeat with the red peppers.
6 Wash, top and tail (but don't peel) the aubergine and chop it into finger-thick chunks. Add to the pan together with the rest of the oil and continue to sauté for a further 5 minutes.
7 Wash, top and tail the courgettes, cut them into finger-thick slices and add to the pan. Stir them in and leave the mixture to cook for 5 more minutes, stirring occasionally.
8 Meanwhile, skin the tomatoes (page 259), coarsely chop them and add them to the pan. Stir in and bring the mixture to a simmer for at least another 5 minutes. Add salt and pepper to taste and serve.

Each serving (of 6) provides: 276 kcal, 4 g protein, 21 g fat, 18 g carbohydrate, 7 g fibre.

The secret of this traditional Provençal dish is to add the vegetables in the sequence given. The resulting stew is a wonderful *mélange* of subtle flavours and colours which is equally good hot or cold. It keeps well – in fact it seems to *improve* if kept for a day or two and then reheated.

This recipe is how one of us was taught to make it in a little country restaurant in Provence. Serve it with lots of wholewheat bread and red wine.

CAULIFLOWER CATALAN STYLE
allow 40 minutes to prepare

To Serve 4–6

Imperial (Metric)		American
1	large cauliflower	1
1 tsp	salt	1 tsp
¼ lb (125 g)	tofu	½ cup
3 tbs (45 ml)	sunflower oil	3 tbs
8 fl oz (200 ml)	soya milk	2 cups
2 tsp	vanilla essence	2 tsp
1 tsp	mustard powder	1 tsp
1 oz (30 g)	pine kernels	2 tbs

1 Cut the cauliflower into its main florets and finely dice the remaining stem. Plunge into fiercely-boiling salted water until just tender (about 5 minutes). Remove from heat and drain.
2 Coarsely dice the tofu and put it in a blender.
3 Add the oil, water, soya milk, vanilla essence and mustard powder and blend to a smooth cream.
4 Arrange the cauliflower in a shallow ovenproof dish and sprinkle the pine kernels over it. Pour the blended cream over and bake in a moderate oven (350°F/177°C/gas mark 4) for 20 minutes. Serve immediately.

Each serving (of 6) provides: 142 kcal, 5 g protein, 13 g fat, 3 g carbohydrate, 3 g fibre.

It's encouraging to think that this vegan version of a traditional dish from Catalonia is actually better for you than its cholesterol-laden original which is made, of course, with masses of fresh dairy cream. Its attraction is that each of its three main ingredients – cauliflower, cream sauce and pine kernels – has a subtle, delicate flavour that is all too easy to swamp, but put together they complement each other perfectly.

It is extremely rich and filling and is best served with a *Basic Green Salad* (page 121) or green vegetables.

BROCCOLI AND LASAGNE
allow 1 hour to prepare

To Serve 4–6

Imperial (Metric)		American
8 lengths	wholewheat lasagne	8 lengths
6 tbs (90 ml)	oil	6 tbs
½ lb (¼ kg)	onions	2 medium
1½ lb (¾ kg)	broccoli	1½ lb
1 lb (½ kg)	fresh or tinned tomatoes	1 lb
2 tsp	marjoram	2 tsp
	salt and pepper to taste	
½ lb (¼ kg)	tofu	1 cup
3 tbs (45 ml)	soya sauce	3 tbs
3 tbs	tomato paste	3 tbs
3 tbs (45 ml)	oil	45 ml
¼ pint (125 ml)	water	½ cup
1 tsp	freshly-ground pepper	1 tsp

1 Fill a large saucepan with water, add a little salt and a few drops of oil and bring to the boil. Add the lasagne. Allow to come back to the boil then reduce heat and simmer till tender (about 12 minutes). Stir often to prevent the pasta from sticking. Drain, rinse in cold water and set aside.

2 Put 6 tablespoonfuls of oil in another large saucepan over a low heat. Skin and chop the onions and sauté them in the oil till transparent.

3 Meanwhile, wash the broccoli, then cut off the florets and set aside. Finely chop the leaves and stalks and add them to the onions. Sauté for about 5 minutes before adding the skinned tomatoes (page 259), marjoram, salt and pepper to taste. Cook for another 5 minutes, stirring often and then add the broccoli florets and cook till they are tender.

4 Crumble the tofu into a blender, add all the remaining ingredients and blend to a smooth, creamy sauce.

5 Arrange the vegetables, lasagne and sauce in alternate layers in a lightly-greased, ovenproof dish (a rectangular one is easiest). Finish with a layer of lasagne and sauce.

6 Heat through in the middle of a moderate oven (350°F/177°C/gas mark 4) for about 20 minutes and serve immediately.

Each serving (of 6) provides: 408 kcal, 13 g protein, 27 g fat, 29 g carbohydrate, 9 g fibre.

This tasty dish is fairly substantial and filling, so it's best to serve it with something light – green vegetables or one of the salad recipes, for example.

SAVOURY RICE
allow 1 hour to prepare

To Serve 4–6

Imperial (Metric)		American
½ lb (¼ kg)	brown rice (dry weight)	1¼ cups
3 oz (90 g)	margarine	⅓ cup
2	cloves garlic	2
½ lb (¼ kg)	onions	2 medium
½ lb (¼ kg)	red pepper	1 large
½ lb (¼ kg)	courgettes	½ lb
¼ lb (125 g)	cashew nuts	1 cup
3 tbs (45 ml)	soya sauce	3 tbs
2 tsp	fresh chopped dill (or 1 tsp dried dill)	2 tsp
	freshly-ground black pepper to taste	

1 Put the rice on to cook (*Plain Rice*, page 94).
2 Meanwhile, melt the margarine in a large frying-pan (or wok), skin and crush the garlic, skin and finely chop the onions, put them in the pan and sauté till tender (about 10 minutes).
3 Cut the pepper in half lengthwise and remove any seeds before washing and finely chopping it. Add to the pan with the onions and stir well in. Leave to cook over a low heat, stirring occasionally.
4 Meanwhile, wash, top and tail the courgettes (and if they are big, quarter them lengthwise) and chop them into finger-thick chunks. Add to the pan, mix well in and sauté till just tender (about another 10 minutes).
5 Add the cashew nuts, soya sauce and dill and mix well in. As soon as the rice is ready, combine it with the cooked vegetables, add freshly-ground black pepper to taste and serve immediately.

Each serving (of 6) provides: 383 kcal, 7 g protein, 22 g fat, 41 g carbohydrate, 4 g fibre.

Almost any vegetables can be used (at steps 3 and 4) to ring the changes on this dish which is substantial enough to turn plain boiled rice into a main course. Serve it with salads or green vegetables or, if your guests are really hungry, with one of the many savoury tarts or flans.

SPINACH AND MUSHROOM TAGLIATELLE
allow 1¼ hours to prepare

To Serve 4–6

Imperial (Metric)		American
5 tbs (75 ml)	olive oil	5 tbs
2	cloves garlic	2
1 lb (½ kg)	fresh spinach	1 lb
	(or 10 oz [300g] packet of frozen spinach)	
½ lb (¼ kg)	tofu	1 cup
2 tbs	fresh chopped basil	2 tbs
	(or ½ tbs dried basil)	
½ lb (¼ kg)	onions	2 medium
½ lb (¼ kg)	mushrooms	½ lb
½ lb (¼ kg)	wholewheat tagliatelle	½ lb

1 Put 2 tbs oil in a large saucepan over a low heat.
2 Skin and crush the garlic and add it to the pan.
3 Wash and add the spinach. Increase the heat a little and cook till soft (only a few minutes if fresh; about 10 minutes if frozen).
4 Transfer the cooked spinach to a blender, crumble in the tofu, add the basil and blend to a smooth paste. (A little water may be needed to assist in the blending depending on how much water was produced during cooking.) Set aside.
5 Put the remaining oil in a frying-pan over a low heat.
6 Skin and finely chop the onions, add them to the pan and sauté till transparent. Don't let them brown.
7 Wash and finely chop the mushrooms, add them to the pan and sauté till tender (about 10–15 minutes).
8 Meanwhile, add a teaspoonful of salt and a few drops of oil to a large pan of water, bring quickly to the boil, add the tagliatelle, bring back to the boil then reduce heat and simmer till cooked (about 10 minutes). Remove from heat and drain.
9 Now add the spinach sauce and the cooked onions and mushrooms to the saucepan with the tagliatelle and mix well by turning with a large spoon. Season with salt and pepper to taste, transfer to a suitable ovenproof serving-dish and heat through in a moderate oven (350°F/177°C/gas mark 4) for about 20 minutes. Serve immediately.

Each serving (of 6) provides: 337 kcal, 15 g protein, 16 g fat, 35 g carbohydrate, 11 g fibre.

Serve with *Cabbage, Fruit and Nut Salad* (page 124) and *Spiced Potatoes* (page 96) for a substantial and nutritious meal.

TOMATO FLAN
allow 1 hour to prepare
(if you have the pre-baked flan shell)

To Serve 8

Imperial (Metric)		American
1	*Pre-Baked Flan Shell* (page 207)	1
3 tbs (45 ml)	oil	3 tbs
4 tbs	wholewheat flour	4 tbs
½ pint (¼ litre)	soya milk	1¼ cups
½ oz (15 g)	fresh yeast (or 1 tsp dried yeast)	½ tbs
5 tbs	tomato paste	5 tbs
1½ tbs (25 ml)	soya sauce	1½ tbs
2 tsp	lemon juice	2 tsp

1   Heat the oil and flour in a small saucepan for a few minutes while
    stirring continuously. Remove from heat.
2   Add the soya milk a little at a time while stirring continuously till you
    have a smooth, even, thin liquid. Check the temperature with a finger.
    If it is hand warm, crumble in the yeast and stir till thoroughly
    dissolved. If it is still too hot, cool by partially immersing the saucepan
    in cold water first. Cover and set aside for 20 minutes.
3   After 20 minutes the yeast will have worked on the mixture and it will
    be foaming and airy. Stir in the tomato paste, soya sauce and lemon
    juice. Transfer to the flan shell and bake in the middle of a moderate
    oven (350°F/177°C/gas mark 4) for 30 minutes. Serve immediately.

**Each serving (of 8) provides: 310 kcal, 7 g protein, 20 g fat,
27 g carbohydrate, 4 g fibre.**

Only cook this flan when you're sure that your guests are reliable time-
keepers because it really must be served and eaten straight from the oven
when it will have a light, airy texture. Serve it with green vegetables or try
Grated Courgettes with Garlic (page 98) or *Fried Cucumbers* (page 100) or one
of the salad recipes.

MUSHROOM FLAN

allow 1 hour to prepare
(if you have the pre-baked flan shell)

To Serve 8

Imperial (Metric)		American
1	*Pre-Baked Flan Shell* (page 207)	1
½ lb (¼ kg)	mushrooms	½ lb
6 tbs (90 ml)	oil	6 tbs
4 tbs	wholewheat flour	4 tbs
½ pint (¼ litre)	soya milk	1¼ cups
½ oz (15 g)	fresh yeast (or 1 tsp dried yeast)	½ tbs
2 tsp	lemon juice	2 tsp
½ tsp	mustard powder	½ tsp
	salt and pepper to taste	

1 Wash, drain and finely dice the mushrooms and sauté them in the oil in a small saucepan till just tender.
2 Stir in the flour and continue cooking gently for a few minutes. Remove from heat.
3 Now add the soya milk a little at a time while stirring continuously till you have a smooth, even, thin liquid. Check the temperature with a finger. If it is hand warm, crumble in the yeast and stir till thoroughly dissolved. If it is still too hot, cool by partially immersing the saucepan in cold water first. Cover and set aside for 20 minutes.
4 After 20 minutes the yeast will have worked on the mixture and it will be foaming and airy. Stir in the lemon juice, mustard powder, salt and pepper, transfer to the flan shell and bake in the middle of a moderate oven (350°F/177°C/gas mark 4) for 30 minutes. Serve immediately.

Each serving (of 8) provides: 361 kcal, 7 g protein, 27 g fat, 25 g carbohydrate, 5 g fibre.

This is at its best served hot, straight from the oven, when it has a light, airy texture. It will still taste good cold, the next day, but the filling will collapse and look less attractive.

CARROT FLAN
allow 1 hour to prepare
(if you have the pre-baked flan shell)

To Serve 8

Imperial (Metric)		American
1	*Pre-Baked Flan Shell* (page 207)	1
2 lb (1 kg)	carrots	2 lb
2	cloves garlic	2
8 fl oz (225 ml)	soya milk	1 cup
1 tbs (25 ml)	wine vinegar	1 tbs
3 tbs (45 ml)	soya sauce	3 tbs
1 tbs	sesame seeds	1 tbs

1   Bring a large saucepan of water to the boil. Meanwhile, scrub the carrots to remove any mud, then top and tail them and slice them thinly. (Peeling is only really necessary if they have injured or pitted skins.)
2   Plunge the sliced carrots into the fiercely-boiling water, bring back to the boil then reduce heat and simmer, uncovered, till tender (about 10–15 minutes). Remove from heat, drain, and transfer to a blender.
3   Skin and crush the garlic, add it to the blender together with the soya milk, vinegar and soya sauce and blend to a smooth consistency.
4   Transfer the filling to the pastry shell, smooth the top, sprinkle the sesame seeds over and bake in the middle of a moderate oven (350°F/177°C/gas mark 4) for 30 minutes.

Each serving (of 8) provides: 273 kcal, 7 g protein, 15 g fat, 30 g carbohydrate, 7 g fibre.

Serve this hot with *Creamed Mushrooms* (page 107), *Fried Courgettes* (page 95) or *Cauliflower Bhaji* (page 103), or cold with *Mixed Sprout Salad* (page 125), *Avocado and Apple Salad* (page 126) or any salad that doesn't include carrots.

TOMATO AND LENTIL FLAN

allow 1 hour to prepare
(if you have the pre-baked flan shell)

To Serve 8

Imperial (Metric)		American
1	*Pre-Baked Flan Shell* (page 207)	1
½ lb (¼ kg)	red lentils	1¼ cups
1 lb (½ kg)	fresh or tinned tomatoes	1 lb
	salt and pepper to taste	
1	medium onion	1
1½ tbs (25 ml)	lemon juice	1½ tbs
2 oz (60 g)	margarine	4 tbs
1 tsp	*Garam Masala* (page 257)	1 tsp
2 oz (60 g)	wholewheat flakes	1 cup

1   Wash the lentils and put them in a large saucepan.
2   Put the skinned tomatoes (page 259) in a blender with salt and pepper to taste and reduce to a thick cream.
3   Now add the blended tomatoes to the saucepan, stir well in and bring quickly to the boil, then reduce heat and simmer, partially covered, till they are completely cooked and beginning to break down (about 30–40 minutes). Stir from time to time and add a little water if necessary to prevent them from sticking.
4   Meanwhile, skin and finely chop the onion and assemble all the other ingredients.
5   When the lentils have absorbed all the liquid and formed a thickish paste, remove from heat, add the margarine, chopped onion, lemon juice, garam masala mixture and wholewheat flakes and mix thoroughly.
6   Transfer the mixture to the flan shell, smooth the top and bake in the middle of a moderate oven (350°F/177°C/gas mark 4) for 30 minutes.

Each serving (of 8) provides: 407 kcal, 13 g protein, 20 g fat, 45 g carbohydrate, 8 g fibre.

Serve this attractive, copper-coloured flan with green vegetables in winter or one of the salad recipes in summer. It keeps well but tends to dry out if reheated, so it's best to serve it hot, straight from the oven, when you first make it and cold thereafter.

OLIVE AND POTATO FLAN
allow 1 hour to prepare
(if you have the pre-baked flan shell)

To Serve 8

Imperial (Metric)		American
1	*Pre-Baked Flan Shell* (page 207)	1
1½ lb (¾ kg)	potatoes	1½ lb
2 oz (60 g)	margarine	4 tbs
½ pint (¼ litre)	soya milk	1¼ cups
½ lb (¼ kg)	black olives	2 cups
1½ tbs (25 ml)	white wine vinegar	1½ tbs
	salt and pepper to taste	

1   Scrub the potatoes and remove any blemishes but don't peel or scrape them, then cut them into thin slices and plunge them into fiercely-boiling water and cook till tender (about 8–12 minutes). Remove from heat and drain.

2   Meanwhile, stone the olives if necessary. This is easy if you have the right gadget – many garlic presses have one in their handles – or a messy job with a sharp knife if you haven't. They can also sometimes be bought already stoned.

3   Set a few of the stoned olives aside (to use as a decoration) and put the rest, together with all the remaining ingredients and the cooked potatoes, into a mixing-bowl and mash together until well mixed. The result will be a dark, rich, smooth cream, speckled with bits of olive.

4   Transfer the filling to the pastry shell, smooth the top and decorate with a few halved olives and bake in the middle of a moderate oven (350°F/177°C/gas mark 4) for 25 minutes.

Each serving (of 8) provides: 392 kcal, 7 g protein, 23 g fat, 41 g carbohydrate, 9 g fibre.

This can be served hot, straight from the oven, or chilled. It is rich, substantial and filling and so is best served with a light salad or green vegetables.

For variety, try adding a clove or two of crushed garlic at step 3.

FRESH PARSLEY AND TOMATO FLAN

allow 1 hour to prepare
(if you have the pre-baked flan shell)

To Serve 8

Imperial (Metric)		American
1	Pre-Baked Flan Shell (page 207)	1
1½ lb (¾ kg)	potatoes	1½ lb
1	large fresh bunch of parsley	1
2 oz (60 g)	margarine	4 tbs
¼ pint (125 ml)	soya milk	½ cup
1	lemon	1
2	cloves garlic	2
3 tbs	tomato paste	3 tbs
1½ tbs (25 ml)	soya sauce	1½ tbs
	freshly-ground black pepper to taste	

1 Scrub the potatoes and remove any blemishes but don't peel or scrape them, then slice them thinly and plunge them into boiling water and cook till tender (about 8–12 minutes).
2 Meanwhile, finely chop the parsley and set aside.
3 When the potatoes are done, remove from heat and drain in a colander.
4 Put the drained potatoes in a large mixing-bowl and add the margarine and soya milk.
5 Squeeze the lemon and add the juice to the bowl.
6 Skin and crush the garlic and add to the bowl.
7 Add all the remaining ingredients (set some of the chopped parsley aside for decoration) and mash with a fork till smooth and creamy.
8 Transfer the filling to the pastry shell, smooth the top and bake in the middle of a moderate oven (350°F/177°C/gas mark 4) for 25 minutes.
9 Decorate with the remaining chopped parsley and serve.

Each serving (of 8) provides: 373 kcal, 8 g protein, 20 g fat, 42 g carbohydrate, 10 g fibre.

This is delicious made with fresh herbs but not worth bothering with otherwise; but you don't have to use parsley – try mint, or any other fresh herb you like.

It's rich and substantial so serve it with green vegetables or a light salad. It's equally good cold and so is suitable for buffet parties.

MUNG BEAN AND COURGETTE CASSEROLE

allow 1 hour to prepare
(if you have pre-soaked the beans – see page 261)

To Serve 4–6

Imperial (Metric)		American
½ lb (¼ kg)	mung beans (dry weight)	1 cup
¼ pint (125 ml)	olive oil	½ cup
	seeds from 4 cardamon pods	
1 tsp	cumin seeds	1 tsp
½ tsp	chilli powder	½ tsp
1 lb (½ kg)	courgettes	2 large
1	lemon	1
½ tsp	oregano	½ tsp
	salt and pepper to taste	
2 tbs	fresh chopped parsley as a garnish	2 tbs
	(or 1 tbs dried parsley)	

1 Cook the soaked beans in a fresh change of water, partially covered, over a low heat till just tender (about 20–30 minutes).
2 Meanwhile, heat the oil in a frying-pan and add all the spices (except the salt, pepper and oregano) and leave to cook gently over a low heat.
3 Wash, top and tail the courgettes, quarter them lengthwise and then chop them up into finger-thick chunks. Now sauté them in the pan with the spices till they're just beginning to brown. Remove from heat, stir in the lemon juice and oregano and set aside.
4 Drain the beans and put them in a casserole dish (the type with a cover). Add the courgettes together with all the spices, oil and lemon juice, season with salt and pepper to taste and gently toss till well mixed. Cover and reheat in the middle of a moderate oven (350°F/177°C/gas mark 4) for 20 minutes.
5 Garnish with the chopped parsley and serve.

Each serving (of 6) provides: 336 kcal, 10 g protein, 25 g fat, 18 g carbohydrate, 11 g fibre.

This light dish is best served with something substantial such as *Savoury Rice* (page 68), *Mushroom Pie* (page 88) or baked potatoes; or it can be served as a side dish.

For variety, try adding a chopped aubergine at step 3 or stir in 1½ tbs of tomato paste at step 4.

FRUIT AND VEGETABLE CURRY

allow 1 hour to prepare

To Serve 4

Imperial (Metric)		American
5 tbs (75 ml)	sunflower oil	5 tbs
1½ tsp	whole cumin seeds	1½ tsp
1 tsp	whole coriander seeds	1 tsp
4 tsp	*Garam Masala* (page 288)	4 tsp
½ lb (¼ kg)	onion	1 large
½ lb (¼ kg)	carrots	½ lb
1 lb (½ kg)	fresh or tinned tomatoes	1 lb
¾ pint (400 ml)	water	2 cups
½ lb (¼ kg)	potatoes	½ lb
1½ tbs	freshly-grated ginger	1½ tbs
	(or ¾ tbs dried ground ginger)	
½ lb (¼ kg)	courgettes	½ lb
2 oz (60 g)	dried apricots	½ cup
1 oz (30 g)	raisins	1 tbs
3 oz (90 g)	creamed coconut	⅓ cup

1 Put the oil in a large saucepan over a low heat, add the cumin and coriander seeds and the garam masala and cook gently for a few minutes.

2 Skin and chop the onion, add it to the pan and cook till soft (about 5–10 minutes). Meanwhile, wash, top and tail and slice the carrots and skin the tomatoes (page 259) if necessary.

3 When the onion is soft, add the sliced carrots and skinned tomatoes together with the water. (If you're using tinned tomatoes, only add ½ pint [¼ litre/1¼ cups] water.) Bring to the boil then reduce heat and simmer, partially covered, for 5 minutes.

4 Wash and chop the potatoes (and peel them if you wish) and add to the pan together with the ginger. Bring back to the boil then reduce heat and simmer for a further 10 minutes.

5 Wash, top, tail and slice the courgettes into finger-thick pieces and add them to the pan together with the apricots and raisins. Add the creamed coconut and stir in till completely dissolved. Simmer for a final 10–15 minutes, stirring often and serve.

Each serving (of 4) provides: 461 kcal, 6 g protein, 33 g fat, 38 g carbohydrate, 18 g fibre.

Ring the changes on this fruity curry by adding or substituting almost any vegetable of your choice. Serve with *Plain Rice* (page 94), *Cauliflower Bhaji* (page 103) or *Cucumber, Yoghurt and Ginger Salad* (page 139).

WINTER PIE
allow 1½ hours to prepare

To Serve 6–8

Imperial (Metric)		American
1½ lb (¾ kg)	mixed carrots and parsnips	1½ lb
1 pint (½ litre)	water	2½ cups
¼ lb (125 g)	margarine	½ cup
4	cloves garlic	4
½ lb (¼ kg)	onions	2 medium
1	head of celery	1
1 tsp	juniper berries (or *garam masala* (page 257); or mustard powder)	1 tsp
	salt and pepper to taste	
3 tbs	wholewheat flour	3 tbs
2 lb (1 kg)	potatoes	2 lb
¼ pint (125 ml)	soya milk	½ cup
1 oz (30 g)	bread crumbs (or wheatgerm)	3tbs

1   Clean, trim and chop the carrots and parsnips into bite-sized pieces and put them in a large saucepan with (unsalted) water. Bring quickly to the boil, then reduce heat, cover and leave to simmer till just tender. Remove from heat, drain, and reserve the cooking water.

2   Melt half the margarine in another large saucepan. Skin and crush the garlic, skin and chop the onions, wash and chop the celery. Sauté the garlic, onions and celery till just tender, taking care not to let the vegetables brown.

3   Stir in the juniper berries, add a seasoning of salt and pepper and mix well over the heat before sprinkling on the flour. Stir well in and continue cooking gently for a few minutes before adding the cooking water from the carrots and parsnips a little at a time till you have a thinnish sauce. Allow to simmer gently to mature flavours and cook the flour before removing from heat and folding in the cooked carrots and parsnips.

4   Wash and chop the potatoes (peel them if you wish) and cook them separately till soft. Remove from heat, drain, add the rest of the margarine and the soya milk and mash till smooth and fluffy.

5   Pour the vegetable mixture into a suitable ovenproof dish, cover with the mashed potato, sprinkle the breadcrumbs on top, dot with knobs of margarine and bake in a moderate oven (350°F/177°C/gas mark 4) till golden brown on top (about 20–30 minutes).

Each serving (of 8) provides: 302 kcal, 7 g protein, 13 g fat, 42 g carbohydrate, 12 g fibre.

MEXICAN BEANS WITH CHILLI
allow 2 hours to prepare
(if you have pre-soaked the beans – see page 261)

To Serve 6

Imperial (Metric)		American
½ lb (¼ kg)	red kidney beans (dry weight)	1 cup
5 tbs (75 ml)	oil	5 tbs
½ lb (¼ kg)	onions	2 medium
1	medium green pepper	1
1	medium red pepper	1
6	stalks of celery	6
3 tbs	tomato paste	3 tbs
½ lb (¼ kg)	tinned or frozen sweetcorn	1 cup
3 tbs	sultanas	3 tbs
2 oz (60 g)	cashew pieces	½ cup
1 tsp	chilli powder (more or less to taste)	1 tsp
	salt and pepper to taste	

1 Drain the pre-soaked kidney beans and put them in a large saucepan with plenty of clean water over a high heat. Allow to boil fiercely for 10 minutes before reducing heat and simmering, partially covered, till cooked (about 1½ hours).

2 Meanwhile, put the oil in a large frying-pan (or wok) over a low heat. Peel and chop the onions, add them to the pan and sauté till soft.

3 Wash and chop the peppers and celery, add to the pan and continue to sauté till tender (about 10–15 minutes).

4 When the beans are cooked spoon out some of the water if necessary (or add some) so that there is just enough liquid to come level with the beans, then stir in the tomato paste, the cooked vegetables and the remaining ingredients. Mix well and heat for a further 10–15 minutes, stirring occasionally. Serve very hot.

Each serving (of 6) provides: 368 kcal, 14 g protein, 18 g fat, 40 g carbohydrate, 15 g fibre.

This colourful dish reheats well – it actually improves if it's allowed to stand for a while – so it can be made well in advance and then complemented by *Plain Rice* (page 94), green vegetables, or other side dishes prepared just before your guests arrive.

Serve it with dry red wine (see page 266) or try *Lassi* (page 256).

COURGETTE AND CAULIFLOWER CASSEROLE

allow 50 minutes to prepare

To Serve 6

Imperial (Metric)		American
1	large cauliflower	1
1 lb (½ kg)	courgettes	1 lb
2 oz (60 g)	margarine	4 tbs
½ lb (¼ kg)	mushrooms	½ lb
½ tsp	turmeric	½ tsp
1 tsp	whole cumin seeds	1 tsp
1½ tbs	wholewheat flour	1½ tbs
8 fl oz (¼ litre)	dry red wine	1 cup
8 fl oz (¼ litre)	soya milk	1 cup
	salt and pepper to taste	
1 oz (30 g)	wholewheat flakes	½ cup
	or	
1 oz (30 g)	wheatgerm	4 tbs

1 Cut the cauliflower into its main florets and plunge them into fiercely-boiling water for 5 minutes. Remove from heat, rinse in cold water and drain.

2 Wash, top and tail the courgettes and cut them into finger-thick slices. Fry them in a pan with the margarine till they're golden brown on both sides. Remove from pan and arrange in a large casserole dish.

3 Wash and drain the mushrooms and remove the stalks. Set the stalks aside and fry the caps in the same pan till golden brown on both sides. Remove from pan and arrange in the casserole on top of the courgettes.

4 Arrange the cauliflower florets on top of the courgettes and mushrooms with their stalks pointing downwards.

5 Finely chop the mushroom stalks and fry them for a few minutes in the same pan before adding the turmeric, cumin seeds and flour. Continue heating for a few more minutes, stirring continuously.

6 Add the red wine and soya milk and continue heating and stirring till the mixture thickens. (Add more soya milk if necessary to produce a thinnish sauce consistency.)

7 Remove sauce from heat, season with salt and pepper and pour over the cauliflower.

8 Sprinkle the wholewheat flakes on top and bake in the middle of a moderate oven (350°F/177°C/gas mark 4) for 20 minutes. Serve immediately.

Each serving (of 6) provides: 165 kcal, 6 g protein, 7 g fat, 14 g carbohydrate, 7 g fibre.

CARROT CURRY
allow 1 hour to prepare

To Serve 4–6

Imperial (Metric)		American
2 lb (1 kg)	carrots	2 lb
1 tsp	salt	1 tsp
½ pint (¼ litre)	orange juice	1¼ cups
2 oz (60 g)	margarine	4 tbs
	seeds from 5 cardamom pods	
1½ tsp	ground turmeric	1½ tsp
4	whole cloves	4
1½ tbs	whole cumin seeds	1½ tbs
1½ tsp	mustard seeds	1½ tsp
¼ tsp	cayenne pepper	¼ tsp
2 tbs	fine cornmeal	2 tbs
3 tbs	raisins or sultanas	3 tbs
1	ripe banana	1

1 Scrub the carrots to remove any mud then top and tail them and slice them thickly on the slant. (Peeling is only really necessary if they have badly-damaged or pitted skins.)
2 Put them in a large saucepan with the salt and orange juice and bring quickly to the boil, then reduce heat, cover and simmer for 5 minutes. Remove from heat and set aside.
3 Melt the margarine in a separate large saucepan and add all the spices. Heat them gently for a few minutes, stirring from time to time, then add the cornmeal and stir well in. Heat for a few more minutes.
4 Add the carrots and the orange juice, a little at a time, stirring continuously. When all the carrots and juice are in, add the dried fruit and the thinly-sliced banana.
5 Cover and simmer over the lowest possible heat, stirring occasionally to prevent sticking, for ½ hour before serving.

Each serving (of 6) provides: 162 kcal, 2 g protein, 8 g fat, 22 g carbohydrate, 6 g fibre.

We are indebted to Anna Thomas for this delicious curry. Unfortunately it is one of the very few vegan recipes in her otherwise excellent *The Vegetarian Epicure*.

Serve it with *Plain Rice* (page 94), *Cucumber, Yoghurt and Ginger Salad* (page 139) or with green vegetables. *Lassi* (page 256) makes a good accompanying drink.

BUTTER BEAN AND MUSHROOM CASSEROLE

allow 2–3 hours to prepare
(if you have pre-soaked the beans – see page 261)

To Serve 6

Imperial (Metric)		American
¾ lb (350 g)	butter beans (dry weight)	2 cups
½ lb (¼ kg)	mushrooms	½ lb
¼ lb (125 g)	margarine	½ cup
2 oz (60 g)	wholewheat flour	½ cup
8 fl oz (¼ litre)	soya milk	1 cup
8 fl oz (¼ litre)	dry white wine	1 cup
1	lemon	1
1 oz (30 g)	wheatgerm	3 tbs

1 Cook the soaked beans in a fresh change of water, partially covered, over a low heat till just tender (about 1–2 hours). Continue simmering gently while you prepare and cook the mushrooms.

2 Wash the mushrooms, separate the caps from their stalks and set the stalks aside. Now fry the caps, gills upwards, in half of the margarine over a high heat for a few minutes till they begin to brown. Remove from the pan and set aside.

3 Finely dice the mushroom stalks and sauté them in the same fat for a few minutes till tender. Reduce heat, sprinkle the flour into the pan and continue stirring for a few more minutes before adding the soya milk and wine. Continue heating gently and stirring till the mixture thickens. Remove from heat and set aside.

4 Grate the lemon rind and set the grated peel aside. Squeeze the lemon and set the juice aside.

5 As soon as they're done, remove the butter beans from heat, drain and put them into a suitable casserole dish. Now add the rest of the margarine and the lemon juice and stir (gently! – because the beans are easy to damage at this stage) until you're sure that every bean is coated.

6 Pour the sauce over, arrange the mushroom caps on top, sprinkle with wheatgerm and the grated lemon peel, dot with a few knobs of margarine, reheat for 20 minutes in a moderate oven (350°F/177°C/gas mark 4) and serve.

Each serving (of 6) provides: 420 kcal, 17 g protein, 20 g fat, 41 g carbohydrate, 16 g fibre.

This substantial casserole goes best with a simple *Basic Green Salad* (page 121) or try it with *Grated Courgettes with Garlic* (page 98).

BARCELONA BAKE
allow 1½ hours to prepare
(if you have pre-soaked the lentils – see page 261)

To Serve 4–6

Imperial (Metric)		American
½ lb (¼ kg)	green lentils (dry weight)	1¼ cups
1	large aubergine	1
¼ pint (125 ml)	olive oil	½ cup
8 fl oz (¼ litre)	dry red wine	1 cup
3	cloves garlic	3
1½ lb (¾ kg)	onions	3 large
5 tbs (75 ml)	sunflower oil	5 tbs
½ lb (¼ kg)	carrots	½ lb
1½ tbs	fennel seeds	1½ tbs
1½ tbs	pine kernels	1½ tbs
3 tbs (45 ml)	soya sauce	3 tbs
½ lb (¼ kg)	tomatoes	3 large
	salt and pepper to taste	
2 tbs	fresh chopped parsley as a garnish	2 tbs
	(or 1 tbs dried parsley)	

1 Cook the soaked lentils in a fresh change of water, partially covered, over a low heat till just tender (about ½–1 hour).
2 Meanwhile, cut the aubergine into finger-thick slices and fry them in the olive oil in a large saucepan till just brown on both sides. Add the wine and cook for 5 minutes. Remove from heat and set aside.
3 Skin and crush the garlic, skin and chop the onions and sauté together in the sunflower oil in a frying-pan over a low heat till the onions are just transparent.
4 Wash and peel the carrots if necessary and then grate them into the pan with the onions. Stir-fry together for 5 minutes, then stir in the fennel seeds, pine kernels and soya sauce. Remove from heat and set aside.
5 Drain the cooked lentils, add the carrot and onion mixture, season to taste and stir thoroughly before transferring the mixture to a suitable casserole dish. Arrange the aubergine slices on top and pour the remaining wine over them. Slice the tomatoes and arrange decoratively on top and bake in the middle of a moderate oven (350°F/177°C/gas mark 4) for 20 minutes.
6 Sprinkle the chopped parsley on top as a garnish and serve.

Each serving (of 6) provides: 577 kcal, 14 g protein, 40 g fat, 38 g carbohydrate, 12 g fibre.

This substantial dish is best served with a green salad or green vegetables.

SAVOURY AVOCADO TART

allow 40 minutes to prepare
(if you have the pre-baked flan shell)

To Serve 8

Imperial (Metric)		American
1	*Pre-Baked Flan Shell* (page 207)	1
½ lb (¼ kg)	tofu	1 cup
2	large ripe avocados	2
½ pint (¼ litre)	soya milk	1¼ cups
3 tbs (45 ml)	soya sauce	3 tbs
	juice of half a lemon	

1 Coarsely dice the tofu and put it in a blender.
2 Spoon out the flesh of the avocados and add it to the blender together with the soya milk and soya sauce.
3 Squeeze the half lemon and add the juice to the blender. Blend to a thick, creamy consistency.
4 Pour the blended mixture into the flan shell, smooth the top and bake in the middle of a moderate oven (350°F/177°C/gas mark 4) for 30 minutes.

Each serving (of 8) provides: 333 kcal, 9 g protein, 23 g fat, 23 g carbohydrate, 4 g fibre.

This is rich, substantial and filling and so is best served with a light salad or green vegetables. It is also excellent cold and so is suitable for buffet parties.

For variety, try adding a clove or two of crushed garlic or freshly-ground black pepper at step 2.

SAVOURY ONION TART

allow 50 minutes to prepare
(if you have the pre-baked flan shell)

To Serve 8

Imperial (Metric)		American
1	*Pre-Baked Flan Shell* (page 207)	1
1 oz (30 g)	margarine	2 tbs
½ lb (¼ kg)	onions	2 medium
2	cloves garlic	2
½ lb (¼ kg)	firm tofu	1 cup
8 fl oz (200 ml)	soya milk	1 cup
	salt and pepper to taste	
½ tsp	freshly-grated nutmeg	½ tsp

1 Put the margarine to melt in a frying-pan over a low heat.
2 Meanwhile, skin and finely dice the onions, add to the pan and sauté for a few minutes.
3 Skin and crush the garlic and stir it in with the onions.
4 Continue cooking till the onion is just transparent but not yet beginning to brown. Remove from heat and set aside.
5 Coarsely dice the tofu and put it in a blender.
6 Add the cooked onion and garlic to the blender together with the soya milk, salt and pepper to taste and blend to a smooth cream.
7 Pour the onion mixture into the flan shell, smooth the top, sprinkle with the ground nutmeg and bake in the middle of a moderate oven (350°F/177°C/gas mark 4) until the top begins to brown (about ½ hour).

Each serving (of 8) provides: 289 kcal, 8 g protein, 19 g fat, 23 g carbohydrate, 4 g fibre.

This is equally good hot, straight from the oven, or chilled. In summer, try serving it with *Sweet Rice Salad* (page 134), *Peach and Cauliflower Salad* (page 135) or *Potato Salad* (page 131). In winter try *Cauliflower Bhaji* (page 103), *Savoury Buckwheat* (page 106), *Whole Courgettes Italian Style* (page 102) or green vegetables.

LEEK, COURGETTE AND TOMATO TART

allow 50 minutes to prepare
(if you have the pre-baked flan shell)

To Serve 8

Imperial (Metric)		American
1	Pre-Baked Flan Shell (page 207)	1
5 tbs (75 ml)	oil	5 tbs
2	medium leeks	2
½ lb (¼ kg)	courgettes	3 small
½ lb (¼ kg)	tofu	1 cup
½ pint (¼ litre)	soya milk	1¼ cups
3 tbs	tomato paste	3 tbs
3 tbs (45 ml)	soya sauce	3 tbs
3 tbs (45 ml)	lemon juice	3 tbs
2 tsp	fresh chopped marjoram	2 tsp
	(or 1 tsp dried marjoram)	

1 Put the oil in a frying-pan over a low heat. Thoroughly wash and drain the leeks, then finely chop them and sauté in the oil for a few minutes.
2 Thinly slice the courgettes, add them to the pan and sauté till just browning. Remove pan from heat.
3 Coarsely dice the tofu, put it in a blender with all the remaining ingredients and blend to a smooth cream.
4 Transfer the leeks and courgettes to the flan shell, making sure that they're evenly distributed, pour the blended tofu mixture over and smooth the top.
5 Bake in the middle of a moderate oven (350°F/177°C/gas mark 4) till the top begins to brown (about 20–30 minutes). Sprinkle some more chopped marjoram on top and serve.

Each serving (of 8) provides: 355 kcal, 9 g protein, 24 g fat, 27 g carbohydrate, 6 g fibre.

Serve this stunning tart hot from the oven as the centre-piece to a dinner-party accompanied with one or two light side dishes such as *Cauliflower Italian Style* (page 99) or *Spiced Potatoes* (page 96) or a green salad. It is equally good cold and so is suitable for buffet parties.

SAVOURY SUMMER TART

allow 2 hours to prepare
(if you have the pre-baked flan shell
and including setting and chilling time)

To Serve 8–12

Imperial (Metric)		American
1	*Pre-Baked Flan Shell* (page 207)	1
1½ pints (¾ litre)	water	3½ cups
½ lb (¼ kg)	broccoli	½ lb
1	large tomato	1
1½ tbs	yeast extract	1½ tbs
4 tbs	agar flakes	4 tbs

1 Put the water on to boil in a medium saucepan.
2 Meanwhile, wash the broccoli and cut off the florets to about 1 in (2½ cm) long. Discard any leaves and dice the green parts of the stems.
3 Plunge the broccoli into the boiling water and simmer till just tender (about 3–5 minutes). Remove from heat, drain, taking care to preserve the cooking water, and set aside.
4 Thinly slice the tomato and arrange decoratively in the flan case, leaving space around the outside edge for the broccoli florets.
5 Arrange the florets decoratively around the edge of the flan case and the diced broccoli stems in the centre. Set aside.
6 Dissolve the yeast extract in the broccoli cooking water, add the agar flakes, bring back to the boil and simmer for 5 minutes, stirring continuously. Remove from heat and cool by placing the saucepan in cold water for a while.
7 As soon as the agar solution is cool (but before it begins to set!) carefully pour it over the vegetables in the flan case taking care not to disturb your decorative arrangement.
8 Chill in a refrigerator for at least 1 hour before serving.

Each serving (of 12) provides: 151 kcal, 4 g protein, 9 g fat, 15 g carbohydrate, 3 g fibre.

This looks so gorgeous that we've put it in the 'special occasions' section even though it isn't really difficult or complicated to make.

For variety, try cauliflower or asparagus or virtually any vegetable that is good raw or that can be easily blanched, or try adding a tablespoonful of lemon juice to the jelly.

MUSHROOM PIE
allow 1½ hours to prepare
(if you have the shortcrust pastry)

To Serve 8

Imperial (Metric)		American
1½ × qty	*Basic Shortcrust Pastry* (page 207)	1½ × qty
¼ lb (125 g)	margarine	½ cup
2	cloves garlic	2
1½ lb (¾ kg)	button mushrooms	1½ lb
½ lb (¼ kg)	tofu	1 cup
1	lemon	1
	salt and pepper to taste	

1 Melt the margarine in a large saucepan over a low heat.
2 Skin and crush the garlic, add it to the pan and cook gently for a minute.
3 Wash and drain the mushrooms, add them to the pan (whole) and sauté till tender (about 15–20 minutes). Remove from heat.
4 Squeeze the lemon and put the juice in a blender.
5 Strain the juice from the mushrooms into the blender, add the crumbled tofu, salt and pepper to taste and blend to a smooth cream.
6 Pour the sauce over the cooked mushrooms, mix together thoroughly and set aside.
7 Roll out ⅔ of the pastry and line a greased, floured pie or flan dish. Fill with the mushroom mixture.
8 Roll out the rest of the pastry (moisten the edge of the base first) and use to form the pie-crust. Use your forefingers and thumbs to pinch the edges together to seal the lid to the base and form decorative scallops. Decorate the centre with pastry trimmings and cut a few slits with a sharp knife to allow steam to escape.
9 Bake in the middle of a moderate oven (350°F/177°C/gas mark 4) for 40 minutes.

Each serving (of 8) provides: 362 kcal, 8 g protein, 28 g fat, 21 g carbohydrate, 6 g fibre.

This is rich and sumptuous and best served with green vegetables in winter or salads in summer. It doesn't reheat well but is excellent cold.

CASHEW LOAF
allow 3 hours to prepare

To Serve 6–8

Imperial (Metric)		American
6 tbs (90 ml)	oil	6 tbs
3	cloves garlic	3
½ lb (¼ kg)	onions	2 medium
½ lb (¼ kg)	mushrooms	½ lb
6 oz (180 g)	wholewheat flour	1½ cups
¼ lb (125 g)	rolled oats	1¼ cups
3 tbs	soya flour	3 tbs
5 tbs (75 ml)	soya sauce	5 tbs
½ pint (¼ litre)	warm water	1¼ cups
½ lb (¼ kg)	red pepper	1 large
½ lb (¼ kg)	cashew nuts	2 cups
2 tbs	mixed herbs	2 tbs
	freshly-ground black pepper to taste	

1 Put the oil in a frying-pan over a low heat. Skin and crush the garlic and add it to the pan. Skin and finely chop the onions and sauté till transparent.
2 Wash, drain and finely chop the mushrooms, add to the pan and sauté till tender.
3 Meanwhile, put the flour, oats and soya flour in a large bowl and mix well.
4 Tip the contents of the frying-pan in with the flour, add the soya sauce and water and mix thoroughly.
5 Wash the pepper, remove the seeds, finely chop it and add to the bowl. Add the cashew nuts, mixed herbs and pepper to taste and mix all the ingredients thoroughly.
6 Transfer the mixture to a greased, floured 2 lb (1 kg) bread tin and bake in a warm oven (325°F/163°C/gas mark 3) for 1 hour, then turn it on its side still in its tin (this will prevent a hole forming) and bake for a further 1½ hours at the same temperature.
7 Allow to cool on a rack before attempting to remove from the tin.

Each serving (of 8) provides: 433 kcal, 12 g protein, 29 g fat, 36 g carbohydrate, 8 g fibre.

This protein-rich loaf may be served cold – slice it up and arrange it on a plate decorated with parsley – or hot – warm it through again by putting it in a moderate oven for 20 minutes. It's also good sliced and fried.

FESTIVE SAVOURY LOAF
allow 2½ hours to prepare

To Serve 8–12

Imperial (Metric)		American
¼ lb (125 g)	wholegrain rice	½ cup
1½ × qty	*Basic Shortcrust Pastry* (page 207)	1½ × qty
5 tbs (75 ml)	olive oil	5 tbs
1 lb (½ kg)	onions	2 large
½ lb (¼ kg)	carrots	½ lb
1 lb (½ kg)	broken mixed nuts	4 cups
6 tbs (90 ml)	water	6 tbs
5 tbs	tomato paste	5 tbs
2 tsp	yeast extract	2 tsp
2 tsp	oregano	2 tsp
	pepper to taste	

1 Put the rice on to cook (see page 94).
2 Put the oil in a large saucepan over a low heat. Skin and finely chop the onions, add them to the pan and sauté till transparent. Set aside.
3 Clean and finely grate the carrots, add them to the pan with the onions and mix thoroughly.
4 Grind the nuts into small pieces. (Fold them up in a clean tea-cloth and crush them with a rolling-pin. You can try using a blender but there is a danger that it will reduce them to a powder.) Add them to the pan with the onions and carrots and mix well.
5 Put the water into a small saucepan over a low heat, add the tomato paste and yeast extract and stir till completely dissolved.
6 When the rice is well cooked add it to the pan with the onion, carrot and nut mixture, pour the dissolved yeast and tomato paste over, add the oregano and pepper and mix thoroughly.
7 Roll out ¾ of the pastry and line a 2lb (1 kg) bread tin, taking care to seal it well at the corners. Fill to the brim with the mixture and smooth the top. Roll out the remaining ¼ of the pastry and make a lid, taking care to seal it all round. Turn it out on to an ovenproof dish, decorate with pastry trimmings and bake in the middle of a moderate oven (350°F/177°C/gas mark 4) till golden brown on top (about 40 minutes).

Each serving (of 12) provides: 491 kcal, 9 g protein, 36 g fat, 35 g carbohydrate, 7 g fibre.

This stunning loaf can be served hot or cold and makes a perfect centre-piece for festive occasions such as Christmas or Easter.

Side Dishes

*Quicker
or
cheaper
or
simpler*
▼
▼
▼
▼
▼
▼
▼
▼
▼
▼
▼
▼
▼
▼
▼
▼
▼
▼
▼
*slower
or
dearer
or
more
elaborate*

Side Dishes

In France every dish, including the simplest plain boiled vegetable, is served as a course in its own right and although this tends to prolong meals (sometimes to two or three hour sagas) it does mean that every single item is eaten with equal appreciation of its special qualities. (When did you last give your full, concentrated attention to the colour, smell, texture and flavour of a perfectly-cooked Brussels sprout?) So, although most of us in this country prefer to serve the main course of a meal as a combination of a centre-piece dish with accompanying side dishes, remember that there are other ways of doing things.

Having decided that you do want to serve a side dish, how do you pick a suitable one? Well, the very best way to eat vegetables is *raw*, of course, because then you get the benefit of their full complement of vitamins and minerals. So, always begin by looking in the *Salads* section. If you do wish to have a cooked side dish, remember that many vitamins are destroyed by prolonged exposure to heat and many minerals dissolve away in water, so *steaming* is by far the best way of cooking them. If you haven't got a steamer or prefer boiling, *blanch* them – that is, cook them in a large pan of fiercely-boiling water for the minimum possible period of time. The side dishes we've gathered together in this section are all based on this approach, but please treat our recipes as springboards for your own ideas. Remember that any steamed or blanched vegetable can be turned into a more elaborate side dish by the simple addition of a sauce from the *Sauces and Dressings* section.

Remember too, when choosing a side dish, to take advantage of vegetables that are in season because not only will they be cheaper but they are also likely to be fresher and of higher quality.

Finally, the perfect side dish complements its main dish both nutritionally and aesthetically. It goes without saying that a main dish that is substantial and protein-rich should be served with a light, delicate, side dish but don't forget to take account of colours and textures of your dishes as well. Usually it's good to *contrast* colours and textures and even temperatures (though one of our best-received meals was an essay in shades of green!). It's not a matter of rules, but of awareness of a whole meal as a pleasurable experience for your guests.

PLAIN RICE
allow 50 minutes to prepare

To Serve 4–6

Imperial (Metric)		American
½ lb (¼ kg)	wholegrain rice	1¼ cups
1¼ pints (600 ml)	water	3 cups
½ tsp	salt	½ tsp

1 Thoroughly wash and drain the rice and put it with the water and salt in a saucepan with a tight-fitting lid.

2 Bring quickly to the boil then reduce heat and simmer *without lifting the lid* for 45 minutes.

3 Remove from heat and leave to stand for another 5 minutes *still without lifting the lid*.

Each serving (of 6) provides: 148 kcal, 3 g protein, 1 g fat, 31 g carbohydrate, 1 g fibre.

This is the simplest way to get perfectly-cooked, tender, but not sticky, rice every time.

Note that the amount of water is 2½ times the amount of rice *by volume*.

Serve it just as it is with stews or curries as a basic simple side dish, or liven it up with one of the many sauces from the *Sauces and Dressings* section.

Why not make a lot while you're about it – it can easily be reheated by pouring fiercely-boiling water over it, leaving it to stand for a minute or two and then draining thoroughly, or it can be gently fried in oil for a few minutes, or it can be used cold in salads.

FRIED COURGETTES
allow 20 minutes to prepare

To Serve 4–6

Imperial (Metric)		American
2 lb (1 kg)	courgettes	2 lb
6 tbs (90 ml)	olive oil	6 tbs
1	lemon	1

1 Wash, top and tail the courgettes and cut them on the slant into finger-thick slices.
2 Put the oil in a frying-pan over a medium heat and fry the courgette slices till they go deep brown. Turn them and repeat.
3 Transfer them to a serving-dish. Squeeze the lemon, sprinkle the juice over and serve.

Each serving (of 6) provides: 178 kcal, 1 g protein, 17 g fat, 6 g carbohydrate, 3 g fibre.

Courgettes can only really be served in this simple way when they are at their best. Try serving them with something substantial, such as *Olive and Potato Flan* (page 74), *Butter Bean and Mushroom Casserole* (page 82) or *Mushroom Pie* (page 88).

Courgettes that are past their best are still perfectly good in *Ratatouille* (page 65), *Grated Courgettes with Garlic* (page 98) or *Courgette and Cauliflower Casserole* (page 80).

SPICED POTATOES
allow 15 minutes to prepare

To Serve 3–4

Imperial (Metric)		American
1 lb (½ kg)	potatoes (preferably new)	1 lb
½ tsp	salt	½ tsp
2 oz (60 g)	margarine	4 tbs
1 tsp	*Garam Masala* (page 257)	1 tsp

1 Wash the potatoes, quarter or halve them if necessary (and peel them if you wish) and drop them in a large saucepanful of salted boiling water. Bring back to the boil, reduce heat and simmer, uncovered, till tender (about 8–12 minutes, depending on their size). Remove from heat and drain in a colander.
2 Put the margarine in a small saucepan over a low heat and add the curry spices. Heat gently for a few minutes.
3 Add the cooked potatoes and toss them around till they're all well coated with spices and margarine. Transfer them to a (preferably hot) dish and serve immediately.

Each serving (of 4) provides: 218 kcal, 3 g protein, 12 g fat, 26 g carbohydrate, 6 g fibre.

This is a quick easy way to give boiled potatoes a bit of bezaz.

Leftovers can be stored in the fridge till needed and are delicious served cold combined with salads.

Nearly all the vitamins in potatoes are just beneath the skin and most are destroyed by cooking so it's best to cook them as little as possible and only to peel them if the skins are badly-marked or injured. The skins also contain most of the fibre.

BRUSSELS SPROUTS ITALIAN STYLE
allow 15 minutes to prepare

To Serve 4

Imperial (Metric)		American
1 lb (½ kg)	Brussels sprouts	1 lb
½ tsp	salt	½ tsp
2 oz (60 g)	margarine	4 tbs
2 tsp	lemon juice	2 tsp

1 Trim the base of each sprout and remove any injured or discoloured outer leaves. Cut a shallow cross into the base (to help the tougher core to cook as fast as the tender outer leaves).
2 Drop the sprouts in a large saucepan of fiercely-boiling salted water, bring back to the boil then reduce heat a little and cook till just tender (about 5–8 minutes). Remove from heat and drain.
3 Transfer the cooked sprouts to a hot serving-dish, add the margarine and lemon juice and toss gently till they are all coated. Serve immediately.

Each serving (of 4) provides: 142 kcal, 5 g protein, 12 g fat, 3 g carbohydrate, 5 g fibre.

Perfectly cooked Brussels sprouts are bright green in colour. If they've lost their colour it's because you've *over*cooked them! Remember, small, fresh sprouts are delicious raw.

GRATED COURGETTES WITH GARLIC
allow 15 minutes to prepare

To Serve 6

Imperial (Metric)		American
2 oz (60 g)	margarine	4 tbs
1	clove garlic	1
2 lb (1 kg)	courgettes	2 lb

1 Put the margarine to melt in a large (preferably thick) saucepan over a low heat.
2 Meanwhile, skin and crush the garlic and add it to the pan. Cover and leave over a low heat.
3 Wash, top and tail the courgettes and begin coarsely grating them. Add them to the pan as you do them and give the mixture a stir each time.
4 Continue heating gently for a further 5 minutes after you've added the last of the courgettes, and serve.

Each serving (of 6) provides: 99 kcal, 1 g protein, 8 g fat, 6 g carbohydrate, 3 g fibre.

We are indebted to Bob Ames for this recipe, which provides an elegant solution for the problem of imperfect courgettes – those with injured or bitter-tasting skins – but tastes even better with perfect ones.

CAULIFLOWER ITALIAN STYLE
allow 15 minutes to prepare

To Serve 4

Imperial (Metric)		American
1	medium to large cauliflower	1
2 oz (60 g)	margarine	4 tbs
1½ tbs (25 ml)	lemon juice	1½ tbs
2 tbs	fresh chopped parsley (or 1 tbs dried parsley)	2 tbs
	salt and pepper to taste	

1　Bring a large pan of slightly salted water to the boil. Meanwhile, cut the cauliflower into its main florets and finely chop the remaining stems and any suitable leaves. Now plunge them into the fiercely-boiling water, bring back to the boil then reduce heat and simmer, partially covered, till just tender (about 5–6 minutes). Alternatively, the cauliflower can be steamed till just tender.

2　Meanwhile, melt the margarine in a small saucepan over a low heat, add the lemon juice, parsley and salt and freshly-ground black pepper to taste.

3　As soon as the cauliflower is done, remove from heat, drain and arrange in a suitable hot serving-dish. Pour the lemon juice and parsley mixture over and serve immediately.

Each serving (of 4) provides: 127 kcal, 2 g protein, 12 g fat, 2 g carbohydrate, 3 g fibre.

This goes best with something substantial. Try *Spinach and Mushroom Tagliatelle* (page 69), *Mushroom Pie* (page 88) or *Carrot Curry* (page 81).

FRIED CUCUMBERS
allow 25 minutes to prepare

To Serve 4–6

Imperial (Metric)		American
2	large cucumbers	2
3 tbs (45 ml)	olive oil	3 tbs
1½ tbs (25 ml)	soya sauce	1½ tbs
2 tbs	fresh chopped dill (as a garnish)	2 tbs

1 Wash, top and tail the cucumbers and cut them on the slant into finger-thick slices.
2 Put the oil in a large frying-pan over a medium heat, add a batch of the cucumber slices and fry them, turning often, till they are just beginning to brown on both sides. Push the fried slices to the sides of the pan and add another batch. Continue in this way till all the cucumber is done.
3 Transfer the fried slices to a hot serving-dish, sprinkle on the soya sauce and toss around, then garnish with the chopped dill and serve.

Each serving (of 6) provides: 95 kcal, 1 g protein, 9 g fat, 4 g carbohydrate, 1 g fibre.

It's surprising how few people seem prepared to experiment with cooking cucumbers though they make such a welcome change from more conventional vegetable side dishes. This simple recipe goes well with hot savoury tarts and flans or with more substantial dishes such as *Butter Bean and Mushroom Casserole* (page 82), *Winter Pie* (page 78) or *Cashew Loaf* (page 89).

GRATED CARROTS WITH GARLIC

allow 20 minutes to prepare

To Serve 6

Imperial (Metric)		American
2 lb (1 kg)	carrots	2 lb
2 oz (60 g)	margarine	4 tbs
2	cloves garlic	2
	salt and pepper to taste	

1 Scrub, top and tail the carrots and set them aside. (Peeling is only really necessary if they have injured or pitted skins).
2 Melt the margarine in a large saucepan over a low heat.
3 Skin and crush the garlic and add it to the pan.
4 Begin coarsely grating the carrots and stirring them into the pan as you do so.
5 Continue heating gently for a further 10 minutes after you've added the last of the carrots, season with salt and pepper to taste and serve immediately.

Each serving (of 6) provides: 113 kcal, 1 g protein, 8 g fat, 9 g carbohydrate, 5 g fibre.

This is a simple way to turn carrots into a colourful side dish. But beware of overcooking them – remember how good they are raw.

For variety, try stirring in the juice of a lemon just before serving, or adding 1 tbs of soya sauce instead of salt and pepper after step 4.

WHOLE COURGETTES ITALIAN STYLE
allow about 15 minutes to prepare

To Serve 4

Imperial (Metric)		American
1½ oz (45 g)	margarine	3 tbs
3 tbs (45 ml)	water	3 tbs
	salt and pepper to taste	
2 lb (1 kg)	small perfect courgettes (see remarks below)	2 lb
2 tsp	lemon juice	2 tsp
2 tbs	fresh chopped parsley (as a garnish)	2 tbs

1   Melt the margarine in a large (preferably thick) saucepan and add the water, salt and pepper.
2   Wash, top and tail the courgettes and add them (whole!) to the pan. Cover and place over a low heat.
3   Remove cover and turn them occasionally till they are just beginning to soften. Start testing them with a skewer after about 5 minutes; as soon as it goes in easily, remove them from the heat. Above all don't overcook them – remember, courgettes are delicious *raw*. For this dish they are just as delicious and *just* not raw.
4   Add the lemon juice and toss them around a little to coat each courgette, then transfer them to a hot serving-dish and garnish with chopped parsley.

Each serving (of 4) provides: 75 kcal, 1 g protein, 6 g fat, 5 g carbohydrate, 2 g fibre.

Courgettes are baby marrows and you may be astonished at how good they can taste prepared in this simple way. But note that this recipe is only suitable for tiny, unblemished, really fresh courgettes. Older, larger or injured ones need different treatment. For them, try *Grated Courgettes with Garlic* (page 98), *Ratatouille* (page 65) or *Courgette and Cauliflower Casserole* (page 80).

CAULIFLOWER BHAJI
allow ½ hour to prepare

To Serve 4

Imperial (Metric)		American
1	medium to large cauliflower	1
5 tbs (75 ml)	oil	5 tbs
1 tsp	whole cumin seeds	1 tsp
1 tsp	black mustard seeds	1 tsp
½ tsp	ground turmeric	½ tsp
	salt to taste	

1 Bring a large pan of slightly-salted water to the boil. Meanwhile, cut the cauliflower up into bite-sized florets and finely chop the remaining stems and any suitable leaves. Now plunge them into the fiercely-boiling water, bring back to the boil then reduce heat and simmer, partially covered, till just tender (about 5–6 minutes). Remove from heat, drain and set aside. Alternatively, the cut cauliflower can be steamed till just tender.

2 Heat the oil in a large frying-pan, then add the seeds and turmeric and cook gently for 1–2 minutes to release the flavours. Add the cauliflower and toss gently around until it is all warmed through and well coated with the oil and spices. Serve immediately.

Each serving (of 4) provides: 117 kcal, 2 g protein, 11 g fat, 2 g carbohydrate, 3 g fibre.

This goes particularly well with curry dishes. For variety, try the same routine with potatoes, carrots or parsnips. Courgettes and mushrooms are also delicious served this way and don't need the pre-cooking of step 1.

LATKES
(Yiddish Potato Cakes)
allow ½ hour to prepare

To Serve 4

Imperial (Metric)		American
1 lb (½ kg)	potatoes	1 lb
½ lb (¼ kg)	onion	1 large
4½ tbs	wholewheat flour	4½ tbs
	salt and pepper to taste	
2–3 oz (60–90 g)	margarine for frying	4–6 tbs

1 Wash and scrub the potatoes (or peel them if you wish), then coarsely grate them and put them in a mixing-bowl.
2 Skin and coarsely grate the onions and add them to the bowl.
3 Add the flour and seasoning and mix thoroughly.
4 Melt the margarine in a large frying-pan then drop the mixture in the pan a tablespoonful at a time. (Use a spoon or spatula to flatten and shape the spoonfuls into round cake shapes.) Fry till golden brown, then turn over and repeat on the other side. Transfer the latkes to a (preferably hot) serving-dish as you do them. Serve hot.

Each serving (of 4) provides: 246 kcal, 5 g protein, 10 g fat, 36 g carbohydrate, 8 g fibre.

Latkes are traditionally served with *Savoury Apple Sauce* (page 168) and are at their best straight from the pan. But if you have too many guests to cope with this, or if you think you'll be too busy with the main dish, they can be prepared in advance and kept warm in the oven.

They're tasty enough just as they are but, for variety, experiment with adding herbs and spices (such as fresh chopped dill or paprika) at step 3.

They also make a good starter. But beware of serving too many of them or your guests will have no appetite left for the main course!

TOFU CHIPS WITH WALNUTS AND OLIVES

allow 20 minutes to prepare

To Serve 4

Imperial (Metric)		American
5 tbs (75 ml)	olive oil	5 tbs
1	clove garlic	1
1 lb (½ kg)	firm tofu	2 cups
3 tbs (45 ml)	soya sauce	3 tbs
2 oz (60 g)	walnuts	½ cup
1 dozen	stoned black olives	1 dozen

1 Put the oil in a large frying-pan over a medium heat.
2 Skin and crush the garlic, add it to the pan and leave to cook for a few minutes.
3 Meanwhile, cut the tofu into finger-thick chip shapes, add them to the pan, pour the soya sauce over and leave to fry on one side.
4 Break the walnuts into halves or quarters, stone the olives if necessary and halve them also. Add the walnuts and olives to the pan as you do them.
5 Keep turning the tofu chips till they are golden brown on all four sides. Serve immediately.

Each serving (of 4) provides: 347 kcal, 12 g protein, 33 g fat, 3 g carbohydrate, 1 g fibre.

This is marvellous on its own as a snack but try also serving it with *Baked Onion Surprise* (page 116), *Courgette and Cauliflower Casserole* (page 80) or *Winter Vegetable Stockpot* (page 64).

For variety, try adding the juice of half a lemon just before serving, or any finely diced root vegetable you have to hand at step 4.

Note that this must be served immediately it's ready. If you let it stand, even for 10 minutes, the tofu chips will begin to go leathery.

SAVOURY BUCKWHEAT
allow ½ hour to prepare

To Serve 6

Imperial (Metric)		American
½ lb (¼ kg)	roasted buckwheat	1¼ cups
1¼ pints (¾ litre)	water	3 cups
2 oz (60 g)	margarine	4 tbs
½ lb (¼ kg)	onions	2 medium
1½ tbs (25 ml)	soya sauce	1½ tbs
1	lemon	1
2 tbs	fresh chopped mint (or 1 tbs dried mint)	2 tbs

1 Put the buckwheat and water in a large saucepan over a high heat and bring quickly to the boil, then reduce heat and simmer for 5–10 minutes, partially covered, till the buckwheat is cooked and still chewy. Remove from heat and drain.
2 Put the margarine in a frying-pan over a low heat.
3 Meanwhile, skin and chop the onions, add to the pan and sauté till transparent.
4 Add the buckwheat and soya sauce and stir-fry over a low heat for a few minutes.
5 Squeeze the lemon and add the juice (and dried mint if you're using it) and continue to stir-fry for a few more minutes.
6 Remove from heat, stir in the fresh chopped mint and serve.

Each serving (of 6) provides: 239 kcal, 5 g protein, 9 g fat, 33 g carbohydrate, 1 g fibre.

Buckwheat has a full nutty flavour and is good served plain. However, try this recipe when you're in the mood for something more extravagant and don't mind the extra preparation time.

It's fairly light with a delicate flavour so would go well with something rich and substantial; try *Savoury Avocado Tart* (page 84), *Baked Onion Surprise* (page 116) or *Cauliflower Catalan Style* (page 66).

CREAMED MUSHROOMS
allow ½ hour to prepare

To Serve 4–6

Imperial (Metric)		American
3 oz (90 g)	margarine	⅓ cup
1	clove garlic	1
1 lb (½ kg)	mushrooms (preferably button)	1 lb
3 tbs	wholewheat flour	3 tbs
¾ pint (400 ml)	soya milk	2 cups
	salt and pepper to taste	

1 Put the margarine to melt in a large saucepan over a low heat.
2 Skin and crush the garlic, add it to the pan and cook gently for a few moments.
3 Wash and drain the mushrooms, add them to the pan and sauté till tender (about 15–20 minutes). (If you couldn't manage to get button mushrooms, chop them into bite-sized pieces first.)
4 Stir in the flour and allow to cook gently for a few minutes before adding the soya milk, a little at a time, stirring continuously till the mixture thickens. Remove from heat, season and serve.

Each serving (of 6) provides: 158 kcal, 4 g protein, 14 g fat, 4 g carbohydrate, 3 g fibre.

These are rich and sumptuous and go best with something light. Try *Bulgur Bake* (page 59), *Courgette and Tomato Crumble* (page 61) or *Savoury Crunchies* (page 47).

BRAISED FENNEL
allow ½ hour to prepare

To Serve 4

Imperial (Metric)		American
1 lb (½ kg)	fennel	1 lb
1 pint (½ litre)	soya milk	2½ cups
1 tsp	fennel seeds	1 tsp
1 oz (30 g)	margarine	2 tbs
2 tbs	wholewheat flour	2 tbs
	salt and pepper to taste	

1 Wash the fennel, cut off the green, fern-like tops, finely chop them and set aside. Clean and chop the rest and put it in a saucepan together with the soya milk and fennel seeds, bring quickly to the boil, then reduce heat and simmer, partially covered, till just tender (about 10–15 minutes).
2 Meanwhile, melt the margarine in a separate, small saucepan over a low heat. When it's completely melted but before it begins to bubble, add the flour and stir in. Continue to heat gently and stir for 2–3 minutes.
3 As soon as the fennel is done, remove from heat and drain, reserving the liquid. Arrange the cooked fennel in a shallow, ovenproof dish.
4 Slowly add the cooking liquid to the roux, stirring continuously. Continue stirring after you've added the full amount until the mixture thickens. Add salt and pepper to taste (and a little extra soya milk if it seems too thick), pour over the cooked fennel and warm through in a moderate oven (350°F/177°C/gas mark 4) for about 15 minutes.
5 Sprinkle the chopped fennel tops over and serve.

Each serving (of 4) provides: 147 kcal, 8 g protein, 9 g fat, 11 g carbohydrate, 2 g fibre.

This has a delicate flavour but is quite filling. Try serving it with *Butter Bean and Mushroom Casserole* (page 82), *Olive and Potato Flan* (page 74), *Savoury Onion Tart* (page 85) or any other casserole, flan or tart and a green salad.

BRAZIL NUT AND CABBAGE STIR-FRY

allow ½ hour to prepare

To Serve 4–6

Imperial (Metric)		American
1½ lb (¾ kg)	white cabbage	1 small
5 tbs (75 ml)	oil	5 tbs
2 tbs	black mustard seeds	2 tbs
¼ lb (125 g)	Brazil nuts	1 cup
1	lemon	1
	salt to taste	

1 Wash the cabbage and remove any injured or discoloured outer leaves. Thinly shred the rest and set aside.
2 Put the oil in a wok (or large saucepan) over a high heat, add the mustard seeds and leave them to cook for about a minute.
3 Add the shredded cabbage and stir till the mustard seeds are evenly distributed through the mixture. Reduce heat to medium and leave to fry for a while, stirring from time to time.
4 Meanwhile, coarsely chop the Brazil nuts and stir them into the pan, then finely grate the lemon rind directly into the pan and squeeze the lemon and add the juice. Continue to stir-fry for another 5 minutes.
5 Transfer to a hot serving-dish, season with salt to taste and serve.

Each serving (of 6) provides: 270 kcal, 5 g protein, 25 g fat, 6 g carbohydrate, 6 g fibre.

Try this with *Spinach and Mushroom Tagliatelle* (page 69), *Mung Bean and Courgette Casserole* (page 76) or *Fresh Parsley and Tomato Flan* (page 75).

Any leftovers can happily be served cold, for lunch, the following day.

For variety, substitute caraway seeds for the mustard seeds at step 2 or use cider vinegar instead of lemon juice at step 4.

BAKED PARSNIPS
allow 45 minutes to prepare

To Serve 4–6

Imperial (Metric)		American
2 lb (1 kg)	parsnips	2 lb
2 oz (60 g)	margarine	4 tbs
1½ tbs	mustard powder	1½ tbs
3 tbs (45 ml)	apple concentrate	3 tbs
	salt and pepper to taste	

1 Top, tail and peel the parsnips, then cut them into quarters lengthwise. Plunge them into fiercely-boiling water for 4 minutes (but no longer) then drain them and set aside.

2 Put the margarine to melt in a small saucepan over a low heat, then stir in the mustard powder and apple concentrate and season with salt and (preferably freshly-ground) pepper to taste. Remove from heat and set aside.

3 Put the parsnips in an ovenproof dish, pour the sauce mixture over and toss them around until they are all well covered. Bake in the middle of a moderate oven (350°F/177°C/gas mark 4) for ½ hour.

Each serving (of 6) provides: 187 kcal, 3 g protein, 9 g fat, 21 g carbohydrate, 7 g fibre.

The combination of mustard and apple concentrate enhances the parsnip's positive qualities – its sweetness and delicate flavour – while subtly disguising the slight aftertaste that puts some people off them. We have known some self-professed life-long parsnip-haters to ask for second helpings of this dish!

CELERY FRITTERS
allow ½ hour to prepare
(if you have the *Batter Mixture*)

To Serve 4

Imperial (Metric)		American
1	large head of celery	1
1 tsp	salt	1 tsp
1 oz (30 g)	margarine	2 tbs
	Batter Mixture (page 258)	

1 Trim off the leaves and break the celery head into individual stalks and wash thoroughly, then chop the stalks into bite-sized lengths and drop them into a large pan of boiling salted water. When they begin to soften (but are still firm and crisp – about 8–12 minutes) remove them from the heat and drain thoroughly.
2 Put the margarine in a large frying-pan over a low heat.
3 Start dipping the celery pieces in the batter mixture. If the batter won't adhere, roll the celery in flour first.
4 Fry the battered pieces for a few minutes on each side till they're golden brown. Remove from pan and serve.

Each serving (of 4) provides: 418 kcal, 12 g protein, 30 g fat, 27 g carbohydrate, 8 g fibre.

If you have a lot of mouths to feed it's probably simplest to prepare the celery fritters about an hour beforehand and then keep them warm in a casserole dish in the bottom of the oven; but if you have just yourself (and perhaps a special friend!) to feed, they are at their most delicious served straight from the pan and, provided you already have some of the batter mixture made up, are really quite quick and easy to prepare.

GRILLED BROCCOLI
allow 25 minutes to prepare

To Serve 4

Imperial (Metric)		American
1 lb (½ kg)	broccoli	1 lb
6 oz (180 g)	tofu	¾ cup
3 tbs (45 ml)	oil	3 tbs
1½ tbs (25 ml)	soya sauce	1½ tbs
1 tsp	mustard powder	1 tsp
1 tbs	sunflower seeds	1 tbs

1 Wash the broccoli, cut off the florets, dice the stems and plunge it all into fiercely-boiling, unsalted water till just tender (about 5 minutes). Remove from heat and drain, retaining ¼ pint (125 ml/6 tbs) of the cooking water.
2 Crumble the tofu into a blender, add the retained cooking water from the broccoli together with the oil, soya sauce and mustard powder and blend till smooth and creamy.
3 Arrange the cooked broccoli in a heatproof serving-dish, pour the blended mixture over, sprinkle with the sunflower seeds and place under a hot grill until it's just beginning to brown on top. Serve immediately.

Each serving (of 4) provides: 193 kcal, 9 g protein, 16 g fat, 5 g carbohydrate, 5 g fibre.

This is light and delicate and so is best served with something substantial such as baked potatoes or *Savoury Rice* (page 68); or try combining it with several light dishes such as *Savoury Crunchies* (page 47), *Cashew and Mushroom Roast* (page 60), *Mung Bean and Courgette Casserole* (page 76) or *Celery Fritters* (page 111).

AUBERGINE FRITTERS
allow about ¾ hour to prepare

To Serve 4

Imperial (Metric)		American
	Batter Mixture (page 258)	
1 lb (½ kg)	aubergine	1 large
2 tsp	salt	2 tsp
3–4 tbs	wholewheat flour	3–4 tbs
	salt and pepper to taste	
1	lemon	1
	oil for frying (preferably olive)	

1 Make up a thinner batter mixture than usual, using extra soya milk.
2 While the batter mixture is standing, wash (but don't peel) the aubergine and cut it into finger-thick slices. Place these in layers in a bowl, sprinkling each layer with salt, and set aside for ½ hour to sweat.
3 Sprinkle the flour over a plate, add a little salt and pepper if you like, and set aside.
4 Squeeze the lemon and set the juice aside.
5 Put 2–3 tbs oil in a frying-pan over a medium heat.
6 Rinse the aubergine slices in cold water, drain and pat them dry with kitchen paper or a clean tea-cloth.
7 Dip each aubergine slice in turn, first in the flour, then in the batter and finally lay it in the frying-pan and fry on both sides till golden brown. Transfer the fritters to a hot serving-fish as you do them. Add more oil to the pan as necessary.
8 Pour the lemon juice over the fritters and serve.

Each serving (of 4) provides: 372 kcal, 8 g protein, 28 g fat, 23 g carbohydrate, 8 g fibre.

These are at their best served straight from the pan – though it's a bit of a sacrifice to be the one making them and not one of the ones eating them! But if you want to serve them as a side dish in the normal way, it's probably best to make them well in advance and keep them warm in a casserole in the bottom of a warm oven.

CREAMED SPINACH
allow 50 minutes to prepare

To Serve 4–6

Imperial (Metric)		American
1 lb (½ kg)	fresh spinach	1 lb
	(or 10 oz [300 g] frozen spinach)	
¼ pint (125 ml)	oil	½ cup
2	cloves garlic	2
3 tbs	wholewheat flour	3 tbs
½ pint (¼ litre)	soya milk	1¼ cups
½ lb (¼ kg)	tofu	1 cup
1½ tbs (25 ml)	soya sauce	1½ tbs
1	lemon	1
	salt to taste	

1 Put 2 tbs of oil in a large saucepan over a low heat.
2 Wash and add the spinach. Increase the heat a little and cook till soft (only a few minutes if fresh; about 10 minutes if frozen). Remove from heat and set aside.
3 Meanwhile put 3 tbs of oil in another saucepan over a low heat. Skin and crush the garlic, add it to the pan and cook gently for a couple of minutes before stirring in the flour. Continue to cook gently for another few minutes.
4 Set 5 tbs of soya milk aside, then gradually stir the rest into the pan with the flour and garlic. Continue to heat gently and stir to make a thick sauce. Remove from heat and combine the contents of the two saucepans by adding one to the other and stirring gently. Set aside.
5 Put the reserved soya milk (5 tbs) in a blender and crumble in the tofu.
6 Squeeze the lemon and add the juice, 3 tbs oil, salt to taste (about 1 tsp), freshly-ground black pepper and blend to a thick cream. Check the seasoning and adjust if necessary then fold the cream into the spinach and pour the mixture into a lightly-greased ovenproof dish. Bake in the middle of a moderate oven (350°F/177°C/gas mark 4) for 30 minutes.

Each serving (of 6) provides: 270 kcal, 10 g protein, 24 g fat, 5 g carbohydrate, 6 g fibre.

This goes well with *Winter Pie* (page 78), *Festive Savoury Loaf* (page 90), or any of the savoury flans or tarts.

SPICED PEASE PUDDING
allow 1½ hours to prepare

To Serve 4–6

Imperial (Metric)		American
½ lb (¼ kg)	yellow split peas	1 cup
3 tbs (45 ml)	oil	3 tbs
1 tsp	whole cumin seeds	1 tsp
1 tsp	ground turmeric	1 tsp
½ tsp	ground cinnamon	½ tsp
½ tsp	chilli powder	½ tsp
½ tsp	ground cloves (or 6 whole cloves)	½ tsp
½ tsp	ground nutmeg	½ tsp
2 tsp	soya sauce	2 tsp

1 Wash the split peas, put them in a large saucepan, cover well with water, bring quickly to the boil, then reduce heat and simmer, partially covered, till they have completely softened and are beginning to break down (about ½–1½ hours depending on how old they are). Check the water frequently and add more as required.
2 When the peas are almost cooked put the oil and spices (but not the soya sauce) in a small saucepan and heat gently for a few minutes, stirring often.
3 As soon as the peas are done, remove both pans from heat, drain the peas if necessary, add the oil, spices and soya sauce and mash to a smooth, thick cream with a fork. Transfer to a hot dish and serve.

Each serving (of 6) provides: 204 kcal, 9 g protein, 9 g fat, 24 g carbohydrate, 5 g fibre.

The traditional pease puddings of the North-East of England have an extra two stages in which they are put into a buttered basin and steamed for an hour; but in the view of these two lazy cooks, they are tasty enough as they are.

They can be served hot with curries or cold with salads. Any cold left-over pudding can be sliced, fried in margarine and served on toast as a quick snack.

For variety, try green split peas, omit the spices and double the amount of soya sauce. Or, for a quicker dish, substitute lentils for the split peas and make an Indian 'dhal'.

BAKED ONION SURPRISE
allow 1¼ hours to prepare

To Serve 4

Imperial (Metric)		American
4	large onions	4
3 oz (90 g)	margarine	⅓ cup
¼ lb (125 g)	mushrooms	¼ lb
¼ lb (125 g)	black olives	1 cup
1 oz (30 g)	breadcrumbs (or wheatgerm)	3 tbs
2 tsp	fresh chopped marjoram (or 1 tsp dried marjoram)	2 tsp
	salt and pepper to taste	
	ingredients for *Red Wine Sauce* (page 169)	

1 Separately wrap the whole onions in foil (don't peel them first!) and bake till soft in a moderate oven (350°F/177°C/gas mark 4); start testing with a skewer after about 30 minutes. When they are soft right through to the centre, remove from oven, discard the foil and set aside to cool.
2 Put the margarine to melt in a frying-pan over a low heat.
3 Wash and dice the mushrooms, add to the pan and sauté till tender. Remove from heat.
4 Top and tail the onions and remove their outer skins. Slice off the top thirds and set aside, then scoop out the hearts with a teaspoon, dice them and add to the pan with the mushrooms.
5 Stone the olives if necessary, then finely dice them and add them to the pan together with the breadcrumbs, marjoram, salt and pepper. Mix thoroughly.
6 Stuff the onions with the mixture and replace their top thirds as 'lids'. There should be plenty of the mixture left over to make a sauce.
7 Replace the stuffed onions in the oven for a further 15 minutes at the same temperature.
8 While they are reheating, prepare a sauce from the remains of the stuffing mixture. (*Red Wine Sauce*, page 169)
9 Remove the onions from the oven, transfer to a hot serving-dish, pour the sauce over, sprinkle on some more of the chopped marjoram and serve.

Each serving (of 4) provides: 437 kcal, 10 g protein, 29 g fat, 27 g carbohydrate, 7 g fibre.

These look sumptuous and are rich and filling, so they should be served with something light – try *Whole Courgettes Italian Style* (page 102) or *Savoury Buckwheat* (page 106) or a green salad.

Salads

Salads

Salads can be served as starters, side dishes, main dishes on their own or they can provide the basis of a complete, delicious, satisfying and healthy meal with the simple addition of wholewheat bread spread with nut-butters, tahini, yeast extract or one of the spreads from the *Spreads* section or dips from the *Starters* section and fresh fruit to finish. Add a glass of wine and you have a feast.

We have given a range of combinations to get you started, but experiment with others. More than 6000 plants have been identified as edible so the possibilities are literally endless.

Why not make a *Basic Green Salad* every day for lunch, simply adding raw *bean sprouts, broccoli, cabbage, carrots, cauliflower, chives, courgettes, cucumber, dill, leeks, mint, mushrooms, parsley, peppers, radishes, spring onions, tomatoes watercress, etc.*, depending on what is in season and what you have to hand.

A word or two about raw food. It may not be known at what point in our long stay on this amazing planet we human beings first began *cooking* our food, but we had certainly fully developed our present digestive systems before we did. If as seems probable our habitat of origin was the tropical rain forest (it must have been *warm* or how else could we have survived naked?) then perhaps our 'natural' diet was similar to that of our cousins the apes and chimpanzees who still live there, predominantly on fruits, leaves and grasses, seeds, nuts, honey when they can find it and, on the rare occasions when they can catch them with their bare hands, insects and small mammals – but *all eaten raw*. Our sweet tooth is a further clue that supports the idea that this must have been our original 'natural' diet since sweetness is an indication of ripeness – i.e. maximum food value – in fruit.

We've put 'natural' in inverted commas because this word has been so used, misused and abused in recent years that it's doubtful if it still has any meaning left, other than to signify general approval. But don't go feeling superior when you hear advertisers chucking it at you as they extol the virtues of some factory-made product. Remember, there isn't anything 'natural' about a field of wheat either, let alone a loaf of bread baked from 100 per cent wholewheat flour in a gas, electric or microwave oven! In the twentieth century all our food is the product of agriculture and this means *big business*.

Nevertheless, it is undeniable that our digestive systems evolved to cope with *raw* food and so this must be as near to 'natural' as we can now get.

So, for truly radiant health, it is important that some raw food should be eaten at every meal.

This needn't be as difficult as it sounds. A bowl of muesli with your breakfast can include seeds, nuts and dried fruits. A daily salad of the kind described above can provide the basis for lunch and even dinner can include a green salad as one course and be rounded off with fresh fruit. If the population at large were to follow this simple formula, there would be a radical improvement in the nation's health.

BASIC GREEN SALAD
allow 10 minutes to prepare

Per Serving

Imperial (Metric)		**American**
1½ tbs (25 ml)	*French Dressing* (page 178)	1½ tbs
3–4 leaves	Cos, Webb or similar lettuce	3–4 leaves

1 Put 1½ tbs (25 ml) of dressing per person in a large salad bowl.
2 Discard only the really damaged outer leaves of the lettuce as necessary (see below), then break off 3–4 leaves per person, wash them thoroughly and drain.
3 Fold them up in a clean tea-cloth (or kitchen paper) and pat them dry. (Or use a centrifugal hand dryer.)
4 Tear the leaves into bite-sized pieces, put them into the bowl, toss till they are all well coated with the dressing and serve.

Each serving provides: 200 kcal, 1 g protein, 20 g fat, 2 g carbohydrate, 2 g fibre.

If you are serving a big, rich meal, always include a simple green salad as one course. It aids digestion and increases the fibre content as well as contributing many essential minerals and vitamins to the diet. Raw lettuce is particularly rich in vitamins A and C but note that cutting the leaves with a steel knife destroys some of the vitamin C (by oxidation) so always *tear* them. Note also that the darker green outer leaves contain up to 50 times more vitamin A than the inner white ones.

Nearly all the calories are in the dressing so if you're trying to keep down your calorie count, use *Yoghurt Salad Dressing* (page 182) instead.

LEMON CARROT SALAD
allow 15 minutes to prepare

To Serve 6

Imperial (Metric)		American
2 lb (1 kg)	carrots	2 lb
2	lemons	2

1 Scrub the carrots to remove any mud, then top and tail them (peeling is only really necessary if they have badly-damaged or pitted skins).
2 Finely grate or shred them (the finer the better) and put them into a suitable serving-bowl.
3 Grate the lemons and set the grated peel aside.
4 Squeeze the lemons, add the juice to the bowl and mix thoroughly.
5 Sprinkle the grated peel on top and serve.

Each serving (of 6) provides: 41 kcal, 1 g protein, 0 g fat, 10 g carbohydrate, 6 g fibre.

Considering how quick and easy it is to prepare, this simple salad is amazingly delicious to eat. It is also very good for you. Raw carrots are particularly rich in vitamins A and C – vitamin A is actually called *carotene* after them. Note that mature carrots contain twice as much of it as young ones.

MIXED PEPPER SALAD
allow 15 minutes to prepare

To Serve 4–6

Imperial (Metric)		American
1 lb (½ kg)	red peppers	2 large
1 lb (½ kg)	green peppers	2 large
1 lb (½ kg)	yellow peppers	2 large
¼ lb (125 g)	black olives	1 cup
¼ pint (125 ml)	*French Dressing* (page 178)	½ cup

1 Wash the peppers and remove the seeds before slicing them into bite-sized pieces.
2 Put the dressing into a suitable serving-bowl, add the sliced peppers and toss till well mixed.
3 Stone the olives if necessary (some garlic presses have a gadget for the purpose in their handles), arrange them on top of the peppers and serve.

Each serving (of 6) provides: 301 kcal, 5 g protein, 23 g fat, 18 g carbohydrate, 5 g fibre.

This quick salad is an attractive addition to any meal with its range of bright primary colours each of which has a different taste, the yellow being the sweetest.

CABBAGE, FRUIT AND NUT SALAD
allow 15 minutes to prepare

To Serve 4–6

Imperial (Metric)		American
2 lb (1 kg)	red cabbage	½ large
1 lb (½ kg)	eating apples	1 lb
¼ lb (125 g)	pecans (or walnuts)	1 cup
¼ pint (125 ml)	*French Dressing* (page 178)	½ cup

1 Shred the cabbage as finely as possible and put into a suitable serving-bowl.
2 Wash and core the apples (but don't peel them), then dice and add them to the bowl.
3 Add the pecan nuts and salad dressing, toss till well mixed and serve.

Each serving (of 6) provides: 356 kcal, 6 g protein, 29 g fat, 17 g carbohydrate, 9 g fibre.

This salad will look most attractive if you can buy *green* eating apples such as *Granny Smiths* to offset the rich red of the cabbage. For variety, try adding sultanas or chopped dates.

MIXED SPROUT SALAD
allow 20 minutes to prepare

To Serve 6–8

Imperial (Metric)		American
½ lb (¼ kg)	mung bean sprouts	½ lb
½ lb (¼ kg)	lentil sprouts	½ lb
¼ lb (125 g)	alfalfa sprouts	¼ lb
½ lb (¼ kg)	red pepper	1 large
12 tbs (175 ml)	*Tahini Dressing* (page 180)	12 tbs

1 Put all of the mung bean and lentil sprouts and half of the alfalfa sprouts into a suitable serving-bowl and mix well together.
2 Wash the pepper and remove the pith and seeds. Cut off a few strips and set aside to use as decoration. Finely chop the remainder, add it to the bowl, together with the dressing and mix thoroughly.
3 Decorate the top with the rest of the alfalfa sprouts and the strips of red pepper and serve.

Each serving (of 8) provides: 157 kcal, 4 g protein, 14 g fat, 5 g carbohydrate, 4 g fibre.

Any kind of bean sprout can be used to ring the changes on this delicious, crunchy salad. A wide range is available in most wholefood shops, but perfectionists will, of course, wish to sprout their own. (See page 262 for advice on how to proceed.)

AVOCADO AND APPLE SALAD
allow 20 minutes to prepare

To Serve 4–6

Imperial (Metric)		American
2	large avocados	2
1 lb (½ kg)	eating apples	1 lb
1	bunch watercress	1
¼ lb (125 g)	salted peanuts	1 cup
¼ pint (125 ml)	*French Dressing* (page 178)	½ cup

1 Scoop out the flesh of the avocados and cut into finger-thick slices. Put them in a suitable serving-bowl.
2 Wash and core the apples (but don't peel them), then dice them and add to the bowl.
3 Chop the watercress into bite-sized pieces and add to the bowl together with the salted peanuts.
4 Add the dressing, toss till thoroughly mixed and serve.

Each serving (of 6) provides: 486 kcal, 9 g protein, 44 g fat, 13 g carbohydrate, 6 g fibre.

This is a summery salad which you can serve all year, the fresh taste of the apples and watercress perfectly complementing the richness of the avocados. It looks best if you use *red* apples to offset the greens of the other ingredients. The peanuts are included to add a bit of protein and crunch.

CELERIAC SALAD
allow 20 minutes to prepare

To Serve 4

Imperial (Metric)		American
1 jar (275 ml)	*Mayonnaise* (page 185)	1 jar
1	large celeriac	1
1 tsp	caraway seeds	1 tsp

1 Put the mayonnaise in a suitable serving-bowl.
2 Peel and slice the celeriac and then grate it as finely as possible directly into the bowl with the mayonnaise. Stop from time to time to toss the grated mixture to coat it with dressing.
3 Sprinkle the caraway seeds on top and serve.

Each serving (of 4) provides: 222 kcal, 4 g protein, 19 g fat, 5 g carbohydrate, 9 g fibre.

Everyone likes the taste of the bottom bit of sticks of celery – the root part – yet few seem prepared to buy celeriac though it tastes similar and consists of nothing else. This recipe is simple to prepare and makes a delicious winter salad. Serve it with savoury flans and tarts, at buffet parties or as a simple starter to a hot meal.

Celeriac discolours very quickly once cut and although this does not affect its taste, it does reduce its visual appeal. Mixing it with the dressing as you go along, as suggested, solves this easily.

CARROT AND COCONUT SALAD
allow 20 minutes to prepare

To Serve 4–6

Imperial (Metric)		American
1 lb (½ kg)	carrots	1 lb
2 oz (60 g)	chopped dates	½ cup
2 oz (60 g)	desiccated coconut	½ cup
2	lemons	2
1½ tbs (25 ml)	apple concentrate	1½ tbs
2 tbs	sesame seeds	2 tbs

1 Finely grate the carrots, put them in a suitable serving-bowl and mix them with the chopped dates and desiccated coconut.
2 Squeeze the lemons and add the juice to the bowl together with the apple concentrate. Mix thoroughly.
3 Put the sesame seeds in a dry pan over a low heat and stir them until the seeds are toasted and begin to pop.
4 Add the toasted sesame seeds to the bowl with the other ingredients, mix once more and serve.

Each serving (of 6) provides: 150 kcal, 3 g protein, 9 g fat, 14 g carbohydrate, 7 g fibre.

The rich variety of flavours in this unusual salad makes it suitable for special occasions even though it is so quick and easy to prepare. Serve it with something substantial such as *Cashew Loaf* (page 89) or *Festive Savoury Loaf* (page 90).

CELERY, CARROT AND SPROUT SALAD

allow ½ hour to prepare

To Serve 6–8

Imperial (Metric)		American
1	head of celery	1
1 lb (½ kg)	carrots	1 lb
¼ lb (125 g)	bean sprouts	2 cups
	Spicy Peanut Sauce (page 172)	

1 Break the celery into individual stalks and wash thoroughly before chopping them into bite-sized pieces. Put them in a suitable serving-bowl.
2 Wash the carrots (or peel, as necessary) then finely grate them into the bowl with the celery.
3 Add the bean sprouts and the peanut sauce, mix well together and serve.

Each serving (of 8) provides: 178 kcal, 4 g protein, 16 g fat, 6 g carbohydrate, 5 g fibre.

This crunchy, spicy salad is delicious served by itself as a starter, or as an accompaniment to a hot main dish.

For variety, try *Tahini Dressing* (page 180) or, if it's a really special occasion, try gently heating the peanut sauce and pouring it over the top of the salad just before serving.

Any kind of bean sprout will do and many varieties can be bought in most wholefood shops but perfectionists will of course prefer to sprout their own. (See page 262 for advice.)

AVOCADO AND GRAPEFRUIT SALAD

allow 1¼ hours to prepare
(including 1 hour to chill)

To Serve 4–6

Imperial (Metric)		American
2	large grapefruit	2
3	large avocados	3
1	lemon	1
3 tbs	fresh chopped mint (or 1 tbs dried mint)	3 tbs

1 Peel the grapefruit, divide them into their individual segments, then slice these into bite-sized pieces, taking care to remove any pips.
2 Scoop out the flesh of the avocados, cut into finger-thick slices and add to the bowl. (Don't mix yet!)
3 Squeeze the lemon, pour the juice over the avocado slices and then gently toss to spread the juice evenly through the mixture. (This will prevent the avocado from discolouring.)
4 Add most of the chopped mint, toss again to mix well, then sprinkle the rest on top as a decoration.
5 Chill for at least an hour before serving.

Each serving (of 6) provides: 187 kcal, 4 g protein, 17 g fat, 6 g carbohydrate, 3 g fibre.

This wonderfully delicate, fresh-tasting salad is the perfect way to start a summer dinner-party.

Note that, despite the routine with the lemon juice, the avocado will gradually discolour and although this will not affect its nutritional value or its taste, it does spoil the appearance of the salad, so it's not a good idea to make a lot.

POTATO SALAD
allow 1½ hours to prepare
(including 1 hour to chill)

To Serve 4–6

Imperial (Metric)		American
1½ lb (¾ kg)	potatoes (preferably new)	1½ lb
1 jar (275 ml)	*Mayonnaise* (page 185)	1 jar
1	bunch chives	1

1 Scrub the potatoes and halve or quarter them depending on their size (and peel them if you wish). Drop them in a large saucepan of fiercely-boiling salted water. Bring back to the boil, then reduce heat and simmer, uncovered, till just tender (about 8–12 minutes depending on how small you've cut them). Remove from heat, rinse thoroughly in cold water and drain in a colander.
2 Put the cooled, drained potatoes in a suitable serving-bowl, add a jarful of mayonnaise and toss till well coated.
3 Finely chop the chives, add them to the bowl (saving a few for decoration) and toss again. Chill for at least an hour.
4 Sprinkle the rest of the chives on top and serve.

Each serving (of 6) provides: 239 kcal, 3 g protein, 13 g fat, 27 g carbohydrate, 6 g fibre.

This keeps well, so why not make a lot and stash it in the fridge for the occasional, unexpected visitor?

Serve it as a side dish to cold savoury flans or tarts in summer or as a starter to a hot meal in winter. It's also suitable for buffet parties.

For variety, try *Tahini Dressing* (page 180) or *Spicy Peanut Sauce* (page 172) instead of the mayonnaise. Almost any fresh chopped herb can be used instead of chives.

LEEK SALAD

allow 1½ hours to prepare
(including 1 hour to chill)

To Serve 4–6

Imperial (Metric)		American
2 lb (1 kg)	leeks	2 lb
1 tsp	salt	1 tsp
¼ pint (125 ml)	*French Dressing* (page 178)	½ cup
2 tbs	fresh chopped mint (or 1 tbs dried mint)	2 tbs

1 Wash and chop the leeks and plunge them into fiercely-boiling salted water till just tender (about 5–10 minutes depending on their size). Drain and then immediately plunge into cold water. Leave them for a few minutes to cool before draining in a colander.
2 When the water has completely drained out transfer them to a suitable serving-bowl, pour the dressing over and toss gently till they are all well coated.
3 Sprinkle the chopped mint on top and refrigerate for at least an hour before serving.

Each serving (of 6) provides: 226 kcal, 4 g protein, 19 g fat, 10 g carbohydrate, 6 g fibre.

This salad is particularly good served with cold savoury flans or tarts in summer, at buffet parties in winter, or as a starter to a meal any time.

WHEATBERRY AND BEAN SALAD
allow 1½ hours to prepare

To Serve 8–10

Imperial (Metric)		American
½ lb (¼ kg)	wholewheat berries	1 cup
½ lb (¼ kg)	mung beans	1 cup
1	head of celery	1
1½ tbs (25 ml)	soya sauce	1½ tbs
¼ pint (125 ml)	*French Dressing* (page 178)	½ cup
1 tsp	ground cinnamon	1 tsp

1　Put the wheatberries in a large saucepan, well covered with water, bring quickly to the boil, then reduce heat and simmer, partially covered, till tender (about 1 hour). Check from time to time to see if the water needs topping up. Note that even when they are cooked, wheatberries are still firm and rather chewy.
2　Put the mung beans in a separate large saucepan, also well covered with water, bring quickly to the boil, then reduce heat and simmer till tender (about 20 minutes).
3　When the beans and berries are done, remove from heat and drain thoroughly before mixing them together in a suitable serving-bowl.
4　Wash and chop the celery into bite-sized pieces, add to the bowl together with the soya sauce, dressing and cinnamon, mix thoroughly and serve.

Each serving (of 10) provides: 248 kcal, 10 g protein, 12 g fat, 27 g carbohydrate, 9 g fibre.

This unusual and attractive salad, with its shades of greens and browns, has the advantage of providing an almost perfect protein balance. It keeps well and so is suitable for buffet parties.

It's odd that people who habitually cook and eat rice – which has to travel a long way to get to our shops – never think of cooking and eating wholewheat berries – which grow right on our doorsteps.

SWEET RICE SALAD
allow about 2 hours to prepare
(including 1 hour to cool)

To Serve 4–6

Imperial (Metric)		American
½ lb (¼ kg)	wholegrain rice	1¼ cups
½ pint (¼ litre)	orange juice	1½ cups
½ pint (¼ litre)	water	1½ cups
1 tsp	ground turmeric	1 tsp
2 oz (60 g)	sultanas	2 tbs
1	red pepper	1
2 oz (60 g)	cashew pieces	½ cup
¼ pint (125 ml)	*Orange Juice Dressing* (page 179)	½ cup

1 Wash and drain the rice and put it together with the orange juice, water and turmeric into a large saucepan. Bring quickly to the boil, reduce heat, cover and simmer over the lowest possible heat without lifting the lid for 45 minutes. Remove from heat and leave to stand for 5 minutes before lifting the lid. (Don't worry if there's a little juice left in the bottom.)
2 Sprinkle the sultanas over the surface of the rice, re-cover and set aside to cool. (This softens the sultanas.)
3 Finely dice the red pepper, mix with the cashew pieces and set aside.
4 When the rice has completely cooled, turn it out into a suitable serving-bowl, add the chopped pepper and cashew pieces and the dressing, mix till you're satisfied that every grain of rice is coated and serve.

Each serving (of 6) provides: 311 kcal, 5 g protein, 13 g fat, 44 g carbohydrate, 2 g fibre.

The simplicity of the dressing adds an agreeable lightness to this colourful and unusual salad which, as it may be prepared well in advance, is suitable for buffet parties as well as everyday use.

PEACH AND CAULIFLOWER SALAD

allow 50 minutes to prepare
(including ½ hour to chill)

To Serve 6

Imperial (Metric)		American
1	large cauliflower	1
6	peaches	6
1	carton mustard and cress	1
2 oz (60 g)	wheatgerm	¾ cup
1 jar (275 ml)	*Mayonnaise* (page 185)	1 jar

1 Cut the cauliflower into bite-sized florets and put them in a suitable serving-bowl. Finely dice the remaining stems and add them to the bowl.
2 Stone and slice the peaches and add them to the bowl.
3 Cut the mustard and cress as near to the roots as possible and add to the bowl.
4 Add the wheatgerm and mayonnaise and mix all the ingredients thoroughly.
5 Chill for at least half an hour before serving.

Each serving (of 6) provides: 221 kcal, 8 g protein, 14 g fat, 16 g carbohydrate, 6 g fibre.

This unusual salad is at its best in the late summer when the seasons for peaches and cauliflowers happily overlap. Raw cauliflower is particularly rich in vitamin C, but even lightly cooking it destroys more than two-thirds of it.

For variety, try nectarines instead of peaches, or broccoli instead of cauliflower.

SALSIFY SALAD

allow 1 hour to prepare
(including ½ hour to chill)

To Serve 4–6

Imperial (Metric)		American
2 lb (1 kg)	salsify	2 lb
10 tbs (150 ml)	*Mayonnaise* (page 185)	10 tbs
2 tbs	chives (preferably fresh, chopped)	2 tbs

1 Peel, top and tail the salsify and cut them on the slant into bite-sized pieces. (The simplest way is to hold them under cold water and use a potato peeler.)
2 Plunge the cut pieces into a large saucepanful of fiercely-boiling unsalted water until they begin to soften (about 8–12 minutes). Remove from heat, rinse in cold water and drain in a colander.
3 Put them in a suitable serving-bowl, add the mayonnaise and toss to mix.
4 Garnish with chopped chives and chill for at least ½ hour before serving.

Each serving (of 6) provides: 101 kcal, 4 g protein, 7 g fat, 5 g carbohydrate, negligible fibre.

This is a simple way to make an unusual salad. Salsify has a delicate flavour similar to asparagus but at only half the cost. Nevertheless it is still expensive and that is why we've put this recipe in the 'special occasions' section. Unfortunately it is only rarely seen in street markets but can be obtained in tins.

ASPARAGUS SALAD

allow 1 hour to prepare
(including ½ hour to chill)

To Serve 4

Imperial (Metric)		American
1	bunch asparagus spears	1
1½ tsp	salt	1½
3 tbs (45 ml)	French Dressing (page 178)	3 tbs
1 lb (½ kg)	tomatoes	4 large
12	stoned black olives	12

1 Prepare the asparagus spears by tying them in bundles of about a dozen. (They are often sold already prepared.)

2 Drop the bundles in a large pan of fiercely-boiling salted water. (Check before you boil the water that the pan is wide enough for the bundles to lie down flat – if it isn't and you have to cut off some of the fibrous ends, don't throw them away! See below.) Bring the water quickly back to the boil, then reduce heat and continue to simmer, uncovered. After about 10 minutes, begin testing the spears by pushing a thin, sharply-pointed knife into their bases. As soon as they begin to soften, remove from heat and drain. Cut the string and lay them out on a clean cloth or kitchen paper to cool.

3 Thinly slice the tomatoes and arrange decoratively round the edge of a large, flat serving-dish. Lay out the cooled asparagus spears in the centre and carefully pour the dressing over them, making sure that every spear is coated. Garnish with the olives and chill for at least half an hour before serving.

Each serving (of 4) provides: 149 kcal, 5 g protein, 12 g fat, 4 g carbohydrate, 4 g fibre.

This is not a complicated or time-consuming recipe to prepare. The only reason we've put it in the 'special occasions' section is the price of asparagus!

For variety, try *Mayonnaise* (page 185) or *Yogurt Salad Dressing* (page 182).

If you have a lot of the fibrous ends left over, you can make asparagus soup by gently boiling them in soya milk for about 15 minutes and discarding them before serving it, seasoned with a little salt and pepper.

AUBERGINE AND TOMATO SALAD
allow 2½ hours to prepare
(including 1 hour to demoisturize the aubergine
and 1 hour to chill)

To Serve 4

Imperial (Metric)		American
1 lb (½ kg)	aubergine	1 large
1 tsp	salt	1 tsp
1 lb (½ kg)	tomatoes	4 large
¼ pint (125 ml)	olive oil	½ cup
7 fl oz (200 ml)	dry red wine	1 cup
1	clove garlic (crushed)	1
2 tbs	parsley (preferably fresh, chopped)	2 tbs

1 Peel the aubergine, remove the stalk and cut into finger-thick slices. Place in layers in a bowl with a sprinkle of salt over each layer. Set aside for an hour.
2 Skin the tomatoes (see page 259) and arrange round the edge of a large serving dish.
3 Put some of the oil in a large frying-pan over a low heat. As you transfer each slice of aubergine to the pan, pat it dry with kitchen paper. Fry each slice just long enough on both sides to begin to colour, then push it to the side of the pan to make room for more. As you add each new batch of slices, add more oil. (They'll drink up enormous quantities, so if you prefer you can use a cheaper vegetable oil, but do put at least 3 tbs of olive oil as this is important for the finished flavour.) When you've fried all the slices on both sides, add the wine, crushed garlic and parsley, mix everything together thoroughly and simmer for 5 minutes.
4 Remove the cooked aubergine slices and arrange them in the middle of the tomatoes on your serving-dish. Pour the contents of the pan over as a sauce.
5 Garnish with more fresh parsley and chill for at least an hour before serving.

Each serving (of 4) provides: 349 kcal, 2 g protein, 31 g fat, 7 g carbohydrate, 6 g fibre.

This is a perfect starter for an alfresco summer dinner-party. As it can be prepared well in advance, it is also suitable for buffet parties, in which case you should double or triple the quantities and allow extra preparation time.

CUCUMBER, YOGHURT AND GINGER SALAD

allow 2½ hours to prepare
(including demoisturizing and chilling time)

To Serve 6

Imperial (Metric)		American
3	large cucumbers	3
1½ tbs	salt	1½ tbs
1 pint (½ litre)	*Vegan Yoghurt* (page 244)	2½ cups
2 tbs	freshly grated ginger (or 1 tbs dried ground ginger)	2 tbs
	salt and pepper to taste	

1 Wash the cucumbers (or peel them if you wish) and cut them into quarters lengthwise. Slice them into finger-thick chunks, put them in a bowl in layers and sprinkle each layer liberally with salt. Set aside for an hour.
2 Rinse the cucumber chunks in cold water and drain. (If you're a perfectionist, dry them by patting between layers of kitchen paper.) Put them in a suitable serving-bowl.
3 Put the grated ginger and salt and pepper to taste in the yoghurt container and stir well in. Pour over the cucumber chunks and mix thoroughly.
4 Chill for at least an hour before serving.

Each serving (of 6) provides: 70 kcal, 4 g protein, 2 g fat, 6 g carbohydrate, 2 g fibre.

This is a delightful, fresh-tasting summer salad which also goes well with hot curries.

Do try to use *fresh* ginger if you can – it lifts the flavour into a unique taste experience.

If the batch of yoghurt you're using is too bland in taste, add a few drops of lemon juice.

MARINATED MUSHROOM SALAD
allow at least 4½ hours to prepare
(including 4 hours marination time)

To Serve 4–6

Imperial (Metric)		American
1 lb (½ kg)	button mushrooms	1 lb
¼ pint (125 ml)	olive oil	½ cup
5 tbs (75 ml)	white wine vinegar	5 tbs
½ tsp	salt	½ tsp
½ tsp	pepper	½ tsp
1 tsp	mustard seeds	1 tsp
¼ tsp	cayenne pepper	¼ tsp
1 tbs	juniper berries	1 tbs

1 Wash, drain and slice the mushrooms and put them in a suitable serving-bowl.
2 Make a marinade from all the remaining ingredients (the easiest way is to put them all in a jam jar, seal and shake well) and pour over the mushrooms. Toss lightly for a few moments till every single slice of mushroom is coated.
3 Chill for at least 4 hours.
4 Toss again to remix and serve.

Each serving (of 6) provides: 198 kcal, 2 g protein, 20 g fat, negligible carbohydrate, 2 g fibre.

As the only problem with this salad is the marination time, it is particularly suitable for buffet parties, where it can be one of the first things you make. Note that during the marination the mushrooms will shrink to about half their volume.

For variety, try using capers instead of juniper berries.

Don't slice the mushrooms too thin. We did this the first time we tried it and as a result they produced too much juice which diluted the marinade and had to be drained off. Slice them about ¼ in (60 mm) thick and you'll be all right.

Desserts

Desserts

Fresh fruit is the healthiest everyday dessert as well as the simplest and cheapest, and a good habit we might acquire from Latin countries is the serving of a bowlful at every meal. It's odd that in this country many people seem to think of fresh fruit as an ornament to be displayed on the sideboard and eaten only as a snack between meals.

Nevertheless there are, of course, good reasons for making more elaborate desserts occasionally – indeed, if you want to give a sense of occasion to a meal, they are essential. And, it has to be said, just as many vegans as omnivores are gluttons. (It's a curious fact that few of the population at large can begin to comprehend that one can be a gourmet, a glutton and a vegan without difficulty!) But the unexpected bonus with vegan food is that the most sensual delights imaginable are *not* cholesterol bombs and indeed that, provided you do not overindulge in them, they are often actually a good, healthy form of nutrition.

A word or two about trifles. All the ingredients for a delicious vegan trifle are given in this book but we haven't given a specific recipe. Simply use any of the biscuit or cake recipes that take your fancy as the base, add some fresh soft fruit, then make up a *Fruit Juice Jelly* (page 144) and top the whole thing with *Vanilla Dessert* (page 147), *Vegan Cream* (sweet or sour, page 238) or *Custard* (page 175). If you want to be really self-indulgent, pour some rum over the biscuit or cake base before adding the jelly, decorate the top with *Vegan Piping Cream* (page 241) and sprinkle with desiccated coconut or chopped nuts. Chill for at least two hours before serving.

FRUIT JUICE JELLY
allow 1½ hours to prepare
(including setting and chilling time)

To Serve 4

Imperial (Metric)		American
3 tbs	agar flakes	3 tbs
1 pint (½ litre)	fruit juice	2½ cups

1 Put the agar flakes into a small saucepan and add about a quarter of the fruit juice. Bring quickly to the boil then reduce heat and simmer for at least 5 minutes, stirring continuously. Remove from heat.
2 Add the rest of the fruit juice and stir well. Pour into individual serving-dishes.
3 Refrigerate till set.

Made with orange juice each serving (of 4) provides: 43 kcal, 1 g protein, 0 g fat, 11 g carbohydrate, 0 g fibre.

The individual jellies can be decorated with slices of fruit, topped with *Vegan Sour Cream* (page 240), *Cashew Cream* (page 242) or *Coconut Cream* (page 243), or simply served plain.

For parties and special occasions, make a layered jelly from two or three different juices, set in a ring mould. You can pile a fruit salad in the middle and decorate the whole thing with *Vegan Piping Cream* (page 241) and you will have an impressive party dish.

FRESH FRUIT FOOL
allow 40 minutes to prepare
(including ½ hour to chill)

To Serve 4

Imperial (Metric)		American
1	lemon	1
¼ pint (125 ml)	soya milk	½ cup
5 tbs (75 ml)	sunflower oil	5 tbs
1 lb (½ kg)	any suitable fresh fruit (see below)	1 lb

1 Grate the lemon rind and set the grated peel aside.
2 Squeeze the lemon and put the juice in a blender.
3 Add the soya milk and sunflower oil.
4 Core and peel the fruit (as necessary), then coarsely chop it, add it to the blender and blend till smooth and creamy.
5 Transfer the blended mixture to individual serving-dishes, sprinkle the grated lemon peel on top and chill for at least ½ hour before serving.

Each serving (of 4, with eating apples) provides: 243 kcal, 1 g protein, 19 g fat, 16 g carbohydrate, 3 g fibre.

Almost any fruit can be used to make this light, creamy fool – from eating apples to mangoes – and although it's so quick and easy to make it's succulent enough to serve at any gourmet meal – but note that fruit with a high water content such as melons will produce more like a milk shake consistency than a fool.

CREAMED APRICOTS
allow 10 minutes to prepare
(the day before serving)

To Serve 4

Imperial (Metric)		American
6 oz (180 g)	dried apricots	1½ cups
½ pint (¼ litre)	soya milk	1½ cups

1   Finely chop the apricots, divide them equally between four individual serving-dishes, pour a quarter of the soya milk into each and refrigerate overnight.
2   Serve chilled.

Each serving (of 4) provides: 100 kcal, 4 g protein, 1 g fat, 20 g carbohydrate, 11 g fibre.

This simple dessert works because the apricots gradually absorb liquid from the soya milk, turning it into a rich, thick, apricot-flavoured cream in the process. It's good just as it is, but try adding one of the following as a topping: *Vegan Sour Cream* (page 240), *Vanilla Dessert* (page 147) or *Fruit Juice Jelly* (page 144).

VANILLA DESSERT

allow 1¼ hours to prepare
(including 1 hour to chill)

To Serve 3–4

Imperial (Metric)		American
2 tbs	arrowroot powder	2 tbs
1 pint (½ litre)	soya milk	2½ cups
2 oz (60 g)	dark muscovado sugar	2 tbs
2 tbs (30 ml)	vanilla essence	2 tbs

1 Put the arrowroot in a small saucepan, add a little of the (cold) soya milk and stir until completely dissolved. Gradually add the rest of the soya milk, stirring continuously.

2 Stir in the other ingredients and bring to a simmer over a medium heat, still stirring continuously until the mixture thickens. Remove from heat, pour into individual serving-dishes and set aside to cool.

3 Refrigerate till needed. Serve chilled.

Each serving (of 4) provides: 121 kcal, 5 g protein, 2 g fat, 18 g carbohydrate, 2 g fibre.

Serve this simple dessert, just as it is, or pour it over sliced fresh fruit, muesli, chopped nuts, or use it as a topping for sweet flans, tarts or trifles.

For variety, add a tablespoonful of cocoa or carob powder at step 2. The addition of 3 tbs of rum or brandy lifts it into another category altogether.

BAKED BANANAS
allow ½ hour to prepare

To Serve 4

Imperial (Metric)		American
4	bananas	4
1	lemon	1
2 oz (60 g)	chopped nuts	3 tbs
1 oz (30 g)	margarine	2 tbs
3 tbs (45 ml)	red wine (optional)	3 tbs

1 Peel the bananas and lay them side by side in a shallow ovenproof dish.
2 Squeeze the lemon and pour the juice over the bananas.
3 Sprinkle the nuts over the bananas, dot with knobs of margarine and, if you wish, sprinkle with wine.
4 Bake in the middle of a fairly hot oven (375°F/190°C/gas mark 5) till deep brown (about 20–30 minutes).

Each serving (of 4) provides: 190 kcal, 2 g protein, 13 g fat, 15 g carbohydrate, 4 g fibre.

This is a simple way to turn 4 bananas into a special treat. Serve just as they are or try pouring *Vegan Single Cream* over (page 238), or serve with chilled *Vegan Yoghurt* (page 244).

BAKED APPLES
allow ¾ hour to prepare

Per Serving

Imperial (Metric)		American
1	large cooking apple	1
1–2 tbs	sultanas	1–2 tbs
1 tsp	maple syrup	1 tsp
½ tsp	lemon juice	½ tsp
	knob of margarine	

1 Wash and core the apples and make a shallow cut in the skin around their 'equators'.
2 Begin stuffing the hole left by the core with the sultanas; when it's about half full, pour in the maple syrup and lemon juice. Continue with the sultanas and press the filling in firmly, top with a knob of margarine and place on a baking-tray or ovenproof dish.
3 Bake in the middle of a moderate oven (350°F/177°C/gas mark 4) till the apples are just beginning to brown on top (about 30–40 minutes).

Each serving provides: 175 kcal, 1 g protein, negligible fat, 44 g carbohydrate, 9 g fibre.

These are good served hot, straight from the oven, just as they are, or topped with *Custard* (page 175), *Brandy Sauce* (page 177) or *Vegan Single Cream* (page 238) but they are also good chilled and decorated with *Piping Cream* (page 241).

PEACH PUDDING
allow 1 hour to prepare

To Serve 6

Imperial (Metric)		American
	Batter Mixture (page 258)	
3 oz (90 g)	raw demerara sugar	5 tbs
6	large peaches	6

1 Make up a batter mixture, add the sugar and stir till thoroughly dissolved.
2 Wash, stone and coarsely chop the peaches and stir them into the batter mixture.
3 Preheat an oven to very hot (450°F/232°C/gas mark 8).
4 Lightly grease a shallow, ovenproof dish with margarine.
5 Pour in the fruit mixture and bake in the middle of the oven for 35 minutes. Serve hot or cold.

Each serving (of 6) provides: 292 kcal, 8 g protein, 11 g fat, 40 g carbohydrate, 6 g fibre.

This is moist enough to serve on its own but try it also with *Brandy Sauce* (page 177), *Vegan Cream* (page 238) or *Custard* (page 175). Any leftovers can either be served chilled or used in a trifle.

For variety, try fresh apricots, plums or any soft summer fruit instead of peaches.

APPLE AND BANANA CRUMBLE
allow 1¼ hours to prepare

To Serve 8

Imperial (Metric)		American
1 lb (½ kg)	cooking apples	2 large
2	bananas	2
2 oz (60 g)	raisins	2 tbs
1½ tbs (25 ml)	apple concentrate	1½ tbs
½ lb (¼ kg)	wholewheat flour	2 cups
2 oz (60 g)	sunflower seeds	½ cup
1½ tbs	raw demerara sugar	1½ tbs
¼ lb (125 g)	margarine	½ cup
2 tbs	sesame seeds	2 tbs

1   Wash, core and chop the apples (peel them if you wish) and put them in an ovenproof dish.
2   Peel and chop the bananas and add them to the dish together with the raisins and mix thoroughly. Pour the apple concentrate over the fruit mixture.
3   Put the flour, sunflower seeds and sugar into a separate bowl and mix them together. Cut and rub in the margarine till the mixture resembles coarse breadcrumbs.
4   Pour the crumble mixture over the fruit, dot with knobs of margarine, sprinkle with the sesame seeds and bake in a fairly hot oven (375°F/190°C/gas mark 5) for 50 minutes.

Each serving (of 8) provides: 383 kcal, 7 g protein, 20 g fat, 45 g carbohydrate, 7 g fibre.

This makes a substantial dessert which is ideal as a warming winter pudding especially if served with *Brandy Sauce* (page 177).

For variety, try *pear and banana* or *rhubarb and date* for the filling.

APPLE PIE
allow 1 hour to prepare

To Serve 8–10

Imperial (Metric)		American
1½ × qty	*Basic Shortcrust Pastry* (page 207)	1½ × qty
3 oz (90 g)	chopped dates	¾ cup
½ pint (¼ litre)	water	1¼ cups
1½ lb (¾ kg)	cooking apples	3 large
¼ lb (125 g)	raisins	¾ cup
1 tsp	ground cinnamon	1 tsp
4	whole cloves	4
1½ tbs (25 ml)	apple concentrate	1½ tbs

1   While the pastry is chilling in the refrigerator, chop the dates and put them in a large saucepan with the water over a low heat and simmer till they begin to distintegrate.
2   Wash, core and finely chop the apples (peel them if you wish) and add them to the pan together with the raisins, cinnamon and cloves. Stir well, then partially cover and simmer gently for 15 minutes.
3   Remove from heat, stir in the apple concentrate and set aside.
4   Roll out ⅔ of the pastry and line a greased, floured pie or flan dish. Fill with the apple mixture.
5   Roll out the rest of the pastry and, after moistening the rim of the pastry base with cold water, use to form the pie crust. Use your forefingers and thumb to pinch the edges together to seal the lid to the base and form decorative scallops. Decorate the centre with the pastry trimmings and cut a few slits with a sharp knife to allow steam to escape.
6   Bake in the middle of a moderate oven (350°F/177°C/gas mark 4) for 30 minutes.

Each serving (of 10) provides: 259 kcal, 4 g protein, 11 g fat, 38 g carbohydrate, 6 g fibre.

This is delicious served hot, straight from the oven, with chilled *Vegan Yoghurt* (page 244), *Vegan Double Cream* (page 239) or cold with *Hot Chocolate Sauce* (page 176).

CARAMEL CREAM PUDDING

allow about 1½ hours to prepare
(including 1 hour to chill and set)

To Serve 6

Imperial (Metric)		American
¼ lb (125 g)	raw muscovado sugar	5 tbs
3 tbs (45 ml)	water	3 tbs
5 oz (150 g)	tofu	⅔ cup
4 tsp	vanilla essence	4 tsp
1 pint (½ litre)	soya milk	2½ cups
1½ tbs	agar flakes	1½ tbs

(Note: if you haven't made caramel creams before, read the remarks below before trying to turn them out of their moulds.)

1 Put the sugar and water in a small saucepan over a low heat, bring to the boil (stirring often) and simmer for 5 minutes, uncovered, to make a caramel mixture.
2 Crumble the tofu into a blender, add 1 tablespoon of the caramel mixture and the vanilla essence, and set aside.
3 Pour the rest of the caramel mixture equally into six individual moulds (or small bowls, or cups) and rotate each in turn to coat the base and sides. Set aside.
4 Pour the soya milk into the same saucepan, add the agar flakes, bring quickly to the boil then reduce heat and simmer for 5 minutes, stirring continuously.
5 Add the hot soya milk to the crumbled tofu in the blender and blend to a smooth cream.
6 Pour the blended mixture equally in each of the moulds and set aside to cool.
7 Refrigerate till set.
8 Turn out on to individual dishes (saucers are ideal) and serve chilled.

Each serving (of 6) provides: 108 kcal, 4 g protein, 2 g fat, 17 g carbohydrate, 2 g fibre.

To get the puddings out of their moulds, proceed as follows: first tip and rotate each mould till the caramel mixture separates the filling from the side; then place your chosen dish on top of the mould taking care to position it exactly in the centre; invert the whole thing, raise it up to shoulder high, bring it down again to waist high and stop it suddenly. You should hear it drop on to the dish. Be sure to position the mould carefully in the centre of the dish because once the pudding has dropped you won't be able to move it again.

ORANGE AND CHOCOLATE MOUSSE

allow 1½ hours to prepare
(including 1 hour to chill)

To Serve 6

Imperial (Metric)		American
1	orange	1
2 tsp	lemon juice	2 tsp
1 pint (½ litre)	soya milk	2½ cups
3 tbs (45 ml)	maple syrup	3 tbs
1 tsp	vanilla essence	1 tsp
5 tbs	unsweetened cocoa powder	5 tbs
¼ pint (125 ml)	sunflower oil	½ cup

1 Finely grate the orange and put the grated peel in a blender.
2 Squeeze the orange and add the juice to the blender together with the lemon juice.
3 Add all the remaining ingredients except the oil and blend till thoroughly mixed.
4 Slowly add the oil a little at a time while continuing to blend until the mixture thickens.
5 Pour into individual serving-dishes and chill for at least an hour before serving.

**Each serving (of 6) provides: 282 kcal, 4 g protein, 23 g fat,
11 g carbohydrate, 1 g fibre.**

This is at its best served on the day of its preparation, garnished with a twist of orange. If you have leftovers that begin to separate, stir with a spoon just before serving.

For variety, try carob powder instead of cocoa.

AVOCADO AND COCONUT WHIP

allow 1¼ hours to prepare
(including 1 hour to chill)

To Serve 4–6

Imperial (Metric)		American
3 oz (90 g)	creamed coconut	⅓ cup
¼ pint (125 ml)	boiling water	½ cup
2	large ripe avocados	2
¼ pint (125 ml)	soya milk	½ cup
3 tbs (45 ml)	maple syrup	3 tbs
2 tsp	fresh chopped mint (or 1 tsp dried mint)	2 tsp

1 Put the creamed coconut and the boiling water in a small bowl and stir till completely dissolved.
2 Scoop out the flesh of the avocados and put it in a blender together with all the other ingredients (including the melted coconut) and blend to a smooth rich cream.
3 Pour into individual serving-dishes and decorate each with sprigs of fresh mint. Chill for at least an hour before serving.

Each serving (of 6) provides: 240 kcal, 4 g protein, 22 g fat, 7 g carbohydrate, 6 g fibre.

Avocados are unusual among fruit in being rich in both vegetable oils and protein so, as your guests indulge themselves in this sumptuous pale green dessert, they can comfort themselves with the thought that, unlike so many comparable non-vegan dishes, it isn't *bad* for them!

If you can't get fresh mint, use dried in the recipe and decorate with chopped nuts, pomegranate seeds or thin slices of lemon or orange.

Note that it doesn't keep well so don't make more than you need.

FRESH FRUIT TART

allow 2 hours to prepare
(including 1 hour to set and chill)

To Serve 8–12

Imperial (Metric)		American
¼ lb (125 g)	wholewheat flour	1 cup
¼ lb (125 g)	ground almonds	1 cup
1 oz (30 g)	raw demerara sugar	1 tbs
1 oz (30 g)	sesame seeds	2 tbs
5 oz (150 g)	margarine	⅔ cup
3	kiwi (or other soft tropical) fruit	3
½ lb (¼ kg)	black grapes	½ lb
1 pint (½ litre)	white grape juice	2½ cups
3 tbs	agar flakes	3 tbs

1 Put the flour, ground almonds, sugar and sesame seeds in a bowl and mix thoroughly. Cut in the margarine and rub together till well blended.
2 Transfer the mixture to a greased, floured flan dish (about 9 in [23 cm] is the right size). Gently push down and smooth out the mixture till it lines the side and base of the dish, using your forefingers and thumb to shape the edge into decorative scallops. Bake in the middle of a moderate oven (350°F/177°C/gas mark 4) for 15 minutes. Remove from oven and leave to cool on a rack.
3 Meanwhile, peel and slice the kiwi fruit, and halve and pip the grapes. When the flan case is cool, arrange the fruit decoratively to cover the whole base.
4 Put ¼ pint (125 ml/½ cup) of the grape juice in a small saucepan with the agar flakes, bring quickly to the boil then reduce heat and simmer for 5 minutes, stirring continuously. Remove from heat, add to the rest of the grape juice and mix thoroughly.
5 Taking care not to disturb your artistic arrangement, slowly pour the grape juice into the flan case.
6 Refrigerate for at least an hour before serving.

Each serving (of 12) provides: 253 kcal, 4 g protein, 17 g fat, 21 g carbohydrate, 3 g fibre.

This looks gorgeous and, unlike many of the things you see in cake-shop windows, isn't even bad for you! If you want to make it even more fancy, decorate it with *Piping Cream* (page 241).

For variety, try other combinations of juice or fruit. For example, peaches with red grape juice, or strawberries with apple juice; or use cherries instead of grapes (they need to be stoned, though).

BANANA TART
allow 1½ hours to prepare
(if you have the pre-baked flan shell and including 1 hour to chill)

To Serve 8

Imperial (Metric)		American
1	*Pre-Baked Flan Shell* (page 207)	1
3	large ripe bananas	3
5 tbs	fine cornmeal (or cornflour)	5 tbs
2 oz (60 g)	raw demerara sugar	3 tbs
1 pint (½ litre)	soya milk	2½ cups
1 tsp	vanilla essence	1 tsp

1 Slice one of the bananas and arrange the slices on the base of the pre-baked flan shell. Mash the other two and set aside.
2 Put the cornmeal and sugar into a saucepan and mix together thoroughly before slowly adding the soya milk and combining to a creamy consistency. Place over a low heat and stir continuously till the mixture thickens. Remove from heat.
3 Stir in the vanilla essence and the mashed bananas and mix well before pouring into the flan shell. Smooth the top and chill for at least an hour before serving.

Each serving (of 8) provides: 308 kcal, 6 g protein, 14 g fat, 40 g carbohydrate, 5 g fibre.

The only reason we've put this tart in the 'special occasions' section is that it is a bit too rich for everyday use, but it is certainly not time consuming or expensive to make. Try decorating it with chopped nuts or, for an exotic finish to a really special dinner-party, add a generous topping of *Coconut Cream* (page 243).

CHOCOLATE TART

allow 2½ hours to prepare
(if you have the pre-baked flan shell and including 2 hours to chill)

To Serve 8

Imperial (Metric)		American
1	Pre-baked Sweet Pastry Shell (page 208)	1
2 oz (60 g)	cocoa powder (unsweetened)	8 tbs
2 oz (60 g)	fine cornmeal (or cornflour)	8 tbs
5 oz (150 g)	raw sugar	1 cup
1½ pints (¾ litre)	soya milk	3½ cups
1 tsp	vanilla essence	1 tsp

1 Put the cocoa powder, cornmeal and sugar into a large saucepan and mix thoroughly.

2 Add the soya milk a little at a time and mix to a smooth creamy consistency taking care to break down any lumps.

3 Stir in the vanilla essence.

4 Use a low heat to bring the mixture to the boil very very slowly, stirring continuously. Simmer and continue stirring till the mixture thickens (about 5–10 minutes). Then as quickly as you can remove from heat and pour into the pastry shell. (With practice, you can get it to form attractive scallops by revolving the shell as you pour.) Set aside to cool for half an hour.

5 Chill for at least 1½ hours before serving.

Each serving (of 8) provides: 344 kcal, 8 g protein, 15 g fat, 46 g carbohydrate, 5 g fibre.

Serve this delicious tart with *Vegan Cream* (page 238), freshly-brewed black coffee and brandy to round off a special dinner-party and your guests will wonder where they ever got the idea that vegans were practising a masochistic form of self-denial!

For variety, use carob powder instead of cocoa or try piping the tart with *Vegan Piping Cream* (page 241).

FRUIT FLAN
allow 1½ hours to prepare
(including 1 hour to cool and set but assuming
you have the pre-baked flan shell and have
pre-soaked the dried fruit: if not, see below)

To Serve 8

Imperial (Metric)		American
1	Pre-Baked Flan Shell (page 207)	1
1½ pints (¾ litre)	water	3½ cups
½ lb (¼ kg)	dried apricots	2 cups
6 oz (180 g)	prunes	1½ cups
½ pint (¼ litre)	soya milk	1¼ cups
2½ tbs	agar flakes	2½ tbs
1 oz (30 g)	chopped nuts (for decoration)	1½ tbs

1　Cover the apricots and prunes with the water and leave to soak for several hours or overnight.
2　Remove the stones from the now soft prunes and discard them. Put the prune flesh, the apricots, the soya milk and half of the remaining soaking liquid into a blender and blend to a smooth cream.
3　Add the agar flakes to the rest of the soaking liquid (adding a little extra water if necessary) and bring quickly to the boil then reduce heat and simmer for 5 minutes while stirring continuously.
4　Combine the blended mixture with the agar solution and stir thoroughly.
5　Pour into the flan shell, decorate with chopped nuts and refrigerate till set. Serve chilled.

Each serving (of 8) provides: 321 kcal, 7 g protein, 14 g fat, 45 g carbohydrate, 15 g fibre.

The only complicated thing about this flan is remembering to soak the dried fruit the previous night. But even if you forgot, you can still make it: simply *stew* the fruit in the recipe liquid till it's soft and then proceed from step 2 above.

The filling is moist enough for the flan to be delicious served on its own, but try also serving it with *Custard* (page 175), *Brandy Sauce* (page 177), *Vegan Cream* (page 238), *Cashew Cream* (page 242) or *Vegan Yoghurt* (page 244).

BANANA CURD CAKE
allow 3 hours to prepare
(including 2 hours to set and chill)

To Serve 8–12

Imperial (Metric)		American
3 oz (90 g)	wholewheat flour	¾ cup
3 oz (90 g)	ground almonds	¾ cup
1 oz (30 g)	raw sugar	1 tbs
¼ lb (125 g)	margarine	½ cup
¾ lb (350 g)	tofu	1½ cups
4	ripe bananas	4
½ pint (¼ litre)	soya milk	1¼ cups
7 tbs (100 ml)	sunflower oil	7 tbs
	juice of 1 lemon	
½ pint (¼ litre)	apple juice	1¼ cups
3 tbs	agar flakes	3 tbs

1 Put the flour, ground almonds and sugar in a bowl and mix thoroughly. Cut in the margarine and rub together till well blended.

2 Transfer the mixture to a greased, floured cake or similar tin with a loose bottom, about 8 in (20 cm). Gently smooth out and push down the mixture till it evenly covers the base of the tin. Bake in the middle of a moderate oven (350°F/177°C/gas mark 4) for 15 minutes. Remove from oven and leave to cool in the tin.

3 Crumble the tofu into a blender, add the peeled and chopped bananas, soya milk, sunflower oil and lemon juice and blend till smooth and creamy.

4 Put the apple juice and agar flakes into a small saucepan and bring quickly to the boil then reduce heat and simmer for 5 minutes, stirring continuously. Remove from heat, add to the blended banana and tofu mixture and stir till thoroughly combined.

5 Now pour the mixture on to the pastry base in the tin and refrigerate till set and chilled (about 2 hours).

Each serving (of 12) provides: 281 kcal, 6 g protein, 23 g fat, 14 g carbohydrate, 3 g fibre.

Serve this with freshly-brewed black coffee as a dessert course, or as a snack any time.

The top may be decorated with thin slices of lemon, chopped nuts or *Piping Cream* (page 241).

LEMON CHEESECAKE
allow 3 hours to prepare
(including baking and chilling times)

To Serve 12–16

Imperial (Metric)		American
1	Basic Sweet Pastry mix (page 208)	1
4	lemons	4
1¼ lb (575 g)	firm tofu (see below)	2½ cups
¼ pint (125 ml)	soya milk	½ cup
¼ pint (125 ml)	sunflower oil	½ cup
¼ lb (125 g)	raw demerara sugar	¾ cup
1½ tbs (25 ml)	vanilla essence	1½ tbs

1   While the pastry is chilling in the refrigerator, finely grate the lemon rinds and put the grated peel in a blender, then squeeze the lemons and add the juice.
2   Add all the other ingredients and blend together till the mixture is smooth and creamy.
3   If you have a 9 in (23 cm) baking-ring, put it on an ovenproof plate, roll out the pastry and line the base with it. Otherwise a pie, flan or cake tin with a loose bottom may be used. Pour in the blended mixture, smooth the top and bake in the middle of a warm oven (325°F/163°C/gas mark 3) for 1¼ hours. The finished cake will be a rich, golden brown on top.
4   Allow to cool on a rack and then chill thoroughly before attempting to remove from the baking-ring.
5   Decorate the top with thin slices of lemon, chopped nuts or toasted sesame seeds.

Each serving (of 16) provides: 225 kcal, 5 g protein, 15 g fat, 18 g carbohydrate, 3 g fibre.

We had some problems getting this exactly right. If you don't use *firm* tofu the finished cake may ooze water which, although it doesn't in any way detract from the pleasure of eating it, does complicate presenting and serving it. If you can't get firm tofu, press ordinary tofu between two boards for an hour to remove some of the excess water. Another problem we had was getting it to cook right through to the centre without burning the top and it may be that the timing will need to be adjusted to suit your particular oven.

However, the end result thoroughly justifies our effort. It tastes wonderful and, unlike its non-vegan counterpart, contains nothing that is bad for you. Nor does it sit heavily on the stomach if you succumb to the temptation to eat too much of it!

Serve it as a dessert course with freshly-brewed black coffee and it will turn a light meal into a feast.

RUM AND CHOCOLATE CHEESECAKE
allow 3 hours to prepare
(including baking and chilling time)

To Serve 12–16

Imperial (Metric)		American
¼ lb (125 g)	wholewheat flour	1 cup
¼ lb (125 g)	ground almonds	1 cup
7 oz (225 g)	raw demerara sugar	1¼ cups
5 oz (150 g)	margarine	scant ⅔ cup
1½ lb (¾ kg)	firm tofu	3 cups
6 fl oz (175 ml)	sunflower oil	¾ cup
6 fl oz (175 ml)	dark rum	¾ cup
¼ pint (125 ml)	soya milk	½ cup
2 oz (60 g)	unsweetened cocoa powder	7 tbs
½ tbs	vanilla essence	½ tbs

1 Put the flour, ground almonds and 1 tbs of the sugar in a bowl and mix well together, then rub in the margarine to form a firm dough.

2 If you have a 9 in (23 cm) baking-ring, put it on an ovenproof plate. Flatten the dough between your hands, put it in the baking-ring and press it down firmly to form a smooth, thick base. Alternatively, use a pie, flan or cake tin.

3 Crumble the tofu into a blender, add all the remaining ingredients and blend together till smooth and creamy. (You may need to do this in two goes.)

4 Pour the blended mixture over the pastry base and bake in the middle of a warm oven (325°F/163°C/gas mark 3) for 1¼ hours.

5 Allow to cool on a rack and then chill thoroughly before attempting to remove from the baking-ring or tin.

Each serving (of 16) provides: 368 kcal, 8 g protein, 26 g fat, 19 g carbohydrate, 3 g fibre.

This tastes wonderful just as it is without any decoration but you may wish to arrange halved strawberries around the rim and sprinkle chopped nuts in the centre. If you want to serve it as a spectacular finale to a really special meal, ice it with *Piping Cream* (page 241) as well.

Sauces and Dressings

Sauces

Dressings

Sauces and Dressings

Our object in this section is to demonstrate that it is perfectly feasible – even easy – to make a wide range of vegan sauces and dressings. Indeed, it's an area in which it is a pleasure to be inventive and imaginative. And it is well worth the effort, for a good sauce can turn any simple steamed or blanched vegetable into a memorable dish.

We've given a range of savoury and sweet sauces and dressings to get you started and advise you not to be put off by the mystique that seems in some quarters to be associated with sauce-making – as if they were in a different category from ordinary cooking. This is nonsense. They are as easy to make as anything else provided you're prepared to follow simple instructions. The only secret, if you can call it that, of smooth, lump-free sauces is *continuous stirring*. But they do spoil quickly so always make them last – just before serving the dish they are to accompany.

For the most part we have used 100 per cent wholewheat flour as a thickening agent. Why is *whiteness* in a sauce supposed to be superior? Sauces made with 100 per cent wholewheat flour are not only better for you but actually have an attractive, nutty flavour of their own.

We have also occasionally specified *arrowroot* when we wanted a thin or transparent sauce. This is available in most wholefood shops (sometimes for some mysterious reason labelled with its Japanese name '*kuzu*') and also in some grocery stores – though we suspect that chemical preservatives may have been added in this case.

Finally, a word or two about salad dressings. Vitamins A, D, E, and K are all oil-soluble. This means they are only assimilable if some oil is eaten at the same time, so there is a sound nutritional reason for serving a salad of raw vegetables with an oil-based dressing.

Sunflower oil has probably the most pleasant and unobtrusive flavour, is cheap and widely available and is completely free of saturated fat (unlike palm or coconut oils). So it's a good basis for most dressings where other oils aren't specifically mentioned. But cold-pressed olive oil is essential for some dishes for the unique taste it contributes. We have used it sparingly only because it is so expensive in this country. But if you should find yourself travelling in the Mediterranean region, don't forget to bring back as large a tin of it as you can carry and stash it away in your larder for a sunny day.

BASIC PLAIN SAUCE
allow 5–10 minutes to prepare

To Make 4–6 Average Servings

Imperial (Metric)		American
1 oz (30 g)	margarine	2 tbs
3 tbs	100 per cent wholewheat flour	3 tbs
½ pint (¼ litre)	soya milk	1¼ cups

(Note: if you haven't made a sauce before, read the introductory remarks on page 165 before beginning.)

1 Melt the margarine in a (preferably thick) saucepan over a low heat.
2 When it has completely melted but before it begins to bubble, add the flour and stir in. Continue to heat gently and stir for 2–3 minutes.
3 Add the soya milk a little at a time, stirring continuously. Continue stirring after you've added the full amount until the mixture thickens.
4 The sauce is now ready for the appropriate flavouring.

Each serving (of 6) provides: 61 kcal, 2 g protein, 5 g fat, 3 g carbohydrate, 1 g fibre.

This makes a thick, plain sauce to which you can add flavourings as desired. It forms the basis of several recipes. To make a thinner sauce, simply use more milk.

BASIL AND TOMATO SAUCE
allow 10 minutes to prepare

To Make 4 Average Servings

Imperial (Metric)		American
1 lb (½ kg)	fresh or tinned tomatoes	1 lb
1 oz (30 g)	margarine	2 tbs
1½ tbs	wholewheat flour	1½ tbs
2 tbs	fresh chopped basil (or 1 tbs dried basil)	2 tbs
1 tsp	freshly-ground black pepper	1 tsp
1 tsp	salt	1 tsp

1 Liquidize the skinned tomatoes (page 259) in a blender and set aside.
2 Melt the margarine in a small saucepan over a low heat, stir in the flour and cook gently for a few minutes.
3 Stir in the liquidized tomatoes a little at a time. Now add the remaining ingredients, stirring continuously. Bring to the boil then reduce heat and simmer, still stirring, till the mixture thickens slightly. Serve immediately.

Each serving (of 4) provides: 80 kcal, 1 g protein, 6 g fat, 5 g carbohydrate, 2 g fibre.

This strong, richly-coloured sauce is at its best made with fresh basil but is still very good made with dried. Serve it with lightly-boiled new potatoes, or any other steamed or blanched vegetable that takes your fancy. It's also good with *Plain Rice* (page 94) or *Olive and Potato Flan* (page 74).

SAVOURY APPLE SAUCE
allow 25 minutes to prepare

To Make 4 Average Servings

Imperial (Metric)		American
1	medium cooking apple	1
¼ pint (125 ml)	water	½ cup
2 tsp	celery seeds	2 tsp
¼ pint (125 ml)	soya milk	½ cup
	salt and pepper to taste	

1 Peel, core and chop the apple, put it in a small saucepan together with the water and celery seeds, bring to the boil then reduce heat and simmer, uncovered, till the apple has gone to a mush (about 15 minutes).
2 Remove from heat, stir in the soya milk, season with salt and pepper to taste and serve.

Each serving (of 4) provides: 34 kcal, 1 g protein, 1 g fat, 6 g carbohydrate, 1 g fibre.

This light sauce goes well with simple steamed or blanched vegetables such as cauliflower, broccoli, Brussels sprouts, or even potatoes. It is also a good accompaniment to any main dish that seems a bit dry, such as *Cashew Loaf* (page 89) or *Bulgur Bake* (page 59), or rice or any cooked grain.

RED WINE SAUCE

allow 5–10 minutes to prepare

To Make 4–6 Average Servings

Imperial (Metric)		American
1 oz (30 g)	margarine	2 tbs
3 tbs	wholewheat flour	3 tbs
8 fl oz (¼ litre)	dry red wine	1 cup
¼ pint (125 ml)	soya milk	½ cup
	salt and pepper to taste	

1 Melt the margarine in a small saucepan over a low heat.
2 When it's completely melted but before it begins to bubble, add the flour and stir in. Continue to heat gently and stir for 2–3 minutes.
3 Add the red wine a little at a time, stirring continuously, then begin adding the soya milk a little at a time. Continue stirring after you've added the full amount until the mixture thickens.
4 Add salt and pepper to taste and serve.

Each serving (of 6) provides: 77 kcal, 1 g protein, 4 g fat, 3 g carbohydrate, 1 g fibre.

This is a good, simple sauce just as it is, but try also adding finely chopped mushrooms, onions or mixed herbs; or stir in 2 tbs of peanut butter after step 3.

It goes well with any steamed or blanched green vegetable, sautéed mushrooms or any root vegetable to make an appetizing side dish.

LEMON CURRY SAUCE

allow 10 minutes to prepare

To Make 4 Average Servings

Imperial (Metric)		American
¾ tbs	arrowroot powder	¾ tbs
½ pint (¼ litre)	soya milk	1¼ cups
1½ tbs (25 ml)	lemon juice	1½ tbs
2 tsp	*Garam Masala* (page 257)	2 tsp
½ tsp	ground turmeric	½ tsp
½ tsp	salt	½ tsp

1 Put the arrowroot into a small saucepan, add a little cold soya milk and stir till completely dissolved, then stir in the rest of the milk.
2 Stir in all the remaining ingredients and bring the mixture slowly to the boil, stirring continuously, then reduce heat and simmer till the sauce thickens. Serve immediately.

Each serving (of 4) provides: 42 kcal, 3 g protein, 1 g fat, 4 g carbohydrate, 1 g fibre.

This low-fat sauce is excellent with any steamed or blanched vegetable, cooked grain or pulse, but is particularly good with boiled potatoes.

Leftovers are good served chilled as a starter.

SWEET AND SOUR SAUCE
allow 10 minutes to prepare

To Make 4–6 Average Servings

Imperial (Metric)		American
1½ tbs (25 ml)	oil	1½ tbs
2	cloves garlic	2
2 tbs	freshly grated ginger (or 1 tbs dried ginger)	2 tbs
¾ tbs	arrowroot powder	¾ tbs
½ pint (¼ litre)	water	1¼ cups
1½ tbs (25 ml)	cider vinegar	1½ tbs
1½ tbs	tomato paste	1½ tbs
1½ tbs (25 ml)	soya sauce	1½ tbs
3 tbs (45 ml)	apple concentrate or raw demerara sugar	3 tbs

1 Put the oil in a small saucepan over a low heat. Skin and crush the garlic and add it to the pan. Finely grate the ginger and add it to the pan. Heat gently for a few minutes, stirring occasionally.
2 Meanwhile, dissolve the arrowroot in the cold water then add all the remaining ingredients and stir till well combined.
3 Pour the arrowroot mixture in the saucepan and bring to a simmer, stirring continuously, till the mixture thickens.

Each serving (of 6) provides: 74 kcal, 1 g protein, 4 g fat, 4 g carbohydrate, **negligible fibre.**

This can be poured over stir-fried vegetables to make the traditional Chinese dish, or over any steamed or blanched vegetable to turn it into a tasty and unusual side dish.

Perfectionists may wish to sieve the sauce (after step 3) prior to serving in order to remove the small pieces of grated garlic and ginger, but these two lazy cooks prefer to leave them in.

SPICY PEANUT SAUCE
allow 10 minutes to prepare

To Make 6 Average Servings

Imperial (Metric)		American
1	clove garlic	1
2 tbs	freshly grated ginger (or 1 tbs dried ginger)	2 tbs
1	lemon	1
7 tbs (100 ml)	sunflower oil	7 tbs
1½ tbs (25 ml)	soya sauce	1½ tbs
½ tsp	chilli powder	½ tsp
3 tbs	peanut butter	3 tbs
1½ tbs (25 ml)	water	1½ tbs

1 Skin and crush the garlic and put it in a blender.
2 Grate the ginger in with the garlic.
3 Squeeze the lemon and add the juice.
4 Add all the other ingredients and blend to a rich, creamy texture. If it seems too thick, add a little more water and blend again. Check the seasoning and adjust if necessary before serving.

Each serving (of 6) provides: 210 kcal, 2 g protein, 21 g fat, 3 g carbohydrate, 1 g fibre.

This can be served cold, but is equally good gently heated in a small saucepan and poured hot over a mixed salad. Other suggestions are given under individual recipes.

Try also serving it as a dip – with *Plain Oatcakes* (page 220) or with sticks of raw carrot, fennel or celery.

ORANGE AND COCONUT SAUCE

allow 10 minutes to prepare

To Make 4–6 Average Servings

Imperial (Metric)		American
1 oz (30 g)	margarine	2 tbs
1½ tbs	wholewheat flour	1½ tbs
½ pint (¼ litre)	orange juice	1¼ cups
½ tsp	salt	½ tsp
3 oz (90 g)	creamed coconut	⅓ cup

1   Melt the margarine in a small saucepan over a low heat.
2   When it's completely melted but before it begins to bubble, add the flour and stir in. Continue to heat gently and stir for 2–3 minutes.
3   Add the orange juice a little at a time, stirring continuously to avoid lumps.
4   Add the salt and coconut and continue to stir until all the coconut is dissolved. Bring to a simmer and serve.

Each serving (of 6) provides: 139 kcal, 1 g protein, 12 g fat,
6 g carbohydrate, 3 g fibre.

This is an unusual and fruity sauce that will liven up any steamed or blanched vegetable to give you a delicious side dish. Try it with cauliflower, broccoli or Brussels sprouts. It's also good poured over hot cooked grains such as rice or bulgur.

TOASTED ALMOND SAUCE
allow 20 minutes to prepare

To Make 4–6 Average Servings

Imperial (Metric)		American
¼ lb (125 g)	almonds	1 cup
½ pint (¼ litre)	soya milk	1¼ cups
1½ tbs (25 ml)	soya sauce	1½ tbs
1 tbs (15 ml)	red wine vinegar	1 tbs
	juice of ½ lemon	
½ tsp	mustard powder	½ tsp
½ tsp	ground nutmeg	½ tsp

1 Coarsely chop the almonds, put them in a dry pan over a medium heat and stir continuously till they are lightly toasted (about 5 minutes). Remove from pan and place in a blender.
2 Add all the other ingredients and blend till smooth.
3 If the sauce is to be used in a casserole and baked, it can be used just as it is. Otherwise, transfer to a small saucepan and heat gently till warmed through.

Each serving (of 6) provides: 136 kcal, 5 g protein, 12 g fat, 2 g carbohydrate, 4 g fibre.

This is good poured over steamed or blanched green vegetables just before serving or over a casserole before baking to get a crunchy topping.

For variety, use lemon juice instead of vinegar or ground cloves instead of nutmeg.

CUSTARD

allow 15 minutes to prepare

To Make 4–6 Average Servings

Imperial (Metric)		American
1½ tbs	arrowroot powder	1½ tbs
1 pint (½ litre)	soya milk	2½ cups
2 oz (60 g)	raw demerara sugar	3 tbs
1 tbs (15 ml)	vanilla essence	1 tbs
1½ tbs (25 ml)	lemon juice	1½ tbs

1 Put the arrowroot in a small saucepan, add a little of the cold soya milk and stir till completely dissolved. Now gradually add the rest of the milk, stirring continuously.
2 Stir in the sugar and vanilla essence and bring to a simmer over a medium heat, still stirring continuously, till the mixture thickens slightly. Reduce to a minimum heat.
3 Using a fork or whisk, beat in the lemon juice as slowly as possible till it's all in. Remove from heat and serve.

Each serving (of 6) provides: 84 kcal, 3 g protein, 1 g fat, 13 g carbohydrate, 2 g fibre.

This may be served hot, just as it is, poured over sweet flans and tarts, or poured into individual serving-dishes, chilled and decorated with slices of fresh fruit, or it can be used in trifles.

HOT CHOCOLATE SAUCE
allow 10 minutes to prepare

To Make 3–4 Average Servings

Imperial (Metric)		American
1 oz (30 g)	margarine	2 tbs
1½ tbs	fine cornmeal	1½ tbs
3 tbs	cocoa powder	3 tbs
3 tbs	raw demerara sugar	3 tbs
¾ pint (400 ml)	soya milk	2 cups

1 Melt the margarine in a small saucepan over a low heat, then add the cornmeal and cook gently for 2 minutes, stirring continuously.
2 Add the cocoa powder and sugar and continue to heat gently for a few more minutes, still stirring all the time.
3 Begin adding the soya milk a little at a time, still stirring continuously, till all the milk is in. Continue to stir and heat gently till the mixture thickens.

Each serving (of 4) provides: 132 kcal, 4 g protein, 9 g fat, 9 g carbohydrate, 1 g fibre.

Serve this rich creamy sauce hot with *Apple Pie* (page 152), *Apple and Banana Crumble* (page 151), *Fruit Juice Jellies* (page 144) or *Plain Ice-Cream* (page 246), or cold with fruit or in trifles. It can also be poured into individual serving-dishes, allowed to cool and then served chilled with a topping of chopped nuts.

BRANDY SAUCE
allow 10 minutes to prepare

To Make 3–4 Average Servings

Imperial (Metric)		American
1½ oz (45 g)	margarine	3 tbs
1½ tbs	fine cornmeal	1½ tbs
½ pint (¼ litre)	soya milk	1¼ cups
1½ tbs (25 ml)	maple syrup	1½ tbs
3 tbs (45 ml)	brandy	3 tbs
1 tsp	vanilla essence	1 tsp

1 Melt the margarine in a small saucepan over a low heat then add the cornmeal and cook gently for 2 minutes, stirring continuously.
2 Continuing to stir, add the soya milk a little at a time, then the maple syrup. Continue to heat gently and stir till the mixture thickens.
3 Remove from heat, stir in the brandy and vanilla essence and serve.

Each serving (of 4) provides: 140 kcal, 2 g protein, 10 g fat, 7 g carbohydrate, 1 g fibre.

This is delicious served hot with *Plain Ice Cream* (page 246), *Fruit Flan* (page 159), *Chocolate Tart* (page 158) or *Apple and Banana Crumble* (page 151); try it also cold with cold *Baked Apples* (page 149) or *Peach Pudding* (page 150). Any left over makes a delicious addition to trifle.

BASIC FRENCH DRESSING
allow 5–10 minutes to prepare

To Make a Jarful (275 ml)

Imperial (Metric)		American
1	lemon	1
1	clove garlic (optional)	1
1 tsp	salt	1
1 tsp	freshly-ground black pepper	1 tsp
½ tsp	mustard powder	½ tsp
	enough olive oil to fill a jam jar	

1 Squeeze the lemon and put the juice in a suitable jar – jam jars are perfect.
2 Skin and crush the garlic and add it to the jar.
3 Add the salt, pepper and mustard powder and fill the jar nearly to the top with olive (or other suitable vegetable) oil.
4 Seal the jar and shake well till all the ingredients are thoroughly mixed.

Each (2 tbs) serving provides: 252 kcal, negligible protein, 27 g fat, negligible carbohydrate, negligible fibre.

This dressing will keep well for days if stored in the fridge. When you finish a jar, immediately prepare another and this way you'll always have a dressing ready for your green and other salads.

For variety, try white wine vinegar, or cider vinegar, instead of lemon juice – each adds its own distinct flavour.

FRUIT JUICE DRESSING
allow 5 minutes to prepare

To Make 4–6 Average Servings

Imperial (Metric)		American
3 tbs (45 ml)	sunflower oil	3 tbs
5 tbs (75 ml)	orange (or other suitable) juice	5 tbs

1   Put the ingredients in a jar and mix thoroughly by shaking.

**Each serving (of 6) provides: 79 kcal, negligible protein, 8 g fat,
1 g carbohydrate, 0 g fibre.**

Most fruit juices can be used to make light and unusual dressings which go particularly well with the more substantial kinds of salad produced when you include grains, rice or potatoes; they also make a welcome change from the conventional savoury varieties. Orange, apple and grapefruit are especially suitable, but why not experiment with other, more exotic kinds? Perfectionists would, of course, use freshly-squeezed juice.

TAHINI DRESSING
allow 10 minutes to prepare

To Make a Jarful

Imperial (Metric)		American
1	lemon	1
5 tbs (75 ml)	tahini	5 tbs
5 tbs (75 ml)	olive oil	5 tbs
5 tbs (75 ml)	water	5 tbs
1½ tbs (25 ml)	soya sauce	1½ tbs

1 Squeeze the lemon and put the juice into a suitable jar. (Jam jars are perfect.)
2 Add all the other ingredients, seal the jar and shake till thoroughly mixed. Refrigerate till needed.

Each (3 tbs) serving provides: 272 kcal, 4 g protein, 27 g fat, 5 g carbohydrate, 2 g fibre.

This goes well with any kind of sprout salad, but try it also with potato salad, sliced raw courgettes, cauliflower or shredded cabbage.

TOFU DRESSING
allow 10 minutes to prepare

To Make a Jarful

Imperial (Metric)		American
¼ lb (125 g)	tofu	½ cup
2	cloves garlic	2
1	lemon	1
5 tbs (75 ml)	oil	5 tbs
5 tbs (75 ml)	water	5 tbs
1 tbs (15 ml)	soya sauce	1 tbs
½ tsp	mustard powder	½ tsp
½ tsp	salt	½ tsp
½ tsp	freshly-ground black pepper	½ tsp

1 Crumble the tofu into a blender.
2 Skin and crush the garlic and add it to the tofu.
3 Squeeze the lemon and add the juice.
4 Add all the remaining ingredients and blend to a thick, smooth, creamy consistency.

Each (3 tbs) serving provides: 154 kcal, 2 g protein, 16 g fat, 1 g carbohydrate, negligible fibre.

Use this dressing to turn almost any raw, chopped or grated vegetable into a delicious starter. Try it with finely chopped cucumbers, grated carrots or sliced courgettes. Or try pouring it over a steamed or blanched green vegetable as a side dish to a rich and substantial main course.

For variety, try adding a herb you particularly like, or a pinch of cayenne pepper to give it a spicy kick.

YOGHURT SALAD DRESSING
allow 5 minutes to prepare
(if you have the yoghurt)

To Make 4–6 Average Servings

Imperial (Metric)		American
¼ pint (125 ml)	*Vegan Yoghurt* (page 244)	½ cup
1 tsp	freshly grated ginger (or ½ tsp dried ginger)	1 tsp
	salt and pepper to taste	

1 Put all the ingredients in a salad bowl and mix thoroughly before adding the salad itself.

Each serving (of 6) provides: 13 kcal, 1 g protein, 1 g fat, 1 g carbohydrate, negligible fibre.

This is excellent with potato salad, cucumber, sliced raw courgettes, asparagus (page 137), cauliflower, or avocados. For variety, try using ground cinnamon or cloves instead of ginger.

CUCUMBER DRESSING
allow 10 minutes to prepare

To Make a Jarful (275 ml)

Imperial (Metric)		American
½	large cucumber	½
2 oz (60 g)	tofu	¼ cup
3 tbs (45 ml)	oil	3 tbs
1½ tbs (25 ml)	lemon juice	1½ tbs
1 tsp	mint	1 tsp
½ tsp	salt	½ tsp
½ tsp	freshly-ground black pepper	½ tsp

1 Coarsely chop the cucumber (peel it if you wish) and put it in a blender.
2 Crumble in the tofu.
3 Add the remaining ingredients and blend till smooth.
4 Transfer to a suitable storage jar (jam jars are perfect) and refrigerate till needed.

Each (3 tbs) serving provides: 65 kcal, 1 g protein, 7 g fat, 1 g carbohydrate, negligible fibre.

This is mild and refreshing and goes best with strong tastes such as tomatoes, carrots or peppers.

For variety, try using grapefruit instead of lemon juice.

CASHEW CREAM DRESSING

allow 5 minutes to prepare

To Make a Jarful

Imperial (Metric)		American
3 oz (90 g)	cashew pieces	¾ cup
¼ pint (125 ml)	soya milk	½ cup
	juice of 1 lemon	
1 tbs (15 ml)	soya sauce	1 tbs
½ tsp	freshly-ground black pepper	½ tsp

1 Put all the ingredients in a blender and blend to a thick, smooth, creamy consistency.
2 Transfer to a suitable storage jar (jam jars are perfect) and refrigerate till needed.

Each (3 tbs) serving provides: 82 kcal, 2 g protein, 7 g fat, 3 g carbohydrate, 2 g fibre.

This is rich, creamy and slightly sweet. Fill avocado halves to the brim with it and sprinkle on some celery seeds to make a starter, or serve it poured liberally over thinly-sliced tomatoes.

For variety, try white wine vinegar instead of lemon juice, or add a pinch of mustard.

MAYONNAISE
allow 10 minutes to prepare

To Make a Jarful

Imperial (Metric)		American
1	lemon	1
¼ pint (125 ml)	soya milk	½ cup
1 tbs (15 ml)	soya sauce (or ½ tsp salt)	1 tbs
5–6 tbs (75–90 ml)	olive oil	5–6 tbs

1 Squeeze the lemon and put the juice into a blender.
2 Add the soya milk and soya sauce (or salt).
3 Blend together while very slowly adding the oil till the mixture thickens.
4 Transfer to a suitable storage jar (jam jars are perfect) and chill till needed.

Each (3 tbs) serving provides: 140 kcal, 1 g protein, 14 g fat, 1 g carbohydrate, 1 g fibre.

The mayonnaise can be stored for several days sealed in its jar in the refrigerator.

Serve it on salads or as directed in recipes. Try it, for example, with potato salad, garnished with fresh chopped dill.

AVOCADO DRESSING
allow 10 minutes to prepare

To Make a Jarful

Imperial (Metric)		American
½	large ripe avocado	½
1	lemon	1
¼ pint (125 ml)	soya milk	½ cup
½ tsp	mixed spice	½ tsp
½ tsp	salt	½ tsp
½ tsp	freshly-ground black pepper	½ tsp

1 Scoop out the flesh of the avocado and put it in a blender.
2 Squeeze the lemon and add the juice.
3 Add all the remaining ingredients and blend to a rich, smooth, thick, creamy consistency.
4 Transfer to a suitable storage jar (jam jars are perfect) and refrigerate till needed.

Each (3 tbs) serving provides: 47 kcal, 2 g protein, 4 g fat,
1 g carbohydrate, 1 g fibre.

This sumptuous, pale-green dressing can be used exactly as you would use mayonnaise. It is at its best served immediately after making as, despite the presence of the lemon juice, it gradually darkens, though this does not affect its taste.

If you want to make it a little thinner, simply use some extra soya milk at step 3.

For variety, try adding 1 tbs freshly-grated ginger.

Spreads

Savoury Spreads

Tahini Spread   191
Cashew and Sunflower Spread   192
Savoury Spread   193
Tomato Spread   194
Savoury Apple Spread   195
Walnut and Garlic Spread   196
Chutney   197

Sweet Spreads

Carob and Banana Spread   198
Apple Butter   199
Almond and Apricot Spread   200
Date Spread   201

Spreads

Some of our vegan friends have remarked that the one thing they really miss from their pre-vegan days is *cheese* which they used to eat with bread as a quick snack or as one course of a large meal. Vegans often use peanut butter or tahini as a substitute, but we hope this section shows that it is easy to make a wide range of different savoury and sweet vegan spreads that can be served with wholewheat bread in just such a way.

Spreads are also good as travel food because if you take a jarful with you, all you need to acquire locally is some wholewheat bread and some fresh fruit and you're kitted out to remain blissfully vegan in an omnivore world.

Although wholefood shops seem to be providing an increasing number of vegan spreads these days, they do all appear to be extremely expensive. This is unjustified. The ingredients are cheap and readily obtainable and the preparation isn't difficult. Since most of these commercially produced spreads have the French word *'pâté'* on the tin, we suspect that they are simply cashing in on the snob-appeal of *pâté de foie gras* – traditionally taken, along with caviar, to represent the epitome of high living. So we hope our readers will permit us a digression on the subject. Literally translated, *pâté de foie gras* means 'Fatty Liver Paste' and it is in our view one of the most appalling products of the food industry. It is made by force-feeding geese literally by *screwing six pounds (three kilos) of fat-enriched maize down their throats at a time.* (This would be the equivalent in human terms of being force-fed twenty-eight pounds (thirteen kilos) of oily spaghetti!) The birds are restrained between sessions of this torture in cages so tiny that they cannot move – to prevent them from working off any of the fat by exercising. This mindless cruelty continues for weeks till their livers have nearly quadrupled in weight and they are then killed. How anyone could want to eat the diseased livers of these unfortunate, innocent creatures after such treatment beggars the imagination and those who buy even one jar of the end product should reflect that they are guilty of helping to perpetuate this unsavoury trade.

In any case it is completely unnecessary. Excellent spreads can be made without recourse to any animal remains whatever, as we hope we have adequately shown in this section.

Although many of our spread recipes take a bit of time to prepare, there are several that are really quick to make. Once you've made them, of course, you have them around to eat for days, even weeks, afterwards.

We've given a range of different techniques to get you started and hope that you'll soon be encouraged to start inventing your own – especially as jars of home-made spread make wonderfully welcome presents for vegan and omnivore friends alike.

TAHINI SPREAD
allow 10 minutes to prepare

To Make a Jarful

Imperial (Metric)		American
1	lemon	1
5 tbs (75 ml)	tahini	5 tbs
5 tbs (75 ml)	water	5 tbs
2 oz (60 g)	sunflower seeds	6 tbs
1½ tbs	miso	1½ tbs

1 Squeeze the lemon and put the juice in a blender.
2 Add the remaining ingredients and blend to a smooth, thick paste.

**Each (3 tbs) serving provides: 200 kcal, 7 g protein, 15 g fat,
11 g carbohydrate, 2 g fibre.**

This is strong and piquant and should be spread sparingly on plain biscuits
or bread. It also makes a good sandwich filling.

CASHEW AND SUNFLOWER SPREAD
allow 10–15 minutes to prepare

To Make a Jarful

Imperial (Metric)		American
4	spring onions (or 3 tbs freshly-chopped chives)	4
¼ lb (125 g)	cashew pieces	1 cup
¼ lb (125 g)	sunflower seeds	1 cup
¼ pint (125 ml)	water	½ cup
	salt and pepper to taste	

1 Wash, trim and chop the onions and put them in a blender.
2 Add all the other ingredients and blend to a thick, smooth paste.
  Transfer to a suitable storage jar and refrigerate till needed.

Each 100 g provides: 229 kcal, 6 g protein, 18 g fat, 12 g carbohydrate, 3 g fibre.

Particularly good in sandwiches, but try it also spread thinly on wholewheat bread, *Plain Oatcakes* (page 220) or crispbread; it also makes a good dip, served with sticks of celery, fennel or carrot.

SAVOURY SPREAD
allow ½ hour to prepare

To Make 3–4 Jarfuls

Imperial (Metric)		American
1 lb (½ kg)	potatoes	1 lb
¼ lb (125 g)	margarine	½ cup
2	medium onions	2
2	cloves garlic	2
½ lb (¼ kg)	mushrooms	½ lb
2 tbs	freshly ground ginger (or 1 tbs dried ground ginger)	
2 tsp	ground cloves	2 tsp
1½ tsp	ground nutmeg	1½ tsp
3 tsp	thyme	3 tsp
3 tbs (45 ml)	soya sauce	3 tbs
3 tbs	buckwheat flour	3 tbs
3 tbs	soya flour	3 tbs
	salt and pepper to taste	

1 Scrub the potatoes and remove any blemishes (and peel them if you wish), then slice and plunge them into a large pan of (unsalted) boiling water. Reduce heat and simmer till tender (about 8–12 minutes). Remove from heat and drain in a colander.
2 Put the margarine to melt in a large saucepan over a low heat. Meanwhile, skin and finely dice the onions and add them to the pan. Skin and crush the garlic and stir it in with the onions. Continue to sauté until the onion goes transparent.
3 Meanwhile, wash and finely dice the mushrooms and add them to the pan. Continue to cook gently, stirring often.
4 Grate the ginger directly into the pan, then stir in the cloves, nutmeg and thyme and continue heating gently and stirring for a few more minutes.
5 Remove from heat, add the soya sauce and cooked potatoes then the two flours and mash all the ingredients together till you have a smooth, creamy texture.
6 Season with salt and pepper to taste and transfer to suitable storage jars. Allow to cool before serving.

Each 100 g provides: 174 kcal, 2 g protein, 12 g fat, 12 g carbohydrate, 3 g fibre.

This is delicious in sandwiches, spread on *Plain Oatcakes* (page 220) or on crispbread. It also makes a good filling for pasties or individual savoury tarts.

For variety, try different combinations of herbs and spices.

TOMATO SPREAD
allow ½ hour to prepare

To Make 3–4 Jarfuls

Imperial (Metric)		American
1 lb (½ kg)	potatoes	1 lb
¼ lb (125 g)	margarine	½ cup
2	medium onions	2
¼ lb (125 g)	mushrooms	¼ lb
3 tbs (45 ml)	sunflower oil	3 tbs
6 tbs	tomato paste	6 tbs
2 tsp	marjoram (preferably freshly chopped)	2 tsp
2 tsp	basil (preferably freshly chopped)	2 tsp
½ tsp	cayenne pepper	½ tsp
3 tbs (45 ml)	soya sauce	3 tbs
3 tbs	buckwheat flour	3 tbs
3 tbs	soya flour	3 tbs
	salt and pepper to taste	

1 Scrub the potatoes and remove any blemishes (peel them if you wish), then slice and plunge them into a large pan of (unsalted) boiling water. Reduce heat and simmer till tender (about 8–12 minutes). Remove from heat and drain in a colander.

2 Put the margarine in a large saucepan over a low heat.

3 While it is melting, skin and finely dice the onions, add them to the pan and sauté until transparent.

4 Wash and finely dice the mushrooms, add to the pan with the sunflower oil and sauté till tender.

5 Stir in the tomato paste, marjoram, basil and cayenne and continue heating gently for a few more minutes.

6 Remove from heat, add the cooked potatoes and all the remaining ingredients and mash to a smooth, creamy texture.

7 Check the seasoning and transfer to suitable storage jars. Allow to cool before serving.

Each 100 g provides: 178 kcal, 3 g protein, 13 g fat, 13 g carbohydrate, 3 g fibre.

Use as a sandwich filling, or spread on plain biscuits or crispbread; or try cutting celery into bite-sized sticks and spreading it in the hollows.

For variety, try different combinations of herbs or add 2 tsp *Garam Masala* (page 257) at step 2 and omit the cayenne pepper.

SAVOURY APPLE SPREAD
allow ¾ hour to prepare

To Make 3–4 Jarfuls

Imperial (Metric)		American
½ lb (¼ kg)	brown lentils	1¼ cups
1½ pints (¾ litre)	water	3½ cups
1½ lb (¾ kg)	Bramley cooking apples	3 medium
1	large onion	1
1½ tbs (25 ml)	olive oil	1½ tbs
3 tbs	tahini	3 tbs
	salt and pepper to taste	

1 Put the lentils in a saucepan with the water and simmer, partially covered, till they soften. (Add more water from time to time, as necessary, to prevent them from sticking.)
2 Peel, core and slice the apples, put them in another saucepan with 2 tbs of water and cook to a mush.
3 Skin and finely chop the onion, place it in a frying-pan with the oil and sauté till it begins to brown.
4 Put all the ingredients together in the largest pan, add the tahini and salt and pepper to taste and mix well. The finished spread has a thick, crunchy texture.
5 Transfer the mixture to suitable storage jars (jam jars are perfect), seal and refrigerate till needed.

Each 100 g provides: 108 kcal, 5 g protein, 4 g fat, 15 g carbohydrate, 4 g fibre.

This makes a tasty sandwich filling or can be spread on wholewheat bread or crispbread as a light snack. Try also serving it as a dip with sticks of celery or carrot. It can also be used as a filling for pasties or individual savoury pies.

WALNUT AND GARLIC SPREAD
allow 10 minutes to prepare

To Serve 4–6

Imperial (Metric)		American
2	cloves garlic	2
½ lb (¼ kg)	walnuts	2 cups
7 tbs (100 ml)	olive oil	7 tbs
½ tsp	salt	½ tsp

1 Skin and crush the garlic and put it in a blender.
2 Add all the other ingredients and blend until the walnuts are reduced to tiny pieces.

Each serving (of 6) provides: 369 kcal, 4 g protein, 38 g fat, 2 g carbohydrate, 2 g fibre.

This is so rich that although the recipe makes only a little, it will go a long way. Try spreading it thinly on *Plain Oatcakes* (page 220) or crispbread.

The walnuts can be ground by hand, using a pestle and mortar and then mixed with the other ingredients – if you haven't got a blender.

For variety, try adding 5–6 tbs water at step 1 to make a less rich, smoother, creamier consistency that makes a good sandwich filling.

CHUTNEY
allow 1 hour to prepare

To Make 3–4 Jarfuls

Imperial (Metric)		American
2 tbs	pickling spice	2 tbs
½ pint (¼ litre)	cider vinegar	1¼ cups
1 lb (½ kg)	onions	2 large
1	large cooking apple	1
1 lb (½ kg)	tomatoes (preferably green)	1 lb
2 oz (60 g)	dried apricots	½ cup
2 tsp	mixed spice	2 tsp
¼ tsp	chilli powder	¼ tsp
2 tsp	salt	2 tsp
3 oz (90 g)	raisins	3 tbs
3 tbs (45 ml)	apple concentrate	3 tbs

1 Put the pickling spice and vinegar into a small saucepan, bring to the boil then reduce heat, cover and simmer for 10 minutes.
2 Meanwhile, finely chop the onions and put them in a large (preferably heavy) saucepan.
3 Coarsely chop the apple and the tomatoes and add them to the pan.
4 Strain in the vinegar (the pickling spices may now be discarded) and bring quickly to the boil, then reduce heat and simmer, covered, for 20 minutes, stirring often.
5 Halve the apricots and add them to the pan together with all the remaining ingredients and simmer for a further 20 minutes, still stirring often to prevent sticking.
6 Allow to cool and transfer to suitable storage jars – jam jars are ideal.

Each 100 g provides: 45 kcal, 1 g protein, 0 g fat, 10 g carbohydrate, 2 g fibre.

The vinegar acts as a preservative so you can make lots of this fruity chutney if you want to.

For variety, try adding at step 2 other finely chopped vegetables such as peppers, carrots or cauliflower, or add 1 tbs freshly-ground ginger (or 2 tsp dried ground ginger) or other spices to suit your own taste.

CAROB AND BANANA SPREAD
allow 10 minutes to prepare

To Make a Jarful

Imperial (Metric)		American
1 lb (½ kg)	bananas	3 large
1	lemon	1
¼ lb (125 g)	ground almonds	1 cup
3 tbs	carob powder	3 tbs

1 Peel the bananas and mash them to a pulp in a bowl.
2 Squeeze the lemon and add the juice.
3 Add the ground almonds and carob powder and continue to stir and mash to form a thick, smooth paste.

Each 100 g provides: 179 kcal, 5 g protein, 12 g fat, 15 g carbohydrate, 6 g fibre.

This nutritious spread makes a good substitute for margarine when spread on wholewheat bread.

Store in a sealed jar in the refrigerator and it will keep for a week or two.

For variety, use cocoa instead of carob powder.

APPLE BUTTER
allow 5 hours to prepare

To Make 3–4 Jarfuls

Imperial (Metric)		American
3 lb (1½ kg)	apples (see note)	3 lb
¾ pint (400 ml)	water	2 cups
2	lemons	2
½ lb (¼ kg)	raw sugar	1 cup
2 tsp	ground cinnamon	2 tsp
½ tsp	ground cloves (or 12 whole cloves)	½ tsp
½ tsp	ground nutmeg	½ tsp
2 tsp	ground ginger	2 tsp
2 tbs	raisins or sultanas	2 tbs

(Note: the quantity of sugar specified assumes you are using Bramley cooking apples. If you use sweeter or eating apples, the amount of sugar can be reduced accordingly.)

1 Peel, core and chop the apples and put them in a large saucepan together with the water.
2 Finely grate the lemon rinds into the saucepan, then squeeze the lemons and add the juice.
3 Bring the apples to the boil and simmer, covered, till completely soft (about 20–30 minutes).
4 When the apples are done, remove them from the heat and add the sugar and spices. At this point you can either blend the mixture to make it really smooth, or stir it till any remaining lumps break down. Transfer the mixture to a large, open, casserole dish. Stir in the dried fruit and bake in a cool oven (300°F/150°C/gas mark 2) for 4 hours, stirring every half-hour or so.
5 Prepare suitable storage jars by soaking them in hot water and draining them. Spoon in the apple mixture and seal immediately. Allow to cool before serving. Once opened, the jars should be kept in the refrigerator.

Each 100 g provides: 78 kcal, negligible protein, negligible fat, 19 g carbohydrate, 3 g fibre.

We are indebted to a friendly denizen of San Francisco for this traditional American recipe, though he isn't responsible for the addition of the ground ginger.

ALMOND AND APRICOT SPREAD
(Sugarless Marzipan)
allow ½ hour to prepare

To Make 2 Jarfuls

Imperial (Metric)		American
2 oz (60 g)	dried apricots	½ cup
½ pint (¼ litre)	soya milk	1¼ cups
1 tsp	almond essence	1 tsp
½ lb (¼ kg)	ground almonds	2 cups

1 Finely chop the apricots, put them in a small saucepan with the soya milk and bring to the boil, then reduce heat and simmer, uncovered, till they begin to break down (about 20 minutes). Don't worry if the soya milk separates.
2 Transfer to a blender, add the almond essence and blend to a thick, smooth consistency.
3 Transfer the blended mixture to a mixing-bowl and stir in the ground almonds a little at a time to form a firm paste.
4 Transfer to suitable storage jars (jam jars are perfect) and refrigerate till needed.

Each 100 g provides: 294 kcal, 10 g protein, 25 g fat, 8 g carbohydrate, 9 fibre.

Note that it's important to use high-quality, sweet apricots for this recipe. Wholefood shops often sell a cheaper variety which have a bitter taste and these are fine for savoury dishes but are not suitable here.

It may surprise you to find our recipe for sugarless marzipan in the *Spreads* section, but it makes such a marvellous sandwich filling or extra topping for jam-tarts that it seemed to us a pity to relegate it to annual use as a topping for Christmas cake. You can also make wonderful little sweets by toasting whole almonds and wrapping them in the marzipan to form little egg shapes.

If you want to use it more traditionally to coat a celebration cake, there will be enough here to do a medium-to-large one.

DATE SPREAD
allow 15 minutes to prepare

To Make a Jarful

Imperial (Metric)		American
2 oz (60 g)	dried dates	½ cup
1 oz (30 g)	dried apricots	¼ cup
2 oz (60 g)	margarine	6 tbs
7 tbs	gram flour	7 tbs
¼ pint (125 ml)	apple juice	½ cup

1 Finely chop the dates and apricots and set aside.
2 Melt the margarine in a small saucepan over a low heat. Stir in the flour and cook gently for a few minutes. (It will form a firm dough-like roux.)
3 Slowly stir in the apple juice a little at a time, then add the chopped dates and apricots, still stirring continuously for another minute or two.
4 Remove from heat, transfer to a jar, or covered dish, and allow to cool completely before serving.

Each 100 g provides: 262 kcal, 4 g protein, 18 g fat, 18 g carbohydrate, 11 g fibre.

This sweet, sugar-free spread is excellent as a sandwich filler or simply spread on bread or toast. It can also be used as extra topping for jam-tarts.

Baking

Pastries and Breads

Biscuits and Cakes

Baking

The refined white flour that is used to make most mass-produced bread, biscuits and cakes has had nearly all of its vitamins, minerals and fibre removed and has had added to it chemicals to preserve, stretch, strengthen and bleach it, synthetic vitamins to replace some of those that were taken out during refining, and chalk to make it lighter. The tasteless, spongy, white, plastic substance that is finally baked from this appalling product and called 'bread' could not by any stretch of the imagination be called 'the staff of life'. But it is worse than worthless. There is now increasing evidence that it is positively harmful to health:

> 'It is now generally accepted by the medical profession that a generous intake of dietary fibre is one of the best measures against constipation and many other diseases of the bowel. Dr Hugh Trowell ... suggested that fibre might also protect against diabetes ... that a lack of fibre in the diet may be much more important as a contributory cause in diabetes than an excess of sugar as had previously been thought.' (Dr Jim Mann in the *Diabetics' Diet Book*, Martin Dunitz, 1982.)

Careful attention to diet is just as important for vegans of course. This is why we have used 100 per cent wholewheat flour throughout this section and why, where we have used sugar, we have specified raw varieties which retain much of their vitamin and mineral content. But in any case, in our view, the resulting bread, biscuits and cakes are not only better for your health but actually taste better as well.

We've also specified fresh yeast. This can be bought in many wholefood shops and in some bakers and delicatessens. Dried yeast works perfectly well but is more likely to contribute a 'yeasty' flavour. (If you do have to use it, always use half the quantity specified for fresh yeast.)

A word or two about bread-making. If you've never baked bread before, start with *Basic Wholewheat Bread* (page 209) because this recipe contains the most detailed description of the method. But we recommend *Three Seed Bread* (page 210) for daily use because of its almost perfect protein balance (see page 270).

It's a mystery to us why bread recipes always use sugar to get the yeast going. This is not only unnecessary but one recipe we've seen actually warns that the yeast will be killed if the sugar solution is too strong. Our recipes should provide you with ample proof that you don't need to use sugar at all.

Another way in which our bread recipes differ is that we start with a measured quantity of warm water and add the yeast and flour to it. This is such an easy way to arrive at a dough of perfect consistency that once you've got used to the method you'll probably wonder why you ever did it differently.

It's strange that even proficient and experienced cooks often claim (almost boast) that the one thing they cannot do successfully is make bread. This is nonsense. Bread-making is not only easy, it's also one of the most satisfying forms of cookery there is – good for the soul as well as the body. It's true that it takes a few hours (although most of the time you aren't required to do anything other than wait for the yeast to do its stuff, so that it's easy to do other things at the same time) but there's nothing to compare with it for the sensual pleasure of kneading the dough or the delightful odours that pervade your home once the bread is in the oven.

Finally, a word or two of warning. While it's certainly true that the vegan cakes and biscuits in this section have little in common with the cholesterol and starch bombs that are daily promoted on our television screens, we nevertheless view them as occasional treats to be eaten with restraint. The fact that we've given so many recipes should not be taken as an encouragement to stuff oneself with them but rather as evidence of our wish to lay to rest once and for always the prejudice that vegans are practising a form of self-denial. We refuse to be held responsible for any lack of self-discipline on the part of our readers that might result from the amazing sensual delights we have created!

BASIC SHORTCRUST PASTRY
allow ¾ hour to prepare
(including 20 minutes to chill)

To Make a 8–9 in (20–23 cm) Flan Shell
(for a pie you'll need half as much again)

Imperial (Metric)		American
½ lb (¼ kg)	100 per cent wholewheat flour	2 cups
¼ lb (125 g)	margarine	½ cup
4–5 tbs (60–75 ml)	iced water	4–5 tbs

1 Put a few ice cubes in a jug with a little water.
2 Put the flour and margarine into a large mixing-bowl and, using two knives, chop it up into pea-sized pieces. Quickly use your fingers to rub them in till the mixture resembles coarse breadcrumbs. Try to do it quickly enough to prevent the warmth of your hands from melting the margarine.
3 Pour 1 tbs of the iced water evenly over the mixture and toss the granules of flour to mix it in. Add another 2 tbs in the same way and then try compressing the mixture to see if it will hold together. (If it won't you can add *a maximum of* 1–2 tbs more of water.) Now pick it up in your hands and squeeze it into a ball, then put it back in the bowl and into the fridge for 20 minutes.
4 Prepare a suitable flan case by greasing it with margarine and sprinkling it with flour.
5 Place the dough on a floured surface and, sprinkling it with more flour as necessary, roll it out to the size and thickness you need. Pick it up by rolling it gently round your rolling-pin and then unrolling it again over the prepared flan-case. Repair any small breaks or cracks and shape the edge into scallops between floured fingers and thumbs.
6 Prick the pastry-case all over with a fork and spread some dry beans over it as weights to prevent it from puffing up during baking – it's a good idea to keep a jarful just for this purpose.
7 Bake for 10–12 minutes in the centre of a hot oven (425°F/218°C/gas mark 7). Remove from oven and set aside to cool on a rack before removing the dried beans.

**Each serving (of 8) provides: 213 kcal, 4 g protein, 13 g fat,
21 g carbohydrate, 3 g fibre.**

Any leftover pastry can be used to make jam tarts or pasties, filled with savoury spreads, peanut butter or tahini.

BASIC SWEET PASTRY
allow ¾ hour to prepare
(including 20 minutes to chill)

To Make a 7–8 in (17–20 cm) Shell

Imperial (Metric)		American
¼ lb (125 g)	100 per cent wholewheat flour	1 cup
2 oz (60 g)	rolled oats	¾ cup
1 oz (30 g)	sunflower seeds	3 tbs
1 oz (30 g)	raw demerara sugar	2 tbs
½ tsp	ground cinnamon	½ tsp
3 oz (90 g)	margarine	⅓ cup
3 tbs (45 ml)	iced water	3 tbs

(Note: see *Basic Shortcrust Pastry* (page 207) for a more detailed description of the method.)

1 Put the flour, oats, sunflower seeds, sugar and cinnamon in a large bowl and mix well together.
2 Cut in the margarine and continue rubbing it in till the mixture resembles coarse breadcrumbs.
3 Add the iced water a little at a time until the mixture holds together to form a firm dough. Chill in the refrigerator for at least 20 minutes.
4 Prepare a suitable flan case or dish by greasing it with margarine and dusting it with flour.
5 Flatten the dough between your hands, put it into the prepared flan case and press it into shape till the whole case is evenly lined. (Or roll it out if you prefer.)
6 Prick the base with a fork and bake in the middle of a hot oven (425°F/218°C/gas mark 7) for 10 minutes.
7 Allow to cool on a rack before attempting to remove from the case.

Each serving (of 8) provides: 188 kcal, 4 g protein, 11 g fat, 19 g carbohydrate, 2 g fibre.

Leftover pastry or trimmings can be used to make jam-tarts.

BASIC WHOLEWHEAT BREAD
allow 3 hours to prepare
(including rising times)

To Make 3 × 1 lb (½ kg) Loaves

Imperial (Metric)		American
1¼ pints (650 ml)	hand-warm water	3 cups
1 oz (30 g)	fresh yeast	2 tbs
about 3 lb (1½ kg)	100 per cent wholewheat flour	12 cups
¼ pint (125 ml)	sunflower oil	½ cup
½ tbs	salt	½ tbs

1 Put the hand-warm water in a large mixing-bowl, crumble in the yeast and stir until completely dissolved.
2 Add enough flour to make a thick batter and stir until flour and yeast are thoroughly mixed. Cover and put in a warm place for half an hour.
3 Stir in the oil and salt. Now begin adding more flour and stirring till the dough begins to hold together.
4 Turn the dough out on to a floured surface and knead, adding more flour as necessary, till it becomes smooth and elastic.
5 Sprinkle flour in the mixing-bowl, put the dough back in and sprinkle more flour on top. Cover and put in a warm place to rise. It should double in size in about an hour.
6 Turn the dough out on to the floured surface and knead again for a few minutes before cutting it into 3 equal pieces and kneading each separately for a further few minutes.
7 Shape into loaves, place in greased, floured 1 lb (½ kg) bread tins, cover and leave to rise for a further 20 minutes. Preheat an oven to very hot (450°F/232°C/gas mark 8).
8 Bake in the middle of the oven for 15 minutes, then reduce heat to moderate (350°F/177°C/gas mark 4) for a further 30 minutes. A well-baked loaf rings hollow when tapped. Depending on your oven, you may need to turn them upside down in their tins for the final 10 minutes.

Each 1 oz (30 g) slice provides: 76 kcal, 2 g protein, 2 g fat, 12 g carbohydrate, 2 g fibre.

This is an easy recipe but don't expect it to turn out exactly right first time – remember, practice makes perfect. Seal loaves you don't need immediately in plastic bags and store in the freezer or freezer compartment of your fridge: they'll stay fresh for weeks. Don't ever *wash* bread tins and they won't stick.

Big manufacturers of factory-made wholewheat bread use the cheapest available oils which are usually of animal origin and also put in preservatives, artificial flavouring, colouring agents and sugar. So home-made bread not only tastes better, it's better for your health too.

THREE SEED BREAD
allow 3 hours to prepare
(including rising times)

To Make 3 × 1 lb (½ kg) Loaves

Imperial (Metric)		American
1¼ pints (650 ml)	hand-warm water	3 cups
1 oz (30 g)	fresh yeast	2 tbs
about 3 lb (1½ kg)	100 per cent wholewheat flour	12 cups
2 oz (60 g)	poppy seeds	6 tbs
2 oz (60 g)	sesame seeds	6 tbs
2 oz (60 g)	sunflower seeds	6 tbs
¼ pint (125 ml)	sunflower oil	½ cup
½ tbs	salt	½ tbs

1 Put the hand-warm water in a large mixing-bowl, crumble in the yeast, stir until completely dissolved, then add enough flour to make a thick batter. Cover and put in a warm place for half an hour.
2 Stir in the three seeds, the oil and the salt and mix thoroughly. Now begin adding more flour and stirring. When the dough begins to hold together, turn it out on to a floured surface and knead, adding more flour as necessary, till it becomes smooth and elastic. Put it back into the bowl, cover and put in a warm place to rise. It should double in size in about an hour.
3 Turn the dough out and knead again for a few minutes before cutting it into 3 equal pieces and kneading each separately for a further few minutes.
4 Shape into loaves, place in greased, floured 1 lb (½ kg) bread tins, cover and leave to rise for a further 20 minutes. Preheat an oven to very hot (450°F/232°C/gas mark 8).
5 Bake in the middle of the oven for 15 minutes then reduce heat to moderate (350°F/177°C/gas mark 4) for a further 30 minutes.

Each 1 oz (30 g) slice provides: 89 kcal, 3 g protein, 3 g fat, 13 g carbohydrate, 2 g fibre.

Apart from the fact that the three seeds add a delicious crunchy texture and nutty taste, they also complement the protein content of the flour to make an almost perfect balance of the essential nutrients so this bread really could be described as *the staff of life*.

OAT BREAD
allow 3 hours to prepare
(including rising times)

To Make 3 × 1 lb (½ kg) Loaves

Imperial (Metric)		American
2 oz (60 g)	rolled oats	¾ cup
1½ pints (¾ litre)	water	3½ cups
1 oz (30 g)	fresh yeast	2 tbs
about 3 lb (1½ kg)	100 per cent wholewheat flour	12 cups
¼ pint (125 ml)	sunflower oil	½ cup
½ tbs	salt	½ tbs

1 Put the oats in a small saucepan with just under half the water and bring quickly to the boil, then reduce heat and simmer for 5 minutes, stirring continuously.
2 Remove from heat, stir in the rest of the water and cool down to hand warm (by partially submerging the saucepan in cold water if you like).
3 Pour the oat mixture into a large mixing-bowl, crumble the yeast into it and stir until completely dissolved. Add enough flour to make a thick batter, cover and put in a warm place for half an hour.
4 Stir in the oil and salt. Begin adding more flour and stirring. When the dough begins to hold together, turn it out on to a floured surface and knead, adding more flour as necessary, till it becomes smooth and elastic. Put it back into the bowl, cover and put in a warm place to rise. It should double in size in about an hour.
5 Turn the dough out and knead again for a few minutes before cutting it into 3 equal pieces and kneading each separately for a further few minutes.
6 Shape into loaves, place in greased, floured bread tins, cover and leave to rise for a further 20 minutes. Preheat the oven to very hot (450°F/232°C/gas mark 8).
7 Bake in the middle of the oven for 15 minutes, then reduce heat to moderate (350°F/177°C/gas mark 4) for a further 30 minutes.

Each 1 oz (30 g) slice provides: 77 kcal, 2 g protein, 2 g fat, 12 g carbohydrate, 2 g fibre.

If you try adding raw oats to ordinary wholewheat dough as you make it, you'll find they absorb all the water and make the resulting bread very dry. But this loaf is wonderful – light and creamy in texture and with a nutty, slightly sour-creamy flavour.

ONION BREAD
allow 3 hours to prepare
(including rising times)

To Make 3 × 1 lb (½ kg) Loaves

Imperial (Metric)		American
1¼ pints (650 ml)	hand-warm water	3 cups
1 oz (30 g)	fresh yeast	2 tbs
about 3 lb (1½ kg)	100 per cent wholewheat flour	12 cups
3	medium onions	3
¼ pint (125 ml)	sunflower oil	½ cup
½ tbs	salt	½ tbs

1   Put the hand-warm water in a large mixing-bowl, crumble in the yeast, stir until completely dissolved, then add enough flour to make a thick batter. Cover and put in a warm place for half an hour.
2   Skin and finely chop the onions and add them to the batter. Stir in the oil and salt and mix thoroughly. Now begin adding more flour and stirring. When the dough begins to hold together, turn it out on to a floured surface and knead, adding more flour as necessary, till it becomes smooth and elastic. Put it back into the bowl, cover and put in a warm place to rise. It should double in size in about an hour.
3   Turn the dough out and knead again for a few minutes before cutting it into 3 equal pieces and kneading each separately for a further few minutes.
4   Shape into loaves, place in greased, floured bread tins, cover and leave to rise for a further 20 minutes. Preheat an oven to very hot (450°F/232°C/gas mark 8).
5   Bake in the middle of the oven for 15 minutes, then reduce heat to moderate (350°F/177°C/gas mark 4) for a further 30 minutes.

Each 1 oz (30 g) slice provides: 77 kcal, 3 g protein, 2 g fat, 13 g carbohydrate, 2 g fibre.

This produces a moist, tasty loaf that goes particularly well with savoury tarts and flans but is also good spread with peanut butter, tahini or one of the many savoury spreads from the *Spreads* section.

SPICE BREAD
allow 1½ hours to prepare

To Make a Small 1 lb (½ kg) Loaf

Imperial (Metric)		American
1 tsp	anise seeds	1 tsp
8 fl oz (¼ litre)	boiling water	1 cup
2 oz (60 g)	raw demerara sugar	3 tbs
½ oz (15 g)	fresh yeast	1 tbs
¾ lb (350 g)	100 per cent wholewheat flour	3 cups
3 tsp	ground cinnamon	3 tsp
1 tsp	ground nutmeg	1 tsp
1 tsp	ground cloves	1 tsp
¼ pint (125 ml)	apple concentrate	½ cup

1 Put the anise seeds in a bowl, pour the boiling water over them, cover and set aside to infuse.
2 When the infusion has cooled to hand-warm (and not before!) add the sugar, stir until completely dissolved, then crumble in the yeast. Continue stirring until all the yeast has dissolved before adding about a third of the flour. Mix again thoroughly, cover and set aside for 20 minutes.
3 Now stir in the spices, the apple concentrate and the rest of the flour, and mix to a sticky, wet dough.
4 Transfer the dough to a well-greased, floured bread tin, cover and leave in a warm place to rise for about ½ hour.
5 Push the dough down to make a hollow in the middle and bake in the middle of a hot oven (425°F/218°C/gas mark 7) for 15 minutes then reduce heat to moderate (350°F/177°C/gas mark 4) for a further 25–30 minutes.
6 Turn out on to a rack and allow to cool before serving.

Each slice (of 16) provides: 98 kcal, 3 g protein, negligible fat, 17 g carbohydrate, 2 g fibre.

Serve this cut very thinly and spread with margarine. It's also good toasted.

For variety, try different combinations of spices; or try adding some cut orange peel; or forming the mixture into bun shapes at step 4 to make a sort of tea-cake.

SPICED BISCUITS
allow 40 minutes to prepare

To Make about Two Dozen

Imperial (Metric)		American
6 oz (180 g)	wholewheat flour	1½ cups
2 oz (60 g)	any raw sugar	3 tbs
1 tsp	baking powder	1 tsp
2 tsp	ground cinnamon	2 tsp
1 tsp	ground cloves	1 tsp
1 tsp	ground ginger	1 tsp
½ tsp	ground nutmeg	½ tsp
3 oz (90 g)	margarine	⅓ cup
3 tbs (45 ml)	water	3 tbs

1 Put the flour, sugar, baking powder and all the spices in a bowl and mix thoroughly.
2 Cut in the margarine and continue rubbing it in till the mixture resembles coarse breadcrumbs.
3 Add the water and toss the mixture around till it forms a firm dough.
4 Using liberal amounts of flour, roll the mixture out to about half the thickness of ordinary biscuits and cut into biscuit shapes with a pastry-cutter. Bake on a greased baking sheet in the middle of a moderate oven (350°F/177°C/gas mark 4) for 20 minutes.
5 Allow to cool on a rack before serving.

Each biscuit (of 24) provides: 61 kcal, 1 g protein, 3 g fat, 7 g carbohydrate, 1 g fibre.

LEMON BISCUITS
allow 50 minutes to prepare

To Make about Two Dozen

Imperial (Metric)		American
¼ lb (125 g)	wholewheat self-raising flour	1 cup
¼ lb (125 g)	wholewheat semolina	1 cup
¼ lb (125 g)	raw demerara sugar	¾ cup
2	lemons	2
¼ lb (125 g)	margarine	½ cup

1 Put the flour, semolina and sugar in a bowl and mix well together.
2 Finely grate the lemon rinds into the bowl and mix again.
3 Cut in the margarine, then use your fingers to rub it well in till the mixture resembles coarse breadcrumbs.
4 Squeeze the lemons and add the juice a tablespoonful at a time (up to a maximum of 3) till the mixture holds together.
5 Roll the dough out on a floured surface to about ¼ in (½ cm) thick and cut into biscuit shapes, using a pastry-cutter.
6 Bake on a greased baking sheet in the middle of a fairly hot oven (375°F/190°C/gas mark 5) till golden brown (about 20–30 minutes).
7 Allow to cool on a rack before serving.

Each biscuit (of 24) provides: 94 kcal, 1 g protein, 4 g fat,
12 g carbohydrate, 2 g fibre.

CAROB AND WALNUT COOKIES
allow ¾ hour to prepare

To Make about Two Dozen

Imperial (Metric)		American
6 oz (180 g)	wholewheat self-raising flour	1½ cups
2 oz (60 g)	carob powder	8 tbs
2 oz (60 g)	any raw sugar	3 tbs
¼ lb (125 g)	margarine	½ cup
2 oz (60 g)	chopped walnuts	½ cup
7 tbs (100 ml)	water	7 tbs

1 Put the flour, carob powder and sugar in a bowl and mix well together.
2 Cut in the margarine and continue rubbing it in till the mixture resembles coarse breadcrumbs.
3 Add the chopped nuts and toss around till thoroughly mixed.
4 Now begin adding the water a tablespoonful at a time until the mixture forms a firm dough.
5 The dough may either be rolled out on a floured surface to about ¼ in (½ cm) thick and cut into biscuit shapes with a pastry-cutter, or cut up and formed into biscuit shapes with the hands.
6 Bake on a greased baking sheet in the middle of a moderate oven (350°F/ 177°C/gas mark 4) for 20–25 minutes.
7 Allow to cool on a rack before serving.

Each cookie (of 24) provides: 92 kcal, 2 g protein, 6 g fat, 7 g carbohydrate, 1 g fibre.

ORANGE AND CINNAMON BISCUITS
allow 40 minutes to prepare

To Make about Two Dozen

Imperial (Metric)		American
¼ lb (125 g)	wholewheat self-raising flour	1 cup
5 oz (150 g)	wholewheat semolina	1¼ cups
2 oz (60 g)	rolled oats	¾ cup
2 oz (60 g)	raw demerara sugar	3 tbs
1 tsp	ground cinnamon	1 tsp
1	orange	1
¼ lb (125 g)	margarine	½ cup
2 tsp	lemon juice	2 tsp

1. Put the flour, semolina, oats, sugar and cinnamon in a bowl and mix thoroughly.
2. Finely grate the orange rind and add the peel to the bowl.
3. Put the margarine to melt in a small saucepan over a low heat.
4. Meanwhile, squeeze the orange and stir the juice into the melting margarine. Add the lemon juice and mix thoroughly.
5. Now stir the melted margarine and juice into the bowl of dry ingredients and combine into a smooth dough. (Add an extra tablespoonful of orange juice or water, if necessary, to get a firm consistency.)
6. Roll the dough out on a floured surface to about ¼ in (½ cm) thick and cut into biscuit shapes using a pastry-cutter or, if you prefer, take teaspoonfuls of the dough and flatten out to form biscuit shapes with your hands.
7. Bake on a greased baking sheet in the middle of a moderate oven (350°F/177°C/gas mark 4) till golden brown (about 30–35 minutes).
8. Allow to cool on a rack before serving.

Each biscuit (of 24) provides: 99 kcal, 2 g protein, 5 g fat, 13 g carbohydrate, 2 g fibre.

GINGER SNAPS
allow 50 minutes to prepare

To Make about Two Dozen

Imperial (Metric)		American
¼ lb (125 g)	wholewheat self-raising flour	1 cup
¼ lb (125 g)	wholewheat semolina	1 cup
¼ lb (125 g)	raw demerara sugar	¾ cup
2 tbs	freshly grated ginger	2 tbs
	(or 1 tbs ground dried ginger)	
¼ lb (125 g)	margarine	½ cup
3 tbs (45 ml)	soya milk	3 tbs

1 Put the flour, semolina, sugar and ginger in a bowl and mix thoroughly.
2 Add the margarine and, using two knives, chop it up into pea-sized pieces. Now use your fingers to rub it well into the dry ingredients.
3 Add 2 tbs of the soya milk. If the mixture doesn't bind together, add a third spoonful.
4 Roll the dough out on a floured surface to about ¼ in (½ cm) thick and cut into biscuit shapes, using a pastry-cutter.
5 Bake on a greased baking sheet in the middle of a fairly hot oven (375°F/ 190°C/gas mark 5) till golden brown (about 20–30 minutes).
6 Allow to cool on a rack before serving.

Each biscuit (of 24) provides: 94 kcal, 1 g protein, 4 g fat, 12 g carbohydrate, 1 g fibre.

Although we've given a quantity for ground dried ginger, the fact is that biscuits made with freshly-grated ginger are a revelation. Taste them once and you'll never want to use dried ginger again.

SESAME SHORTBREAD
allow ½ hour to prepare

To Make a 9 in (23 cm) Round

Imperial (Metric)		American
6 oz (180 g)	wholewheat flour	1½ cups
1 oz (30 g)	raw demerara sugar	2 tbs
¼ lb (125 g)	margarine	½ cup
1 tbs	sesame seeds	1 tbs

1 Put the flour and sugar in a bowl and mix well.
2 Put in the margarine and continue rubbing it in till the mixture resembles coarse breadcrumbs.
3 Prepare a suitable flan case, dish or tin by greasing it with margarine and dusting it with flour.
4 Put the mixture into the dish and press it down with your hands until it is an even thickness all over. Prick it all over with a fork and mark it into 16 portions. Sprinkle the sesame seeds on top and press them in lightly.
5 Bake in the middle of a hot oven (425°F/218°C/gas mark 7) until it is just beginning to go golden brown (about 12–15 minutes).
6 Allow to cool on a rack before removing from tin or dish.

Each ¾ oz (20 g) slice provides: 103 kcal, 2 g protein, 7 g fat, 9 g carbohydrate, 1 g fibre.

PLAIN OATCAKES
allow ¾ hour to prepare

To Make about Three Dozen

Imperial (Metric)		American
¼ lb (125 g)	rolled oats	1½ cups
3 oz (90 g)	oatmeal	¾ cup
3 oz (90 g)	wholewheat flour	¾ cup
½ tsp	salt	½ tsp
5 tbs (75 ml)	oil	5 tbs
approx ¼ pint (125 ml)	water	½ cup

1 Put the oats, oatmeal, flour and salt into a large bowl and mix thoroughly.
2 Stir in the oil a little at a time until thoroughly mixed.
3 Slowly stir in the water a little at a time till the mixture forms a firm, sticky dough.
4 Now roll the dough out on a floured surface to about half the thickness of ordinary biscuits and, using a pastry-cutter, cut into small discs.
5 Bake on a greased baking sheet in the middle of a moderate oven (350°F/177°C/gas mark 4) until they begin to brown (about 25 minutes).
6 Allow to cool on a rack before serving.

Each biscuit (of 36) provides: 51 kcal, 1 g protein, 3 g fat, 6 g carbohydrate, 1 g fibre.

These are perfect for scooping up dips; or try spreading them with peanut butter, tahini or any of the home-made spread recipes as a light snack.

COCONUT OATCAKES
allow 40 minutes to prepare

To Make a Dozen

Imperial (Metric)		American
2 oz (60 g)	rolled oats	¾ cup
3 oz (90 g)	oatmeal	¾ cup
3 oz (90 g)	wholewheat flour	¾ cup
¼ lb (125 g)	desiccated coconut	1 cup
3 oz (90 g)	raisins	½ cup
1 oz (30 g)	sunflower seeds	3 tbs
1 oz (30 g)	sesame seeds	3 tbs
5 tbs (75 ml)	oil	5 tbs
¼ pint (125 ml)	apple juice	½ cup

1 Put the oats, oatmeal, flour, coconut, raisins, sunflower and sesame seeds in a large bowl and mix thoroughly.
2 Stir in the oil a little at a time until thoroughly mixed.
3 Slowly stir in the apple juice till the mixture forms a firm dough.
4 Roll the dough out on a floured surface to about ½ in (1 cm) thick and cut into rounds with a pastry-cutter. (If any raisins find their way to the surface, push them back inside the dough or they may burn.)
5 Bake on a greased baking sheet in the middle of a moderate oven (350°F/ 177°C/gas mark 4) till they go golden brown (about 20–30 minutes).
6 Allow to cool on a rack before serving.

Each oatcake (of 12) provides: 239 kcal, 4 g protein, 16 g fat, 21 g carbohydrate, 5 g fibre.

With their balanced mixture of cereals, seeds and fruits, these substantial cakes make perfect snacks for journeys since they provide not only carbo-hydrates, oils, vitamins and minerals, but also have an excellent protein balance.

FRUIT SCONES
allow ½ hour to prepare

To Make About a Dozen

Imperial (Metric)		American
10 oz (300 g)	wholewheat flour	2½ cups
1½ tsp	baking powder	1½ tsp
3 oz (90 g)	sultanas	5 tbs
3 oz (90 g)	margarine	⅓ cup
approx. ¼ pint (125 ml)	soya milk	½ cup

1 Put the flour, baking powder and sultanas into a large mixing-bowl and mix thoroughly.
2 Add the margarine and, using two knives, chop it into pea-sized pieces. Use your fingers to rub it well into the dry ingredients.
3 Add soya milk a little at a time and mix until a firm dough is formed.
4 Roll the dough out on a floured surface to about ½ in (1 cm) thick and use a pastry-cutter to cut it into scone shapes.
5 Bake on a greased baking sheet in the middle of a hot oven (425°F/218°C/gas mark 7) till golden brown (about 10–20 minutes).

Each scone (of 12) provides: 157 kcal, 4 g protein, 7 g fat, 22 g carbohydrate, 3 g fibre.

These are at their best served hot, straight from the oven, sliced open and spread with margarine or, if it's a special occasion, with *Cashew Cream* (page 242) and jam. In the unlikely event that your guests leave you any, store them in an air-tight tin. If they start to dry out, try slicing them in half and toasting the halves separately.

SAVOURY SCONES
allow ½ hour to prepare

To Make about a Dozen

Imperial (Metric)		American
½ lb (¼ kg)	100 per cent wholewheat flour	2 cups
2 oz (60 g)	buckwheat flour	½ cup
2 tsp	baking powder	2 tsp
2 tsp	mustard powder	2 tsp
3 tbs (45 g)	sunflower seeds	3 tbs
3 oz (90 g)	margarine	⅓ cup
3 tbs (45 ml)	soya sauce	3 tbs
	juice of 1 lemon	
7 tbs (100 ml)	soya milk	7 tbs

1 Put the flours, powders and sunflower seeds in a large bowl and mix thoroughly.
2 Add the margarine and, using two knives, chop it up into pea-sized pieces. Use your fingers to rub it well into the dry ingredients.
3 Stir in the soya sauce and the lemon juice, then add the soya milk a little at a time and mix to form a firm dough.
4 Roll the dough out on a floured surface to about ½ in (1 cm) thick and cut into rounds using a pastry-cutter.
5 Bake on a greased baking sheet in the middle of a hot oven (425°F/ 218°C/gas mark 7) till just beginning to brown (about 10–20 minutes).

Each scone (of 12) provides: 165 kcal, 5 g protein, 8 g fat, 20 g carbohydrate, 2 g fibre.

These are at their best served hot, straight from the oven. Slice them in half and spread them with margarine or any of the spreads from the *Spreads* section – they're every bit as good as cheese scones and with none of the cholesterol.

Store them in an airtight container and toast them if they go stale.

POPPY SEED TART
allow 1 hour to prepare

To Serve 8–12

Imperial (Metric)		American
1	*Sweet Pastry Shell* (page 208)	1
3 oz (90 g)	blue poppy seeds	¾ cup
½ pint (¼ litre)	soya milk	1¼ cups
¼ lb (125 g)	ground almonds	1 cup
¼ lb (125 g)	wholewheat flour	1 cup
3 oz (90 g)	raw demerara sugar	5 tbs
3 tbs (45 ml)	oil	3 tbs
½ tsp	almond essence (or more to taste)	½ tsp

(Note: if you haven't already made the sweet pastry shell, do Step 1 below before you do.)

1 Put the poppy seeds in a small saucepan, add the soya milk, bring quickly to the boil, then remove from heat, cover and set aside for 20 minutes.
2 Put the ground almonds, flour and sugar in a bowl and mix thoroughly.
3 Now stir in the oil, the soaked poppy seeds with their soya milk and the almond essence. Mix thoroughly to form a thick paste.
4 Transfer the mixture to the pastry shell, smooth the top and bake in a moderate oven (350°F/177°C/gas mark 4) for 30 minutes.
5 Allow to cool on a rack before serving.

Each serving (of 12) provides: 343 kcal, 8 g protein, 22 g fat, 30 g carbohydrate, 5 g fibre.

Poppy seeds tarts and cakes like this are popular in Austria and Germany but should you find the filling a bit too substantial for your taste, try putting a layer of stewed dried apricots (or wholefruit jam) in the pastry-shell and topping it with half the quantity of the poppy seed mixture.

BANANA AND DATE CAKE
allow 1½ hours to prepare

To Make a Small (6 in/15 cm) Round Cake

Imperial (Metric)		American
10 oz (300 g)	wholewheat flour	2½ cups
1 tbs	baking powder	1 tbs
6 oz (180 g)	dates	1½ cups
3	ripe bananas	3
3 tsp	vanilla essence	3 tsp
¼ pint (125 ml)	soya milk	½ cup
¼ lb (125 g)	margarine	½ cup
	a few whole almonds for decoration	

1 Put the flour and baking powder in a large bowl and mix thoroughly. Roughly chop the dates and mix well in.
2 Put the bananas, vanilla essence and soya milk in another bowl, mash together till thoroughly combined and set aside.
3 Melt the margarine in a small saucepan over a low heat, then stir it into the flour. Now add the mashed bananas and combine the two mixtures thoroughly by stirring and turning with a spoon.
4 Pour the cake mixture into a small, lightly-greased cake tin (a 6 in/15 cm round one is ideal), decorate the top with a few whole almonds or other nuts and bake in the middle of a warm oven (325°F/163°C/gas mark 3) till a knife inserted in the centre comes out cleanly and the cake is golden brown on top (about 1 hour).
5 Allow to cool before removing from tin.

Each 2 oz (60 g) slice provides: 159 kcal, 3 g protein, 7 g fat, 22 g carbohydrate, 3 g fibre.

CARROT AND SULTANA CAKE
allow 1½ hours to prepare

To Make a 1 lb (½ kg) Cake

Imperial (Metric)		American
½ lb (¼ kg)	carrots	½ lb
½ lb (¼ kg)	wholewheat flour	2 cups
1 tbs	baking powder	1 tbs
2 oz (60 g)	sultanas	2 tbs
¼ lb (125 g)	margarine	½ cup
¼ lb (125 g)	raw demerara sugar	¾ cup
1 tbs	sesame seeds	1 tbs

1 Clean, top and tail (and if necessary peel) the carrots then coarsely grate them and set them aside.
2 Put the flour, baking powder and sultanas in a mixing-bowl and mix thoroughly.
3 Melt the margarine in a small saucepan over a low heat then add the sugar and stir until dissolved. Remove from heat and pour over the flour mixture.
4 Add the grated carrots and mix well in.
5 Transfer the cake mixture to a small, lightly greased, cake or bread tin, sprinkle the sesame seeds on top and bake for about 50 minutes in a warm oven (325°F/163°C/gas mark 3) till a knife inserted in the centre comes out cleanly.
6 Allow to cool before removing from tin.

Each 2 oz (60 g) slice provides: 154 kcal, 2 g protein, 7 g fat, 21 g carbohydrate, 3 g fibre.

LEMON SPONGE CAKE
allow 40 minutes to prepare

To Make a 2-Layered 9 in (23 cm) Round Cake

Imperial (Metric)		American
½ lb (¼ kg)	fine-milled 100 per cent wholewheat flour	2 cups
1½ tbs	baking powder	1½ tbs
3 oz (90 g)	raw demerara sugar	5 tbs
¼ lb (125 g)	margarine	½ cup
5 tbs (75 ml)	hot water	5 tbs
1½ tbs (25 ml)	malt extract	1½ tbs
3	lemons	3

1 Sift the flour and baking powder into a bowl, add the sugar and mix well by lifting and sprinkling, using a spoon.
2 Put the margarine to melt in a small saucepan over a low heat. Remove from heat as soon as it's melted.
3 Put the hot water in a jug together with the malt extract and set aside.
4 Finely grate the lemon rinds, add to the dry ingredients and mix in by lifting and sprinkling as before.
5 Squeeze the lemons, add the juice to the water and malt mixture and stir till the malt has completely dissolved.
6 Preheat an oven to fairly hot (400°F/204°C/gas mark 6) and prepare two suitable sponge tins by lightly greasing and flouring them.
7 As quickly as you can, add the melted margarine to the dry ingredients and stir well in, followed immediately by the water, malt and lemon juice mixture. Beat well for a few moments only before transferring equal amounts to each of your two prepared sponge tins and placing them in the preheated oven.
8 Bake till the top goes firm and golden brown (about 20–25 minutes).
9 Allow to cool before removing from the tins.
10 Fill with jam, lemon or orange marmalade or *Vegan Piping Cream*, flavoured with lemon juice (page 241).

Each slice (of 8) provides: 270 kcal, 4 g protein, 13 g fat, 34 g carbohydrate, 5 g fibre.

ALMOND AND APRICOT CAKE
allow 1½ hours to prepare
(if you have pre-soaked the apricots)

To Make a Small (6 in/15 cm) Round Cake

Imperial (Metric)		American
6 oz (180 g)	dried apricots	1½ cups
½ pint (¼ litre)	soya milk	1¼ cups
¼ lb (125 g)	chopped almonds	1 cup
¼ lb (125 g)	wholewheat flour	1 cup
¼ lb (125 g)	ground almonds	1 cup
1½ tbs	baking powder	1½ tbs
¼ lb (125 g)	margarine	½ cup
2 oz (60 g)	raw sugar	3 tbs
1 tsp	almond essence	1 tsp

a few whole almonds for decoration (optional)

1 Finely chop the apricots, put them in a bowl, pour the soya milk over, cover and leave to stand for several hours – preferably overnight.
2 Sprinkle the chopped almonds on an ovenproof plate and put them in the top of a hot oven (425°F/218°C/gas mark 7) till they begin to brown (about 8–12 minutes). Remove from the oven and set aside. Leave the oven door open and reduce heat to warm (325°F/163°C/gas mark 3).
3 Put the flour, ground almonds and baking powder in a bowl and mix thoroughly.
4 Melt the margarine and sugar in a small saucepan over a low heat before adding it to the flour mixture. Mix well in and then add the soaked apricots (together with any remaining liquid), the roasted almonds and the almond essence and combine all the ingredients together thoroughly.
5 Transfer the mixture to a greased, floured cake tin, decorate with more almonds (whole ones look good, if you have them) and bake in the middle of a warm oven (325°F/163°C/gas mark 3) for about 50 minutes till a knife inserted in the centre comes out cleanly.
6 Allow to cool before removing from tin.

Each 2 oz (60 g) slice provides: 210 kcal, 5 g protein, 15 g fat, 14 g carbohydrate, 6 g fibre.

CAROB CAKE
allow 1 hour to prepare

To Make an 8 in (20 cm) Round Cake

Imperial (Metric)		American
½ lb (¼ kg)	100 per cent wholewheat flour	2 cups
¼ lb (125 g)	carob powder	1¼ cups
1½ tbs	baking powder	1½ tbs
¼ lb (125 g)	dark raw muscovado sugar	7 tbs
7 tbs (100 ml)	oil	7 tbs
1½ tbs (25 ml)	malt extract	1½ tbs
1½ tbs (25 ml)	vanilla essence	1½ tbs
½ pint (¼ litre)	warm water	1¼ cups
	Topping	
2 oz (60 g)	margarine	6 tbs
3 tbs	carob powder	3 tbs
2 tbs (30 ml)	maple syrup	2 tbs

1 Sift the flour, carob powder and baking powder into a bowl, add the sugar and mix well by lifting, turning and sprinkling, using a large spoon.
2 Preheat the oven to moderate (350°F/177°C/gas mark 4) and prepare a suitable 8 in (20 cm) round cake tin by lightly greasing with margarine and dusting with flour.
3 As quickly as possible, add the oil, malt extract, vanilla essence and warm water to the bowl and beat together (using an electric mixer if you prefer) till well combined.
4 Pour the mixture into the prepared tin, smooth the top and make a slight hollow in the centre (to prevent splits forming). Bake in the middle of the oven for about 40 minutes till a knife inserted in the centre comes out cleanly.
5 Allow to cool before removing from tin.
6 Cream all the topping ingredients together (using a mixer if you prefer) till thick and smooth. Spread evenly over the cake and smooth out any imperfections using a knife dipped in cold water.

Each slice (of 8) provides: 333 kcal, 7 g protein, 17 g fat, 39 g carbohydrate, 4 g fibre.

CELEBRATION CAKE
allow 3½ hours to prepare
(if you have pre-soaked the dried fruit)

To Make a Large 9 in (23 cm) Round Cake

Imperial (Metric)		American
½ lb (¼ kg)	sultanas	2 cups
½ lb (¼ kg)	raisins	2 cups
¼ lb (125 g)	currants	1 cup
½ pint (¼ litre)	sweet white wine	1¼ cups
¼ lb (125 g)	margarine	½ cup
3 oz (90 g)	raw demerara sugar	5 tbs
3 tbs (45 ml)	molasses	3 tbs
½ lb (¼ kg)	100 per cent wholewheat flour	2 cups
¼ pint (125 ml)	soya milk	1 cup
2 tbs	mixed spice	2 tbs

1 Put all the dried fruit in a bowl, pour the sherry over and leave to soak overnight. Stir from time to time to make sure all the fruit is coated.
2 Put the margarine and sugar in a large mixing-bowl and cream well together before stirring in the molasses, flour, soya milk and mixed spice. An electric mixer may be used if you prefer.
3 Fold in the soaked dried fruit and stir till evenly distributed through the mixture.
4 Line a 9 in (23 cm) round cake tin with grease-proof paper. Pour in the mixture and bake in a cool oven (300°F/150°C/gas mark 2) for about 3 hours till a knife inserted in the centre comes out cleanly.
5 Allow to cool on a rack before removing from tin.

Each slice (of 12) provides: 321 kcal, 4 g protein, 9 g fat, 56 g carbohydrate, 6 g fibre.

This is a perfect cake for really special occasions such as birthdays or Christmas. It's marvellous as it is, but you may wish to cover it with *Sugarless Marzipan* (page 200) and ice it as well – if you prefer not to use sugar icing, try dissolving creamed coconut in a little hot water, pouring it over the cake and smoothing it with a knife dipped frequently in hot water.

The Alternative Dairy

The Alternative Dairy

SOYA MILK

Soya Milk as a Health Food

Soya milk has a high protein, vitamin and mineral content and is naturally low in fat (and what fat there is in it is in any case the unsaturated type). So it is easy to digest and never provokes the allergic symptoms that many people suffer from cow's milk. Cow's milk is mucus-forming and has other dangers too of course – chiefly the result of its high cholesterol level which has now been accepted by the medical profession at large as a major contributory factor in heart disease. (It is not a coincidence that countries that have a low consumption of dairy produce are virtually free from heart disease.)

Availability of Soya Milk

We had long discussions during the preparation of this book on whether we should include a method for making soya milk in the home. (This isn't really difficult, but it takes a lot of space and is messy and time-consuming.) In the end we decided that we didn't need to for the simple reason that even while we were writing the book, two or three more brands came on to the market to add to the several that were already available. It can now be bought in any wholefood or Chinese store and in several of the larger grocery stores. So we really don't anticipate that you're going to have trouble finding it.

Sweetened, Unsweetened or Concentrated

Soya milk is available in these and several flavoured varieties. We haven't specified sweetened or unsweetened in the ingredients lists of individual recipes because the sweetened brands are only very slightly sweet and so it doesn't really matter very much which you use. But as a rule of thumb, *use the unsweetened variety in any recipe, the sweetened only in dessert or sweet recipes.*

A couple of brands of concentrated soya milk are available. We haven't specified these anywhere but if it is all you could get, simply dilute it according to the instructions on the packet and proceed with the recipe as printed. In just a few cases you may like to use it undiluted in order to produce a richer, thicker texture in a particular dish. It can also be used as a kind of single cream and poured over fruit.

Soya Milk as a Drink

If you like milk straight as a drink try adding 2 teaspoons of vanilla essence to 1 pint (½ litre/2½ cups) soya milk. This cancels the slightly 'beany' taste that some people don't like, without giving the milk a vanilla flavour. But most vegans find that after a while they get so used to the taste of soya milk that they cease even to like cow's milk on the rare occasions that they are obliged to drink it.

Soya Milk in Hot Drinks

Added to tea in the normal way, soya milk produces a perfectly good ordinary cuppa. But with coffee, there can be problems. If you make a half and half mixture of hot coffee and cold soya milk, all will be well; but if you like your coffee strong with just a dash of milk, you're out of luck. The acidity and high temperature of the coffee combine to cause the milk to coagulate (actually it's a good demonstration of the first stage of making tofu!) and although this doesn't affect its taste in any way, it does seem to disturb sensitive souls. But then, it doesn't seem such a difficult thing for people who like strong coffee to go all the way and start drinking it black.

MARGARINE

From the health point of view, soft margarines made from cold-pressed oils and containing a high proportion of polyunsaturated fat are best, though they do also tend to be the most expensive. Hard margarines contain a higher proportion of hydrogenized (i.e. 'saturated') fat. We have assumed that you will only use these for biscuit and pastry recipes and that they will not form a large part of your diet. But if you really are addicted to biscuits and pastry and want to eat some every day, it would be a good idea to use soft, polyunsaturated margarine in these recipes too. It produces a friable, crumbly dough that is difficult to handle and roll out, but, once baked, has a wonderful, mouth-watering texture.

Wholefood shops are the best places to buy high-quality, guaranteed vegan margarines. Most of the margarines to be found in such abundance in large supermarkets are not vegan. (Close scrutiny of the list of ingredients usually reveals the presence of *whey*, a product of the dairy industry, dried cow's milk, and often reclaimed animal fats.) However, such stores do usually stock one or two brands of kosher margarines, which are vegan, and these may well prove the easiest to obtain. They also stock several brands of 100 per cent vegetable fats (such as *Trex*) that make acceptable substitutes for margarine in many of the baking recipes. Jewish delicatessens also sell kosher margarines, of course, and so provide another useful source of supply for vegans.

Although you may initially have to spend a certain amount of time scouting out a regular supplier, once you've found the vegan margarines you like you can simply stick to them, and stocking up will be no harder than buying any other ingredient.

TOFU

What is Tofu?

Tofu is the Japanese word for *soya bean curd*. Originating in China, it has been made in the Far East for more than 2000 years and is the chief source of high-quality protein for more than a billion people throughout the world.

It first became widely available in this country in the early 1970s as a result of the upsurge of interest in macrobiotics and this is the probable reason for the adoption of the Japanese name for it here – even though most people's first encounter with it will probably have been in a Chinese restaurant.

It is highly nutritious yet low in calories, 100 grams of tofu providing 8 grams of protein, 4 grams of (polyunsaturated) fat, negligible carbohydrate and only 63 kilocalories.

Buying Tofu

Tofu can be bought in wholefood shops and Chinese stores and it's clear that it is daily becoming more popular so, as with soya milk, we don't anticipate that you'll have any trouble finding it. It comes in a number of different forms, ranging from *silken tofu*, which is the softest, to a firm, hard-pressed tofu which is a bit like cream cheese. *Smoked tofu* is another form which has recently become more widely available in wholefood shops. This is delicious to eat just as it is, or it can be used in savoury recipes where you want a stronger, smoky flavour. There is also a Japanese brand of *instant tofu* (oddly enough, we've seen it only in Chinese supermarkets). We found it horrible and wouldn't recommend it for anything.

Keeping Tofu

Completely fresh tofu is quite odourless and pure white in colour. It can be kept, floated in water in a refrigerator for up to a week, provided the water is changed every day.

Note that if you put tofu in the freezer compartment of your refrigerator, it will keep for ages, but it will also completely change its character, becoming granular and chewy. In this state it will readily soak up marinades, opening up yet another set of cooking possibilities for this versatile ingredient.

Cooking with Tofu

Tofu is the perfect ingredient because it is bland in flavour and so can be led in any direction you choose, making it equally suitable for savoury or sweet dishes. Its texture too lends itself to a range of uses. Firm tofu is best for slicing or cubing; soft (or silken) tofu is best for blending. We haven't specified which kind to use unless it is likely to affect materially the recipe in question. However, if you are working on a recipe that requires firm tofu and you have only soft tofu to hand, you can firm it up by wrapping it in a clean tea-towel and pressing it between two wooden chopping-boards for about 20–30 minutes.

Home-made Tofu

Although it isn't difficult to make tofu in the home (by adding a coagulant such as lemon juice to soya milk, then straining and pressing it) we decided not to include a method for this for the same reasons as those given in the introductory remarks on soya milk (page 233).

VEGAN YOGHURT

How to get 100 per cent Vegan Yoghurt

If you keep soya milk in an open jug in your refrigerator, you will find sooner or later that a jugful 'goes thick'. *Don't throw it away!* Apart from the fact that it still tastes perfectly good and can be used as you would use single cream – on cereals or fruit – it presents a golden opportunity to make 100 per cent vegan yoghurt using either of the two methods given. Once you've made your first-ever batch in this way, you can reserve 2 table-spoonfuls as a starter for the next batch.

How to Make Vegan Yoghurt in a Hurry

If you're too impatient to await the chance arrival of the bacteria described above (which clearly have an affinity for soya milk) you can start your first-ever batch by buying a packet of dried culture (obtainable in most whole-food shops) or even an ordinary plain shop yoghurt. Note that in this case **Method 1** must be used and the resulting yoghurt won't be 100 per cent vegan, of course, because even the dried cultures contain some cow's milk products. Furthermore, the bacteria that are used to culture most cow's (and goats) milk yoghurts *(streptococcus thermophilus* and *lactobacillus bulgaricus)* have the unfortunate effect of making soya yoghurt taste slightly 'beany'. This can be counteracted by stirring in a little vanilla essence; if you get the quantity exactly right, this cancels out the 'beany' taste without giving the yoghurt a vanilla flavour.

The Difference between the two Methods

The two methods given produce quite different flavours and textures. **Method 1** produces a strong, thick yoghurt and will work with both the opportunistic and the bought cultures but it's more trouble. **Method 2** produces a mild, thin yoghurt that goes well with muesli, cereals and fresh fruit and is so trouble free and easy to make that it's surely worth having a jar of it permanently 'ticking over' in your fridge – but it won't work with the bought cultures which like higher temperatures (*thermophilus* means 'warmth-loving').

With both methods the taste will vary from batch to batch. The very first batch will be very mild – whichever method or culture medium you use – but the taste will get stronger from batch to batch and with **Method 1** and bought culture, it may end up too strong for your taste after a number of batches – in which case you'll just have to start again from scratch.

Whatever the life history of the batch you have to hand, if it's too mild in flavour for the use you have planned for it, simply stir in lemon juice a little at a time till you get to the strength you want.

VEGAN ICE-CREAM

A Simple Method for Home-made Vegan Ice-cream

We began our experiments with vegan ice-cream by simply substituting vegan ingredients into the traditional home ice-cream making method involving (endless!) alternating freezings and churnings. But this didn't work well and in any case we found it such a bore that we decided to try a completely different approach instead. Luckily, with fresh fruit ice-creams, this worked the first time and is, in essence, the method given. What you do is simply peel and chop fresh fruit, freeze it into solid chunks, then put these into a blender together with the remaining ingredients listed and blend to a wonderful, instant ice-cream. (Depending on your blender, this may take a few seconds or a few minutes.)

With most fruits, no sweetener is needed but where one is, we've used *maple syrup*. If you're prepared to include honey in your vegan diet, then this can obviously be used instead.

We've given recipes for several variations on this theme, but you can use virtually any fresh fruit, so why not invent ice-creams of your own?

For plain or flavoured ice-creams, of course, another method had to be found which, in the event, proved equally simple. You deep-freeze ⅔ –¾ of the recipe soya milk then blend the resulting ice cubes with the remaining ingredients as before.

These simple methods produce a light texture, half-way between conventional ice-cream and a sorbet, which we find preferable to most commercially-produced ice-creams. But if you want to get nearer the richer, fattier texture of the latter, double the quantity of sunflower oil and use *concentrated soya milk* instead of ordinary.

VEGAN SINGLE CREAM
allow 5 minutes to prepare

To Make 1–2 Jarfuls

Imperial (Metric)		American
¼ lb (125 g)	tofu	½ cup
5 tbs (75 ml)	sunflower oil	5 tbs
¼ pint (125 ml)	water	½ cup
¼ pint (125 ml)	soya milk	½ cup
2 tsp	vanilla essence	2 tsp
1½ tbs (25 ml)	maple syrup (optional)	1½ tbs

(Note: if you're planning to use the cream for a savoury dish you should, of course, omit the maple syrup.)

1 Put all the ingredients in a blender and blend to produce a rich cream.
2 Transfer to suitable storage jars and refrigerate till needed.

Each 100 g provides: 163 kcal, 2 g protein, 16 g fat, 2 g carbohydrate, negligible fibre.

This will enrich your morning cereal and is also good poured over cakes, fruit pies or puddings when you want to add extra moistness without the added calories of *Vegan Double Cream*.

VEGAN DOUBLE CREAM
allow 5 minutes to prepare

To Make 1–2 Jarfuls

Imperial (Metric)		American
¼ lb (125 g)	tofu	½ cup
5 tbs (75 ml)	sunflower oil	5 tbs
7 tbs (100 ml)	soya milk	7 tbs
1 tbs (15 ml)	vanilla essence	1 tbs
1½ tbs (25 ml)	maple syrup (optional)	1½ tbs

(Note: for a thicker cream use half the amount of soya milk. If you're planning to use the cream for a savoury dish you should of course omit the maple syrup.)

1   Put all the ingredients in a blender and blend to produce a rich, thick cream.
2   Transfer to suitable storage jars and refrigerate till needed.

Each 100 g provides: 268 kcal, 4 g protein, 26 g fat, 5 g carbohydrate, 1 g fibre.

This simply-made vegan cream is every bit as sumptuous as its cousin which is habitually stolen from calves but, unlike its cousin, it contains nothing that is bad for you. Tofu is high in protein, low in fats and carbohydrates and contains no cholesterol. So even if you hadn't decided to become vegan, it would make sense to eat it instead of dairy cream, wouldn't it?

Serve it with fresh fruit salads, on *Apple Pie* (page 152), on puddings, fruit tarts or flans, or simply add it to any dessert when you want to make the occasion a little bit special.

If you're on a diet, try making it with only 2 tbs sunflower oil instead of 5.

VEGAN SOUR CREAM
allow 5 minutes to prepare

To Make 1–2 Jarfuls

Imperial (Metric)		American
½ lb (¼ kg)	tofu	1 cup
5 tbs (75 ml)	sunflower oil	5 tbs
7 tbs (100 ml)	soya milk	7 tbs
1½ tbs (25 ml)	vanilla essence	1½ tbs
3 tbs (45 ml)	lemon juice	3 tbs
2 tsp	soya sauce	2 tsp
½ tsp	mustard powder	½ tsp
1½ tbs (25 ml)	maple syrup (optional)	1½ tbs

(Note: omit the maple syrup if you're planning to use the cream for a savoury dish.)

1 Put all the ingredients in a blender and blend to produce a rich, thick cream.
2 Transfer to a suitable storage jar and refrigerate till needed.

Each 100 g provides: 186 kcal, 5 g protein, 17 g fat, 4 g carbohydrate, 1 g fibre.

This is a tasty filler for open baked potatoes, or add extra salt and pepper and fresh chopped chives and serve it as a salad dressing.

Sweetened, it goes well with fresh fruit salads, puddings and desserts.

VEGAN PIPING CREAM
allow 10 minutes to prepare

To Make a Jarful

Imperial (Metric)		American
1½ tbs	fine cornmeal	1½ tbs
¼ pint (125 ml)	soya milk	½ cup
1 tsp	vanilla essence	1 tsp
1 tsp	maple syrup (optional)	1 tsp
2 oz (60 g)	margarine (see below)	4 tbs
3 extra tbs (45 ml)	soya milk (optional)	3 extra tbs

1   Put the cornmeal in a small saucepan and add the soya milk a little at a time, blending in carefully to remove any lumps.
2   Add the vanilla essence (and the maple syrup if you want a sweetened cream) and then begin heating and stirring gently and continuously till the mixture thickens. Remove from heat and stand the saucepan in cold water to cool.
3   Put the margarine in a small bowl or jar and mash it with a fork till it begins to cream. Begin adding the cooled cornmeal mixture and continue mashing and blending till you have a rich, smooth, creamy consistency. (An electric mixer may be used if you prefer.) If it seems too thick, add some extra soya milk – but don't thin it too much or it won't hold its shape when you pipe it.
4   Transfer to a suitable storage jar and refrigerate till needed.

Each 100 g provides: 257 kcal, 2 g protein, 25 g fat, 6 g carbohydrate, 1 fibre.

Note that if you use a soft margarine you'll get a texture similar to whipped double cream whereas a hard margarine will give more that of clotted cream.

The cream is ideal for decorating fruit flans, tarts or cakes as it will hold its shape perfectly when piped. Made thinner, it can be floated on coffee.

Adding cocoa or carob powder not only colours the cream but also makes it flow more smoothly for fine piping effects.

CASHEW CREAM
allow 5 minutes to prepare

To Make a Jarful

Imperial (Metric)		American
6 oz (180 g)	broken cashew pieces	1½ cups
¼ pint (125 ml)	fruit juice	½ cup

1 Put all the ingredients in a blender and blend to produce a rich, thick cream. (Add a little more or less juice to get the consistency you prefer.)
2 Transfer to a suitable storage jar and refrigerate till needed.

Each 100 g (made with orange juice) provides: 197 kcal, 4 g protein, 18 g fat, 8 g carbohydrate, 3 g fibre.

Almost any fruit juice can be used to ring the changes on this rich, thick cream, but apple juice is probably the best one to start with.

It goes particularly well with *Fruit Juice Jelly* (page 144) or fresh fruit salad.

Although whole cashew nuts are expensive, most shops sell broken pieces quite cheaply so this gourmet cream needn't be a rare treat.

COCONUT CREAM
allow 10 minutes to prepare

To Make a Jarful

Imperial (Metric)		American
¼ pint (125 ml)	water	½ cup
¼ lb (125 g)	creamed coconut	½ cup
3 tbs (45 ml)	soya milk	3 tbs
½	lemon	½

1 Put the water in a small saucepan over a low heat.
2 Coarsely chop the creamed coconut to make it easier to dissolve and add it to the saucepan. Stir until there are no lumps left. Remove from heat.
3 Squeeze half a lemon and put the juice into a blender.
4 Add the soya milk to the blender and then the dissolved coconut and blend till the mixture thickens.
5 Transfer to a suitable storage jar and refrigerate till needed.

Each 100 g provides: 239 kcal, 3 g protein, 24 g fat, 3 g carbohydrate, 10 g fibre.

You can buy creamed coconut in any wholefood shop and in some larger stores as well as oriental shops.

Coconut cream made according to this recipe will set quite firm if refrigerated and can be used as a topping for fresh fruit salads, jellies or cakes. It's very very rich, so serve sparingly.

VEGAN YOGHURT – METHOD 1
allow 20 minutes to prepare
6–8 hours to ferment

To Make 3 pints (1½ litres)

Imperial (Metric)		American
3 pints (1½ litres)	soya milk	7½ cups
3–4 tbs	starter culture	3–4 tbs

(Note: if you haven't made yoghurt by this method before, read the remarks below before beginning.)

1 Put the soya milk in a large saucepan and bring it quickly to the boil, stirring continuously. Remove from heat and cool down to hand-warm. (The quickest way is to stand the saucepan in a bowl of cold water while you're getting the containers ready.)
2 Put the starter culture in a jar, add a little hand-warm milk and stir in. Repeat until you have a jarful of thoroughly dissolved culture. Pour it back into the saucepan and stir until thoroughly combined.
3 Transfer to suitable storage jars (jam jars are ideal), seal, put in a warm place, cover and leave for at least 6 hours.
4 Refrigerate till needed.

Each 100 g provides: 52 kcal, 3 g protein, 2 g fat, 2 g carbohydrate, 1 g fibre.

Maintaining the right temperature is the secret of success with this method. If the milk is too hot, you'll kill the starter culture but if it isn't kept warm enough, the fermentation won't get started. Hand-warm is about right. (Perfectionists may like to know that the ideal temperature is 112°F/45°C.) Airing-cupboards are ideal places to store the jars during fermentation but if you haven't got one, don't give up – simply wrap them in several layers of blanket and keep them away from draughts. (You can also use a wide-mouthed vacuum flask, though getting the yoghurt out again can be tiresome.)

With this method you can use any of the following as a culture: a packet of dried culture bought from a wholefood shop, some plain yoghurt bought anywhere, some leftover yoghurt from a previous batch, or an opportunist culture that has decided to move in with you (see introductory remarks to this section).

Note that with this method the *proportions* of the container affect the end result. To get an even, creamy consistency right through it should be about 1½ times as deep as it is wide. (Shop yoghurt tubs are an example of the ideal shape.) If you use a shallow dish you'll get separated curds and whey.

VEGAN YOGHURT – METHOD 2
allow 5 minutes to prepare
1–2 days to ferment

To Make 1 pint (½ litre)

Imperial (Metric)		American
3–4 tbs	starter culture	3–4 tbs
1 pint (½ litre)	soya milk	2½ cups

(Note: if you haven't made yoghurt by this method before, read the remarks below before beginning.)

1 Divide the starter culture equally between 2 or 3 storage jars (jam jars are ideal) then fill each jar with soya milk, seal and shake vigorously.
2 Place in the refrigerator till fermented (1–2 days).

Each 100 g provides: 52 kcal, 3 g protein, 2 g fat, 2 g carbohydrate, 1 g fibre.

Note that this simple method will only work with the opportunistic culture that occasionally arrives to thicken an uncovered jug of soya milk that has been in use for a day or two (see page 236 for more details). Of course, once you've got some and made your first batch, you can reserve 2–3 table-spoonfuls as a starter for the next.

Also note that the very first batch you make will be little more than a thickened, mildly-flavoured milk but the taste will gradually strengthen and the texture gradually thicken from batch to batch. If you want to strengthen the taste of the batch you have to hand, simply stir in a little lemon juice.

With this method there is no need to keep the jars warm during fermentation – once you've filled and shaken them you can simply put them in the fridge to ferment and forget about them for a day or two.

This yoghurt is excellent poured over breakfast cereals, fresh fruit and puddings, or stirred into soups just before serving. It's also all right for making *Lassi* (page 256) though you'll probably need to add a little lemon juice as already mentioned.

PLAIN ICE-CREAM
allow 4–5 hours to prepare
(including freezing time)

To Serve 4–6

Imperial (Metric)		American
¾ pint (400 ml)	soya milk	2 cups
7 tbs (100 ml)	sunflower oil	7 tbs
3 tbs (45 ml)	vanilla essence	3 tbs
3 tbs (45 ml)	maple syrup	3 tbs

1 Pour ½ pint (275 ml/1½ cups) soya milk into ice-cube trays and place in the freezer or freezer compartment of your refrigerator till frozen solid (about 4–5 hours).

2 Put the remaining ¼ pint (125 ml/½ cup) soya milk into a blender together with the sunflower oil, vanilla essence and maple syrup. Add the now-frozen soya milk cubes, blend till very smooth and creamy and serve.

**Each serving (of 6) provides: 216 kcal, 2 g protein, 18 g fat,
10 g carbohydrate, 1 g fibre.**

We had some trouble getting this exactly right. The degree of solidity of the soya milk ice-cubes seems to be critical if you want to be able to serve the ice-cream immediately after making it – too soft and you'll end up with iced milk-shakes; too hard and you may have difficulty getting it to blend completely. Either way, don't even consider giving up! If it seems too soft, simply put it back in the freezer for half an hour to thicken. If the milk cubes are too hard, simply persist with the blending till they have completely broken down. It's worth it because it makes an ice-cream that feels lighter than its dairy counterpart. But if you want to get nearer to dairy ice-cream, increase the quantity of sunflower oil and substitute *concentrated* soya milk (obtainable from most wholefood shops) in step 1.

BANANA ICE-CREAM

allow 4 hours to prepare
(including freezing time)

To Serve 4

Imperial (Metric)		American
1 lb (½ kg)	bananas	3 large
	juice of ½ a lemon	
¼ pint (125 ml)	soya milk	½ cup
5 tbs (75 ml)	sunflower oil	5 tbs
2 tsp	vanilla essence	2 tsp

1 Peel and coarsely chop the bananas, put them into a bowl and place in
   the freezer or freezer compartment of your refrigerator for at least 4
   hours. (It's a good idea to turn the fridge to maximum if possible.)
2 Put all the remaining ingredients in a blender, add the now-frozen
   banana chunks and blend to a rich, thick, smooth consistency.

**Each serving (of 4) provides: 273 kcal, 3 g protein, 18 g fat,
25 g carbohydrate, 5 g fibre.**

If the ice-cream is a little too soft for your taste, put it back in the freezer for
about half an hour or so before serving. In fact, it can be kept in the freezer
for as long as you like provided you remember to defrost it for at least 2
hours, and churn it with a spoon before serving. However, despite the
lemon juice, it will discolour slightly if kept for long though this doesn't
affect the flavour.

PINEAPPLE ICE-CREAM
allow 4 hours to prepare
(including freezing time)

To Serve 3–4

Imperial (Metric)		American
1 lb (½ kg)	pineapple	½ large
5 tbs (75 ml)	sunflower oil	5 tbs
¼ pint (125 ml)	soya milk	½ cup

1 Peel the pineapple, carefully removing all traces of skin and scales, then coarsely chop it, put the pieces into a bowl and place in the freezer or freezer compartment of your refrigerator for at least 4 hours.
2 Put the oil and soya milk into a blender, add the now-frozen pineapple chunks and blend to a thick, smooth, creamy consistency and serve.

Each serving (of 4) provides: 242 kcal, 2 g protein, 19 g fat, 16 g carbohydrate, 2 g fibre.

If the pineapple chunks are frozen so hard that they prove difficult to blend, just persist, adding a little extra soya milk if necessary. The ice-cream may be returned to the freezer and kept for as long as you like provided you remember to get it out at least 2 hours before serving.

This ice-cream doesn't need any sweetener at all. If you can't get fresh pineapple, you can make it with tinned, unsweetened pineapple chunks, but remember to drain them before putting in the freezer for step 1. If you're using tinned pineapple and would rather make a sorbet, simply use the liquid from the tin instead of the oil and soya milk at step 2.

CHOCOLATE ICE-CREAM

allow 4–5 hours to prepare
(including freezing time)

To Serve 4–6

Imperial (Metric)		American
¾ pint (400 ml)	soya milk	2 cups
7 tbs (100 ml)	sunflower oil	7 tbs
3 tbs	unsweetened cocoa powder	3 tbs
1½ tbs (25 ml)	maple syrup	1½ tbs
2 tsp	vanilla essence	2 tsp

1 Pour ½ pint (275 ml/1½ cups) soya milk into ice-cube trays and place in the freezer or freezer compartment of your refrigerator till frozen solid (about 4–5 hours).
2 Put the remaining ¼ pint (125 ml/½ cup) soya milk into a blender together with the remaining ingredients. Add the now-frozen soya milk cubes, blend till completely smooth and serve.

Each serving (of 6) provides: 215 kcal, 3 g protein, 19 g fat, 7 g carbohydrate, 1 g fibre.

If the ice-cream seems a little too soft to serve immediately, put it back in the freezer for half an hour or so. If the soya milk ice-cubes are too hard, continue blending till they're completely soft.

This ice-cream can be stored in your freezer for as long as you like provided you remember to defrost it for at least an hour before serving.

PEACH SORBET
allow 3 hours to prepare
(including freezing time)

To Serve 4

Imperial (Metric)		American
1 lb (½ kg)	ripe peaches	4 large
1	lemon	1
1½ tbs (25 ml)	maple syrup	1½ tbs
2 tsp	vanilla essence	2 tsp
¼ pint (125 ml)	soya milk	½ cup

1 Stone and coarsely chop the peaches, put them in a bowl and place in the freezer or freezer compartment of your refrigerator for at least 3 hours.
2 Squeeze the lemon and put the juice in a blender.
3 Now add all the remaining ingredients together with the now-frozen peach chunks and blend to a thick, smooth consistency. Serve immediately.

Each serving (of 4) provides: 88 kcal, 2 g protein, 1 g fat, 19 g carbohydrate, 3 g fibre.

If you don't want to serve this sorbet immediately, you can refreeze it for as long as you like; but note that you must remember to defrost it for at least 2 hours before serving.

Miscellaneous Recipes

MUSHROOMS ON TOAST
allow 10 minutes to prepare

Per Serving

Imperial (Metric)		American
1½ oz (45 g)	margarine	3 tbs
¼ lb (125 g)	mushrooms	1 cup
2 slices	wholewheat bread	2 slices
	salt and pepper to taste	

1 Melt the margarine in a saucepan over a low heat.
2 While it is melting, wash and slice the mushrooms (or leave them whole if they're the button variety) and add them to the saucepan. Turn them every few minutes with a wooden spoon or slice.
3 Meanwhile, toast the bread and arrange on a plate.
4 As soon as the mushrooms are beginning to brown, add salt and pepper to taste, pour over the slices of toast and serve.

Each serving provides: 474 kcal, 8 g protein, 38 g fat, 25 g carbohydrate, 8 g fibre.

Mushrooms are so good done in this simple way that they really don't need any additions but, for variety, try adding ½ tsp *Garam Masala* (page 257) at step 1, or a little freshly-grated ginger. For a more substantial variation, make *Creamed Mushrooms* (page 107) and pour these over freshly-made toast.

SCRAMBLED TOFU AND HERBS ON TOAST

allow 10 minutes to prepare

Per Serving

Imperial (Metric)		American
1 oz (30 g)	margarine	2 tbs
¼ lb (125 g)	firm tofu	½ cup
2 slices	wholewheat bread	2 slices
½ tsp	mixed herbs	½ tsp
	salt and pepper to taste	

1 Melt the margarine in a small saucepan over a low heat.
2 Now crumble in the tofu and stir gently till it's warmed right through.
3 Meanwhile, toast the bread and arrange it on a plate.
4 Add the mixed herbs and salt and pepper to taste and stir for a few
   seconds before pouring over the slices of toast. Serve immediately.

**Each serving provides: 427 kcal, 15 g protein, 31 g fat, 25 g carbohydrate,
5 g fibre.**

This filling, protein-rich dish can be made in a few minutes when you're
short of time or inclination to cook something more substantial or complicated.

For variety, try adding finely chopped onions and a little more margarine at step 1 or different herbs at step 4; or substitute *Garam Masala* (page
257) for the mixed herbs. Freshly-chopped herbs lift it into a different category altogether and only add another few moments to the preparation
time.

JUICY PORRIDGE
allow 10 minutes to prepare

Per Serving

Imperial (Metric)		American
1½ oz (50 g)	rolled oats	½ cup
½ pint (¼ litre)	fruit juice	1¼ cups
	salt to taste	

1 Put all the ingredients in a small saucepan, bring to the boil, stirring continuously, then reduce heat and simmer, uncovered, till the porridge thickens. Add more juice if necessary to prevent the mixture from becoming too thick. Continue simmering for a few more minutes, still stirring continuously.
2 Remove from heat, transfer to individual bowls and serve with a jug of the same fruit juice, iced, to pour over and cool the porridge.

Each serving (made with orange juice) provides: 283 kcal, 7 g protein, 4 g fat, 58 g carbohydrate, 4 g fibre.

Porridge can be made with most fruit juices. Orange, apple, pineapple and apricot are particularly good. If you have any leftovers, serve them, chilled, as a dessert.

For variety, try adding ¼ tsp ground cinnamon or cloves.

LASSI
(Traditional Indian Sweet or Salty Yoghurt Drink)
allow 5 minutes to prepare

To Serve 4–6

Imperial (Metric)		American
½ pint (¼ litre)	*Vegan Yoghurt* (page 244)	1¼ cups
1½ pints (¾ litre)	iced water	3½ cups
1 tsp	salt (or 1 tbs any raw sugar)	1 tsp

1 Put all the ingredients in a blender and blend for a few seconds till thoroughly mixed.
2 Refrigerate till needed. Serve ice cold.

Each serving (of 6, made with salt) provides: 22 kcal, 1 g protein, 1 g fat, 1 g carbohydrate, negligible fibre.

If you like your curries hot, salt lassi is the drink to serve with them. It has a cooling effect in the mouth and throat that is little short of miraculous. But either salt or sweet lassi can be served any time as a refreshing drink.

Note that it can be made several hours in advance so long as it is kept covered in a refrigerator and is well stirred before serving.

Also note that if the batch of yoghurt you're using happens to be rather bland, it's a good idea to add the juice of a lemon to the mixture.

GARAM MASALA
(Basic Indian Curry Spice Mixture)
allow 5 minutes to prepare

To Make about 2 tablespoonfuls

Imperial (Metric)		American
1 heaped tsp	cardamom seeds	1 heaped tsp
2 in (5 cm)	stick of cinnamon (or 1 tsp ground cinnamon)	2 in
2 tsp	whole cumin seeds (or 1 tsp ground cumin)	2 tsp
½	clove of nutmeg (or ½ tsp ground nutmeg)	½
1 tsp	whole cloves (or ½ tsp ground cloves)	1 tsp
1 tsp	whole black peppercorns (or ½ tsp ground pepper)	1 tsp
1 tsp	ground turmeric	1 tsp

1 Use a coffee-grinder to grind all the whole seeds into a coarse powder.
2 Add the already-ground ingredients and seal in a jar till needed.

Most wholefood shops and good grocery stores keep a wide range of whole seeds and spices but you can also get them in local Indian or Chinese shops. Always use freshly-ground spices if you can – only then will you end up with a dish that is enhanced by the intermingling of many subtle aromas and flavours. But it isn't a good idea to make up large quantities because they soon lose their pungency, even when tightly sealed and kept in a cool, dark place.

For variety, try adding or substituting from the following list: *caraway, coriander, fennel, fenugreek, mustard or poppy seeds, ground ginger,* or *chilli.*

BASIC BATTER MIXTURE
allow 25 minutes to prepare
(including 20 minutes to stand)

To Make about a Dozen Pancakes
or
To Batter about 2 lb (1 kg)
of Fruit or Vegetables

Imperial (Metric)		American
¼ lb (125 g)	100 per cent wholewheat flour	1 cup
2 oz (60 g)	soya flour	¾ cup
2 tsp	baking powder	2 tsp
	salt to taste	
¼ pint (125 ml)	soya milk	½ cup
¼ pint (125 ml)	water	½ cup
3 tbs (45 ml)	oil	3 tbs

1 Put the flours, baking powder and salt to taste into a bowl and mix thoroughly.
2 Now add the milk a little at a time and then the water, stirring continuously until the mixture becomes smooth and creamy. For fritters keep the mix fairly thick; for pancakes, make it thinner: the thinner the mix the lighter the pancakes.
3 Beat in the oil a little at a time with a whisk, a fork or an electric mixer.

Each pancake (of 12) provides: 97 kcal, 4 g protein, 4 g fat, 8 g carbohydrate, 2 g fibre.

This can be prepared several hours in advance if you wish or, if you have some left over, simply cover and store in the fridge for use later.

Use it to make pancakes, fruit or vegetable fritters or sweet or savoury puddings.

SKINNED TOMATOES
allow 10 minutes to prepare 1 lb (½ kg)

(Note: many of our recipes call for skinned tomatoes so here is a simple method of skinning them.)

1 Put the tomatoes in a small mixing-bowl and pour over enough boiling water to cover them completely. Leave to stand for 1 minute.
2 Now pick up each tomato individually with a fork and using a very sharp knife to break the skin, pull it away in swathes.

Whole, tinned tomatoes can be bought relatively cheaply in supermarkets and work well enough in most recipes, but always read the labels to see if any preservatives, flavouring or colouring have been added. If you have a good greengrocer or street market near by, however, or if it is simply against your philosophy of life to use tinned produce under any circumstances, then you will obviously prefer to use fresh ones, in which case this method will be useful. Shops and street markets are occasionally flooded with very cheap but absolutely tasteless, pale-pink tomatoes and when this happens your finished recipe will probably taste better if you use tinned ones.

SKINNED PEPPERS
allow 20 minutes to prepare 1 lb (½ kg)

Method 1

1   Cut the peppers in half lengthways, remove the seeds and then cut them in half lengthways again. Flatten them as much as possible by patting them down on a chopping-board and then place them under a hot grill till the skins have turned completely black. This will take about 10–15 minutes and you'll need to turn them from time to time to get them black all over.

2   As soon as they are, drop them in a bowl of cold water before picking them up one at a time with a fork and peeling the skin off with a sharp knife.

Method 2

1   Pick the peppers up individually by plunging a fork into the stalk end and hold in a flame while turning continuously till the skin goes completely black.

2   Plunge the whole, now black, peppers into cold water for a few moments before peeling with a sharp knife.

3   Cut in half and remove the pith and seeds before chopping or using as directed in the recipe.

This is a bit of a performance, so if you're impatient or pressed for time, it's simpler and in our view quite satisfactory to use tinned ones – but read the labels first to check that they don't contain any preservatives, flavouring or dyes.

SOAKING AND COOKING PULSES
(Dried Peas & Beans)
allow several hours to prepare depending on type (see below)

1 Put the pulses in a large saucepan and pour over enough boiling water to cover. Leave to stand for 5 minutes.
2 Drain and repeat.
3 Drain and repeat but this time leave to stand for 1 hour.
4 (Optional) Drain and repeat and leave to stand overnight.
5 Change water, bring quickly to the boil, then reduce heat and simmer, partially covered, till tender.

Approximate Cooking Times
(assuming pre-soaked as above)

(Note: the time pulses need to cook varies with their age and quality. Generally, the fresher they are, the less time they need. The times given assume fresh pulses, recently bought from a reliable shop.)

20–30 minutes (10 minutes in a pressure-cooker)
aduki beans, field beans, mung beans, dried peas

½ –1 hour (15–20 minutes in a pressure-cooker)
black beans, black-eyed beans, flageolet beans,
lentils (only green need soaking), lima beans, split peas

1–2 hours (½ –1 hour in a pressure-cooker)
broad beans, butter beans, chick peas, haricot beans,
red kidney beans (NB: see warning below!)

3–4 hours (1–1½ hours in a pressure-cooker)
soya beans

All pulses cook quicker if pre-soaked as described above, but the chief object of the method given is to eliminate their one drawback – their well-known and unfortunate tendency to cause flatulence and farting. This is because of the large quantities of potassium oxide salt they contain. It is not harmful and the problem is easily solved by the method given. Alternatively, the effects may be much reduced by adding anise, fennel or caraway seeds to the recipe. We have done this in most cases. If all else fails, make an infusion of any (or all) of these seeds in boiling water and sip it slowly.

If all this puts you off the whole idea of pulses, pause for a moment to consider their virtues. They contain more protein, weight for weight, than almost any other food (including beef steak!) as well as a wide range of minerals and vitamins and a very high fibre content.

Warning: red kidney beans should be boiled rapidly for at least 10 minutes before eating. Never slow casserole them unless they have been boiled for 10 minutes first.

SPROUTING SEEDS AND PULSES
several days to prepare depending on type

(Note: if you haven't sprouted seeds or pulses before, read the remarks below before beginning.)

1 Soak 2–3 oz (60–90 g/2–3 tbs) of your chosen seed or pulse in tepid water overnight.
2 Rinse in cold water and drain. Put the rinsed seeds or pulses in a large jar and cover with muslin, gauze or blotting paper. Store in a cool, dark place.
3 Rinse in cold water daily till ready. If you want them to turn green, set them out in sunlight (or daylight) for their last few hours. This won't affect their nutritional value however.
4 Remove any loose skins (if necessary) by floating them in cold water. Drain thoroughly and serve.

Special Notes on Individual Pulses

Alfalfa Seeds: the most commonly-sprouted seeds, easy and delicious.
Chick Peas: very quick; can be eaten as soon as the first shoot appears or kept for up to 4–5 days; delicious and nutty.
Lentils: must be *whole* (i.e. *brown* not *red*).
Mung Beans: easy but unpredictable; lift out sprouted ones by their shoots and leave others longer; a few will not sprout at all.
Red Kidney Beans: easy and attractive but probably not worth bothering with because *they must be boiled for at least 10 minutes or they remain poisonous even when sprouted.*
Rice: must be *wholegrain* (white rice is *dead*).
Sesame Seeds: can be eaten as soon as a shoot appears but, unlike alfalfa seeds, can't easily be induced to grow for very long.
Soya Beans: easy, rich in protein and minerals (especially calcium and iron) and delicious; need more frequent rinsing – twice daily or more, or they'll go off; eat when they're about 3 in (7 cm) long.
Sunflower Seeds: eat as soon as a shoot appears; they can't be induced to grow for long before going off.
Wheatberries: smell and taste of the countryside in summer but remain rather chewy.

It is a sobering miracle to watch a steel-hard, indigestible raw bean transform itself in a few hours into a crunchy plant-shoot. Why anyone should think it worthwhile to use time and energy to factory-process beans into the simulated mince-meat of TVP is a mystery of an altogether more prosaic kind.

Listed above are the most widely available and easy to use seeds and pulses, but it's always worth experimenting with others.

Purpose-made bean-sprouters can be bought in many wholefood shops. They consist of 2 or 3 stacking dishes to spread the pulses on, a tray to catch the rinsing water and a cover to keep off insects; but a simple jar, covered with muslin held in place with an elastic band serves just as well.

Injured or discoloured pulses won't sprout and may go mouldy and infect the whole batch, so it's better to pick them out first – spreading them on a tray will help you to find them.

Failures can be caused by *chemicals* (wholefood shops are the safest places to buy them), *injuries* (have they been chipped or stripped of their skins?) or *age* (how long have they been in stock?).

NON-ALCOHOLIC FRUIT PUNCH
allow 20 minutes to prepare

To Serve 8–12

Imperial (Metric)		American
2 pints (1 litre)	apple juice	5 cups
2 tsp	ground cinnamon	2 tsp
12	whole cloves	12
2 tbs	freshly grated ginger (or 2 tsp ground dried ginger)	2 tbs
1	lemon	1
1	orange	1
1	lime (or another lemon)	1
2 pints (1 litre)	orange juice	5 cups
2 pints (1 litre)	pineapple juice	5 cups
	a few sprigs of mint	
	ice cubes	

1 Put a quarter of the apple juice in a small saucepan, add the spices, bring quickly to the boil then reduce heat and simmer, uncovered, for 15 minutes.
2 Meanwhile, peel the ginger root and grate it into the saucepan, squeeze the lemon and add the juice. Stir from time to time.
3 Thinly slice the orange and lime (another lemon will do if you couldn't get a lime) and put the slices into a suitable serving-bowl or large jug.
4 Pour all the remaining fruit juices into the bowl, add the contents of the saucepan, a few sprigs of fresh mint and the ice cubes and serve.

Virtually any fruit juice can be used to ring the changes on this fruit cocktail. Serve it on hot summer days (or nights) or as an alternative to alcohol at parties.

WINE PUNCH
allow 20 minutes to prepare

To Serve 12–16

Imperial (Metric)		American
½ pint (¼ litre)	water	1¼ cups
2 tsp	ground cinnamon	2 tsp
12	whole cloves	12
2 tbs	freshly grated ginger (or 2 tsp dried ground ginger)	2 tbs
2 pints (1 litre)	orange juice	5 cups
2 pints (1 litre)	apple juice	5 cups
3–4 bottles	white wine	3–4 bottles
3–4 bottles	red wine	3–4 bottles
1	lemon	1
1	orange	1
3 large bottles	tonic water (optional)	3 large bottles
	ice cubes	
	a few sprigs of mint	

1 Put the water into a small saucepan, add the spices, bring quickly to the boil, then reduce heat and simmer, uncovered, for 15 minutes. Meanwhile, peel and grate the ginger into the saucepan, stirring from time to time.
2 Pour the juices and all the wine into a suitable serving-bowl or large jug.
3 Add the contents of the saucepan to the bowl as soon as it's ready.
4 Thinly slice the lemon and the orange and add the slices to the bowl.
5 Add the tonic water and ice cubes to the bowl and stir well. Decorate with sprigs of mint and serve.

This punch is miles better if you can afford to use *champagne* instead of tonic water, but even if you can't, it gives a welcome lift to the sort of cheap plonk most of us have to drink at parties. If you can't afford even the cheap plonk and have to ask your guests to 'bring a bottle', you can still use the recipe by preparing it beforehand without the wine and simply add it as your guests arrive – though it's probably not a good idea to let them see you adding the tonic water! It sweetens the punch and adds sparkle but some people are puritanical about such things.

A SIMPLE TABLE WINE
allow 7 hours to prepare
5–6 weeks to ferment and mature

Imperial (Metric)		American
	For up to 3 gallons (15 litres)	
2 tsp	wine yeast	2 tsp
1 lb (½ kg)	bananas	1 lb
	Plus for each gallon (5 litres)	
2 pints (1 litre)	grape concentrate (red, white or rosé)	5 cups
1 lb (½ kg)	refined granulated sugar	3 cups
1 tsp	yeast nutrient	1 tsp
2	vitamin B tablets	2

(Note: if you haven't made wine before, read the remarks below before beginning.)

1   Activate the yeast: i.e. half fill a small bottle with hand-warm water, add the wine yeast, shake well, stop with a cotton-wool bung and put it in a warm place. Peel and slice the bananas, put the flesh in a bowl (discard the skins), pour boiling water over, cover and set aside. Put the grape concentrate in a warm place too. Leave for 5–6 hours.
2   Put half the sugar in a suitable fermentation vessel and add enough hot water to dissolve it completely. Strain in the liquid from the bananas (discard the flesh). Add the grape concentrate. Make up the liquid to your chosen amount, using cold water till you get the ideal temperature (hand warm, 77°F/25°C). Add the yeast solution and nutrient and stir thoroughly. Cover the fermentation vessel and leave in a warm place for 4 days.
3   After 4 days, dissolve the rest of the sugar in jugfuls of the must (the correct name for the fermenting grape juice solution), tip it back into the fermentation vessel and stir well in. Leave in a warm place for another week. Stir daily.
4   Siphon the must into gallon (5 litre) demijohns, add 2 crushed vitamin B tablets to each jar and top up with cold water if necessary. Plug the jars with cotton-wool bungs and leave in a warm place for a further 7–10 days. Disturb the must by shaking the jars with a circular motion every day if you can remember.
5   Move the jars to a cool place and leave completely undisturbed till the wine clears (about 2–3 weeks).
6   Siphon into bottles. The wine will continue to improve in flavour and texture for several weeks – if you can resist drinking it!

All you really need for home wine-making is a large vessel to ferment the must in – a plastic bucket will do provided it has a cover – glass demijohns to store it in and a wine-maker's siphoning tube.

Normal kitchen standards of hygiene will suffice unless you plan to keep the wine for a year or more before drinking it, but take great care to keep the must covered at all times to keep out the dreaded vinegar bug. If you want to lay down a long-term cellar, every single implement must be steril-ized before use and the yeast must be de-activated with Campden tablets before the bottling.

This simple recipe works nearly every time, but if you do have problems the rule of thumb is: *if in doubt rack it* – that is, siphon it into a fresh clean demijohn. There isn't room to go into the subject more deeply here, so, if racking does not work, consult one of the many books for beginners.

Note that the bananas don't flavour the wine at all, but do give it a rich, smooth texture – sufficient even to fool some connoisseurs!

RUM TRUFFLES
allow about 2 hours to prepare

To Make about 15

Imperial (Metric)		American
2 oz (60 g)	raisins	3 tbs
3 fl oz (90 ml)	dark rum	⅓ cup
3 oz (90 g)	firm margarine	⅓ cup
¼ lb (125 g)	gram flour	1 cup
3 tbs (45 ml)	maple syrup	3 tbs
5 tbs (50 g)	carob powder	½ cup
3 tbs	desiccated coconut	3 tbs

1 Put the raisins in a small bowl, pour the rum over and set aside for at least ½ hour.
2 Melt the margarine in a small saucepan, stir in the gram flour to make a firm roux and cook gently for 2–3 minutes. Stir in the maple syrup, rum and raisins and continue stirring till thoroughly mixed. Remove from heat.
3 Set 2 tbs of the carob powder aside and add the rest to the saucepan. Mix thoroughly to a thick, slightly sticky, uniformly coloured paste. Set aside for 20 minutes.
4 Put the desiccated coconut and the remaining 2 tbs of carob powder on a plate and mix together till the coconut becomes carob coloured.
5 Now, take teaspoonfuls of the truffle mixture, drop them on to the coconut and roll them around to make well-coated little balls of about 1 in (2 cm) diameter.
6 Refrigerate for at least an hour before serving.

Each truffle (of 15) provides: 135 kcal, 3 g protein, 9 g fat, 7 g carbohydrate, 5 g fibre.

These are about as decadent as we are proposing to get in this book and we advise you not to make too many of them lest your friends should over-dose themselves. Serve them with freshly-brewed black coffee and brandy to round off a really special meal. They also make a delightful, thoughtful present for a vegan friend.

For variety, use brandy or liqueur instead of rum, or finely chopped dates instead of raisins.

Appendix 1
Notes on Vegan Nutrition

FOOD FOR HEALTH

'We are what we eat' goes the well-known platitude. But it's actually a simple statement of fact because all living tissue on our planet is made from the sun's energy via the miracle of plant growth.

For perfect health, the human body needs carbohydrate and fat (for energy), protein (for the building of tissues), fibre (for good digestion), plus tiny amounts of complex substances called vitamins, certain minerals and, of course, water. This brief summary of these individual constituents of our diet describes what they are and how we, as vegans, can make sure that we eat them in the correct proportions.

CARBOHYDRATE

When sunlight falls on green plants, they mysteriously spin their substance from carbon dioxide and water. How they do it is still not fully understood. We take it for granted simply because it happens all the time. Sugars and starches are two forms of plant substance, known as carbohydrates, that the plant produces as a way of storing energy for use when the sun isn't shining and these form the chief source of energy in human food. And only plants can do this – although carnivorous animals such as dogs and lions seldom eat plants directly, they do eat animals that have eaten nothing else. Since these sugars and starches are present in all plants, sugars predominantly in fruit, starches in seeds and roots, there is no difficulty in getting an adequate supply in an exclusively vegan diet.

FAT

There are three main kinds of fat. Two of them, *saturated* and *monounsaturated*, can be made in the body from carbohydrate and so are not essential in the diet. They occur chiefly in animals which store them as an energy reserve (even lean meat contains a lot) and are high in cholesterol. The third kind, *polyunsaturated*, cannot be made in the body but must be taken in the form of plant food. It contains no cholesterol.

'The Royal College of Physicians advocate a generous intake of polyunsaturated fatty acids but a restricted intake of saturated fatty acids for the prevention of coronary heart disease.'

The conclusion seems obvious – not only are vegetable oils necessary, but a healthier way to take the fat we need.

The Health Education Council now recommends that fat should not form more than 30–35 per cent of the total energy intake. Nearly all omnivores and some vegetarians often exceed this figure by 10–20 per cent or more – and it's animal fat at that – but:

'A vegan diet composed mainly of unrefined cereals, pulses and nuts supplemented with smaller amounts of fruit and vegetables will be high in fibre and starch and provide 60–70 per cent of the total energy in the diet from carbohydrate.'

Which is just what the doctor ordered!

PROTEIN

Proteins are enormous molecules which are broken down by the body's digestive processes into their component parts, called amino acids, and used as building blocks for tissues such as skin and muscle. There are several different kinds of these amino acids commonly found in plants and animals but although plants can synthesize all they need, there are eight kinds that humans and other animals are unable to make. These are called the essential amino acids and, as the body is unable to store them, they form a vital part of our daily food.

All these building blocks must be present together for the body to be able to use them and, as their proportions vary from one plant to another, it makes sense to combine two or more plants in a particular dish to ensure 'a good protein balance'. (For example, *Three Seed Bread*, page 210, *Tomato & Lentil Flan*, page 73, *Poppy Seed Tart*, page 224 and so on.)

But, contrary to popular belief, there is no problem at all getting enough of these protein building blocks from plant food.

'Cereals, nuts, potatoes and oil seeds contain about 10 per cent of their available energy as protein and pulses about 30 per cent; fruit, leafy vegetables and roots and tubers (other than potatoes) generally contain very little protein.

'The Department of Health & Social Security recommend that 10 per cent of the daily energy intake should come from protein. This means an intake of 55 grams/day for women and 68 grams/day for men leading a sedentary life. *These recommended intakes can easily be satisfied by a vegan diet based mainly on cereals, potatoes, pulses, nuts and oil seeds and supplemented by smaller amounts of fruit and vegetables.'* (Our italics)

FIBRE

Some of the carbohydrates synthesized by plants are used to form the basic structure of their cell walls. Called cellulose or fibre, these can only be easily digested by herbivores (such as sheep, cows and horses) by a process of fermentation that takes several days and, in the case of cows, requires five stomachs! As a result, fibre was once thought not to be an essential part of the human diet. But more recent research has shown that it is in fact vital for healthy digestion in humans because it provides roughage that helps the food pass through the gut more quickly, thereby preventing constipation and the build-up of toxins. It also helps to control blood sugar levels by slowing down the absorption of sugars and starches – particularly important for diabetics – and keeps down the blood cholesterol level, thereby reducing the risk of heart disease. There is also evidence that it reduces the risk of bowel cancer. Finally, and perhaps most importantly of all, it gives a feeling of fullness without the consumption of more food than is good for you.

VITAMINS

Plants are such a rich source of nearly all the vitamins we need that only two need concern us here: B_{12} and D.

VITAMIN B_{12}

'Vitamin B_{12} is unique among the vitamins being made exclusively by micro-organisms. Cereals, fruit, nuts, pulses, vegetables and other plant foods are apparently free from the vitamin unless contaminated by micro-organisms that produce the vitamin and by insects. Thus vegan diets are most likely to be lacking in vitamin B_{12}. The highest amount of vitamin B_{12} in foods is found in liver and kidney although it is present in all flesh and dairy foods. The vitamin is produced commercially from bacteria and a number of vegan foods, such as Tastex, Barmene, Plamil and Granogen, are now supplemented with the vitamin. The daily requirement for vitamin B_{12} is very small, in the region of 1–3 micro-g/day (1 micro-g is a millionth of a gram), and this makes the study of vitamin B_{12} nutrition very difficult.'

Furthermore, the human body can store up to four years' supply of the vitamin, so that although the body may use 3 micro-gs daily, we don't actually need to *eat* some every day.

It seems likely that in our original 'natural' state, eating rain-washed fruits, roots and berries in the primeval forest, human beings would have developed or absorbed the necessary intestinal flora to synthesize the tiny amounts needed and have had the capacity to absorb them directly from the gut without needing to take them in through the mouth. Even with today's sprayed and fertilized crops, many vegans claim to have remained healthy for years without supplementing their diets with B_{12}.

Luckily, there are natural sources of B_{12} other than dead animal flesh, for it is almost always found in plant products that are the result of fermentation, such as beers (particularly stout), wines, miso, yoghurt, etc.

Amounts may be small, however, and if you plan to be exclusively vegan on a permanent basis, it's probably better to be safe than sorry and take a vitamin B_{12} supplement. Even though you probably won't actually need it, it won't do you any harm! In any case, the vitamin B_{12} tablets available in wholefood shops are produced by fermentation processes similar to those occurring in the production of beer or miso, and have just as much claim to being described as 'natural'.

VITAMIN D

'Plant foods do not contain vitamin D, which is associated with the absorption of calcium and bone development, but individuals can synthesise the vitamin for themselves by the action of sunlight on their skin. Vitamin D deficiency can occur in children reared on a vegan diet if they are not sufficiently exposed to sunlight or not given a dietary source of the vitamin.'

So vegans who shun the sun should make sure they're getting enough of the vitamin in their diet. This isn't difficult in practice since it is added as a supplement to all margarines and to some soya milks. Vitamin D pills are also available. These remarks apply particularly to young children, especially those of Asian families, who tend to keep them out of the sun.

MINERALS

We also need a number of minerals in our diet for good health but since these are widely distributed through a whole range of plants there is generally no problem getting them.

Plant foods, especially fruit and vegetables, contain less salt than foods of animal origin. The correct quantity of salt is a matter of much dispute in the medical profession, but there is some evidence that the typical Western diet contains too much of it and that this leads to problems of high blood pressure and difficulties with the heart and kidneys. So, once again, the vegan diet may alleviate rather than cause symptoms.

SUMMARY

If you eat from a wide range of the recipes given in this book, using the ingredients specified, you are most unlikely to suffer any nutrient, vitamin or mineral deficiency.

But if you are cautious by nature and want to be absolutely sure of your supply of vitamin B_{12}, take care to include some stout beer, yoghurt, wine and miso in your diet on a regular basis and take vitamin B_{12} pills which are themselves, as has been pointed out, produced by a process of natural fermentation.

If you wish to know more on the subject, we recommend you to read *Vegan Nutrition* by T. A. B. Sanders, published by the Vegan Society, which is the source of all the quotes in these brief notes.

Appendix 2
Seven Reasons to be Vegan

1 HEALTH

It would be possible to follow a 100 per cent vegan regime and not be eating healthily – but you'd have to work at it. For example you could have white bread and jam for breakfast, chips and beans for lunch and baked beans on white toast for dinner. Providing you persisted, after a while, if you didn't die of boredom, you'd die of something else.

But people who become vegan generally do so only after a lot of thought and the diet they choose usually consists of high-quality wholefood cereals, grains and pulses supplemented with fresh fruit, salads and vegetables – the diet, in short, that we present in this book and this is what we mean by 'a vegan diet' in this section.

There is increasing evidence that a vegan diet like this is to be strongly recommended on health grounds:

- Animals reared for consumption as meat are now fed on an appalling cocktail of chemicals, hormones and antibiotics. The long-term consequences of consuming these toxic substances in meat isn't known but it can hardly be beneficial.
- The high levels of cholesterol found in all meat and dairy products are now generally thought by the medical profession to be dangerous for human health. 'Natural' meat came from animals that roamed and ran wild. They had virtually no fat on them and what they had was unsaturated. Factory-farmed animals get no exercise at all and their flesh – even the lean – contains up to 50 per cent saturated fat.
- Cow's milk produced by the dairy industry has been found to contain significant quantities of pesticides, antibiotics and teat dip disinfectants. Their effect on humans has not been investigated. Again, it cannot be beneficial.
- A surprisingly large number of people are allergic to cow's milk, especially young children. Eczema, asthma, tonsillitis and gastro-intestinal disturbances are some of the problems that can result. People may suffer from a range of distressing symptoms for years before discovering that the symptoms simply disappear as soon as they stop drinking the cow's milk that caused them.
- The typical Western diet provides about 12 grams of salt a day – about 2 teaspoonfuls – most of it coming from meat and meat products. This is

certainly too much and may lead to high blood pressure and all its associated risks. Vegan diets are relatively low in salt.

 • Vegan and vegetarian foods do not attract the noxious bacteria that
are responsible for salmonella and other forms of food poisoning.

Further evidence was published by the Health Education Council in a leaf-
let in 1985:

'A hundred years ago, most people ate plenty of fibre from bread and
potatoes, but lacked a fully adequate varied diet. Diseases caused by a
lack of vitamins and minerals were common. Today, the problems are
different. Many people now eat too much meat, dairy produce and
sugar, and too little fibre for good health . . .
 'Research has shown links between what we eat and many modern
diseases. For example:

 • Heart disease may be linked with too much fat.
 • Diabetes and tooth decay may be linked with too much sugar.
 • High blood pressure and strokes may be linked with too much
salt.
 • Bowel cancer, constipation and diverticulosis (a common bowel
problem) may be linked with too little fibre.
 • Obesity may be linked with too much fat and sugar, and too little
fibre. Diabetes, high blood pressure, strokes and heart disease are all
associated with obesity too.'

All the fats referred to in this quote are the saturated type, found chiefly in
foods of animal origin. Just over a quarter of the fat eaten in the typical
Western diet comes from meat, butter and margarine provide another
quarter, milk and cooking fats account for another, and the remaining
quarter is made up of cheese and 'hidden' fats in pastry, sweets, ice-creams
and other 'convenience' foods.

*The simple fact of converting to a vegan diet removes all the cholesterol and
nearly all the saturated fat and reduces the total quantity of polyunsaturated fat to
the 30–35 per cent of the total energy intake which is recommended by the Health
Education Council for general good health and the prevention of heart disease.*

If all this leaves you unmoved, consider this: Britain's longest-lived man,
Harry Shoerats, died in February 1984, aged 111. He was born in Russia in
1872 and settled in Britain in 1917. He attributed his longevity primarily to
his vegan diet of fruit, nuts, vegetables and cereals. He did not retire from
his work as a craftsman until the age of 104 and cycled to work daily till his
100th birthday.

2 ECONOMIC

If you follow a diet based on the recipes in this book, you'll certainly find yourself spending a lot less on food on a personal basis, but the consequences of a shift to a vegan diet among the population at large would be considerably more far-reaching.

Animals reared for their meat have been calculated to use 90 per cent of the plant food given to them simply to sustain their own bodily processes. Only 10 per cent finally arrives on the plates of omnivores. It would be hard to imagine a more uneconomic or wasteful way of using the world's resources.

If there were a major shift towards veganism in the industrialized nations, the prices of plant foods would fall everywhere, especially in the Third World.

3 ECOLOGICAL

More than 40 per cent of the world's tropical rain forest has been destroyed this century. The current rate of disappearance is 50 hectares a minute. Most people might think it fatuous to suggest that becoming a vegan could have the slightest effect on this. Yet it is a simple fact that most of the vast areas that are being destroyed and laid down to grass in South America are being levelled for no better reason than the raising of beef cattle for the North American steak and hamburger market. As a result, the world is losing rare species at a frightening and accelerating rate.

Similar pressures apply wherever land is farmed intensively. Britain's countryside is fast being turned into a vast, bleak, prairie-like landscape devoid of hedgerows or trees simply in order to produce yet more contributions to the EEC grain mountains, most of which are sold off as animal feed. Countless species of our wild birds, animals, butterflies and wild flowers are threatened as a result.

At sea, intensive fishing has destroyed the vast herring shoals that once roamed around Britain's shores (and the North Sea fishing industry with them) and everyone knows how near several species of whale have come to extinction.

The list, alas, goes on and on. There are hundreds of other species whose habitats are threatened by the millions of omnivores *our* species counts among its members.

'The average Briton now consumes up to 8 beef cattle, 36 pigs, 36 sheep and 550 poultry birds in the average lifetime.' (*The Animals Report*, Richard North, Penguin, 1983.)

Multiply this by the 55 million people in the UK and you begin to realize the scale of the problem.

Clearly, every single person who becomes vegan immediately ceases their personal contribution to this inexorable demand for the products of the intensive farming of animals. So *everyone who becomes vegan ceases to be part of the problem and becomes part of the solution* – helping to ease the intolerable pressure that humanity now exerts on every other species to the farthest reaches of the globe.

4 ALTRUISTIC

'Why do you people care more about animals than about humans?' is a challenge that is often thrown at vegans and vegetarians by irritated omnivores.

Leaving aside the fact that it is clearly an emotional response, probably stemming from their own feelings of guilt, it is simply not true:

'If Americans were to reduce their meat consumption by only 10 per cent for one year, it would free at least 12 million tons of grain for human consumption – or enough to feed 60 million people . . . Indeed, if Americans were to stop eating grain-fed beef altogether the grain thus released would be enough to feed all the 600 million people in India.' (*Animal Liberation*, Peter Singer, Thorsons, 1983.)

Not to mention the 'few' starving millions in central Africa!

For the truth is that if you wish to put the welfare of humanity first, you can hardly do better than *become vegan*!

So the next time an irritable omnivore challenges you in this way, why not throw the challenge right back by asking: 'Why are you so indifferent to the starving people in the Third World that you selfishly continue to eat more than ten times the grain you need in the form of animal protein?'

If all this sounds a bit too idealistic for you, consider this: since the case for the vegan diet as healthier is now irrefutable (and generally accepted by the medical profession) what better way can there be of showing your love and concern for those closest to you than by preparing for them not only food they will enjoy, but food that is good for their health?

5 COMPASSIONATE

'A human being is a part of a whole, called by us 'Universe', a part limited in time and space. He experiences himself, his thoughts and feelings as something separated from the rest – a kind of optical delusion of his consciousness. This delusion is a kind of prison for us, restricting us to our personal desires and to affection for a few persons nearest to us.

'Our task must be to free ourselves from this prison by widening our circle of compassion to embrace all living creatures and the whole of nature in its beauty.' (Albert Einstein.)

'If true, the Pythagorean principles as to abstaining from flesh, foster innocence; if ill-founded they at least teach us frugality, and what loss have you in losing your cruelty? It merely deprives you of the food of lions and vultures . . . let us ask what is best – not what is customary. Let us love temperance – let us be just – let us refrain from bloodshed.' (Seneca.)

'I, for my part, wonder of what sort of feeling, mind or reason that man was possessed who was first to pollute his mouth with gore, and allow his lips to touch the flesh of a murdered being; who spread his table with the mangled form of dead bodies, and claimed as daily food and dainty dishes what but now were beings endowed with movement, with perception and with voice.' (Plutarch.)

What would such compassionate and thoughtful men as these have said of the catalogue of misery and suffering we now inflict on animals in the name of profit and of science? For the abuses they wrote of were trifling compared with the scale and quality of the practices of factory farming, or the wholesale abuses inherent in the routine testing on innocent and defenceless creatures of the unnecessary, trivial products of the cosmetics industry?

Most omnivores, if they were forced to spend a single day enduring the conditions of the average factory farm would renounce meat-eating for life. It is not lack of imagination that prevents them from discovering this, but a deliberate, conscious decision to remain ignorant for fear that *knowing the full consequences of their demand for cheap meat would be too painful too endure.* Such people are more guilty of the suffering inflicted on animals in their name than any German citizen was, in the Second World War, who sought to prove afterwards that he or she simply 'didn't know' what was going on in the concentration camps.

But if what is done in factory farms is appalling, it pales into insignificance compared with the horrors inflicted in laboratories in the name of science.

'In Britain, where experimenters are required to report the number of experiments performed, official government figures show that 4,443,843 experiments on animals were performed in 1981. In the United States there are no figures of comparable accuracy. Under the Animal Welfare Act [sic] of 1970 the US Department of Agriculture publishes a report listing the number of animals used by facilities registered with it, but this list is incomplete in many ways. It does not include rats, mice, birds, reptiles, frogs, or domestic farm animals used for experimental purposes; it does not include animals used in secondary schools, or by government agencies; and it does not include experiments performed by facilities that do not transport animals interstate or receive grants or contracts from the federal government. According to this very incomplete report, somewhere between 1.6 and 1.8 million animals are used in experimentation each year. The number of dogs is 200,000, cats 50–70,000, primates 50,000, rabbits, hamsters and guinea pigs around half a million each . . .

'Surely one day . . . our children's children, reading about what was done in laboratories in the twentieth century, will feel the same sense of horror and incredulity at what otherwise civilised people can do that we now feel when we read about the atrocities of the Roman gladiatorial arenas or the eighteenth-century slave trade.' (*Animal Liberation*, Peter Singer.)

Ask yourself what possible response can any sane and compassionate person have to this unforgivable lapse on the part of humanity, other than determinedly and single-mindedly to boycott any or all of the products of such practices?

6 ETHICAL

'If man's aspirations towards right living are serious . . . he will first abstain from animal food because . . . its use is simply immoral, as it requires the performance of an act which is contrary to moral feeling – killing.' *The Ethics of Diet*, Tolstoy.

But are humanity's aspirations serious? We often claim to have attained the highest level of consciousness of any living creature on earth. Whether this is true or not – and it must be open to doubt in view of the mindless, institutionalized cruelty of our factory farms, vivisection laboratories and the torture of our own kind in prisons around the world, it is certainly true that we have become the guardians of this planet and of all its life forms. So, with all our faults, we must try to behave as responsibly as we can.

Is factory farming a responsible way to behave? Even the most recalcitrant meat-eater can hardly deny that cruelty and suffering are inherent in it. In an attempt to divert attention away from their own doubts, which often stem from the fear of having to change, such people launch into debates about *how much* pain animals can suffer compared with humans. But this is irrelevant. If we agree that suffering is bad, and that animals do suffer as a consequence of our actions, then it doesn't matter how much they suffer but that they suffer at all. So we must change our actions or stand condemned of callousness.

Nor is it good enough to support the theory but fail to support the practice: 'They pity, and they eat the objects of their compassion.' (*The Citizen of the World*, Oliver Goldsmith, in *Collected Works*, Clarendon Press, Oxford, 1966.)

'If a boycott is the only way to stop cruelty, then we must encourage as many people as possible to join the boycott. We can only be effective in this if we ourselves set the example.' (*Animal Liberation*, Peter Singer.)

'A vegetarian diet is the acid test of humanitarianism.' (Tolstoy.)

7 SPIRITUAL

Orthodox Buddhists and Hindus have always been vegetarian and often vegan for their religions are founded on the belief that life is sacred – not just *human life*, as in Christianity, but *all* life. But, just as importantly, both these great religions also teach that not only is a vegan diet correct in ethical terms, but that it is also more conducive to spiritual peace of mind and the acquisition of the virtues of humility and compassion. Christians have, of course, always admired just these two virtues above all else in their own founder and leader, so it is odd how little heed is paid to his own words on the subject:

'Not by shedding innocent blood, but by living a righteous life shall ye find the peace of God ... Blessed are they who keep this law; for God is manifested in all creatures. All creatures live in God, and God is hid in them ...

'The fruit of the trees and the seeds and of the herbs alone do I partake, and these are changed by the spirit into my flesh and blood. Of these alone and their like shall ye eat who believe in me and are my disciples; for of these, in the spirit, come life and health and healing unto man ...'

(From *The Gospel of the Holy Twelve*, trans. by G. J. Ouseley.)

It would seem that the Jesus in this apocryphal gospel is advocating veganism. In another early gospel, translated into English directly from the Aramaic tongue Jesus is thought to have spoken, there is a specific warning of the dire consequences of the killing and eating of animals:

'And the flesh of slain beasts in his own body will become his own tomb. For I tell you truly, he who kills, kills himself, and whoso eats the flesh of slain beasts, eats the body of death.'

(From *The Gospel of Peace of Jesus Christ by the Disciple John*, Trans. by E. B. Szekely, C. W. Daniel, London 1937.)

But isn't it enough to be vegetarian?
Why do I have to become *vegan*?

The problem is that the industrial production of milk, butter, eggs and cheese is totally dependant on the existence of the rest of the factory farming industry with all its odious practices. Repeated frustrated pregnancies

are required to keep dairy cows lactating and in any case they are slaught-
ered for meat as soon as their milk yield drops, and it is the fate of their unfortunate calves to be removed from their mothers at birth and sent either
straight to the slaughterhouse or to veal production units. Most eggs come
from battery systems of course (including those with names like 'Farm
Fresh') but even free-range egg production entails the killing of the unpro-
ductive – the cocks (only half of a batch of fertile eggs will hatch into hens)
and even the productive hens are sent for slaughter as soon as their laying
days are over.

So we see that even buying a carton of milk in a supermarket or half a
dozen free-range eggs in a wholefood shop, makes a tiny, but significant,
contribution to industrial slaughter.

Well, if these seven reasons haven't convinced you, let us add an eighth!
Neither of the authors of this book found their food even half as enjoyable
before becoming vegan as we have since. So, if you can't bring yourself to
change your diet for health, economic, ecological, altruistic, compassionate, ethical or spiritual reasons, then *change it for the sheer pleasure of eating
the wonderful vegan dishes we have invented for you!*

Appendix 3
Useful Addresses

UNITED KINGDOM

Animal Aid Society   (campaigns to promote animal rights)
7 Castle Street, Tonbridge, Kent, TN9 1BH.
Animal Concern (Scotland)
121 West Regent Street, Glasgow, G2 2SD
Animal Liberation Front   (direct action to rescue animals)
BCM Box 1160, London WC1N 3XX
Animus   (fund-raising for animal rights groups)
34 Marshall Street, London, W1V 1LL.
British Union for the Abolition of Vivisection
16a Crane Grove, London, N7.
Compassion in World Farming   (campaigns against factory farming)
20 Lavant Street, Petersfield, Hampshire, GU32 3EW.
The Dr Hadwen Trust for Humane Research   (alternatives to animal experiments)
6c Brand Street, Hitchin, Herts. SG5 1HX.
Friends of the Earth   (campaigns on ecological issues)
26–8 Underwood Street, London, N1 7JQ.
National Anti-Vivisection Society
51 Harley Street, London, W1N 1DD.
The Vegan   (quarterly magazine of The Vegan Society)
33/35 George Street, Oxford, OX1 2AY.
The Vegan Society   (campaigns to promote a vegan diet)
33/35 George Street, Oxford, OX1 2AY.
Vegan Views (quarterly magazine)
6 Hayes Avenue, Bournemouth, BH7
The Vegetarian Society   (campaigns to promote vegetarianism)
Parkdale, Dunham Road, Altringham, Cheshire WA14 4QG
Vegfam   (famine relief without exploiting animals)
The Sanctuary, Near Lydford, Devon.
World Society for the Protection of Animals   (aims to relieve animal suffering)
106, Jermyn Street, London, SW1Y 6EE.

UNITED STATES OF AMERICA

Action for Life   (opposes factory farming)
Box 5888, Bethesda, Md. 20814, USA.

American Vegan Society   (campaigns to promote the vegan diet)
501 Old Harding Highway, Malaga, N.J. 08328, USA.
Animal Liberation Inc.   (campaigns against factory farming)
319 West 74th Street, New York, N.Y. 10023, USA.
Animal Rights Network
Box 5234, Westport, Ct. 06880, USA.
Beauty Without Cruelty   (American branch of British Group)
175 West 12th Street, New York, N.Y. 10012, USA.
Friends of Animals Inc.   (opposes all cruelty to animals)
11 West 60th Street, New York, N.Y. 10023, USA.
The Fund for Animals Inc.   (opposes seal-hunting and whaling)
140 West 57th Street, New York, N.Y. 10019, USA.
Mobilization for Animals
Box 337, Jonesboro, Tenn. 37659, USA.
People for the Ethical Treatment of Animals (PETA)   (campaigns against laboratory use of animals)
Box 56272, Washington D.C. 20011, USA.
Society for Animal Rights   (direct action in support of animal rights)
421 South State Street, Clarks Summit, Pa. 18411, USA.
United Action for Animals   (campaigns against use of animals in research)
205 East 42nd Street, New York, N.Y. 10017, USA.
Vegetarian Activist Collective   (active political group)
616 6th Street, Brooklyn, N.Y. 11215, USA.

AUSTRALIA

Animal Liberation
c/o Total Environment Centre, 18 Argyle Street, Sydney, NSW.
The Vegan Society
P.O. Box 467, Broadway 2007, NSW.

NEW ZEALAND

Save Animals from Experimentation
P.O. Box 647, Auckland 1.

Appendix 4
Selected Bibliography

Animal Factories, Jim Mason and Peter Singer (Crown, New York, 1980)

Animal Liberation, Peter Singer (Thorsons, Wellingborough, 1983)

Animal Rights and Human Obligations, Tom Regan and Peter Singer (Prentice Hall, New Jersey, 1976)

Animal Rights – A Symposium, David Paterson and Richard Ryder (eds) (Centaur Press, 1979)

Animal Suffering, Marian Stamp Dawkins (Chapman & Hall, London, 1980)

Animal Welfare in Poultry, Pig & Veal Calf Production (HMSO, London, 1981)

Animals, Men and Morals: An Enquiry into the Mal-Treatment of Non-Humans, Stanley and Roslind Godlovitch and John Harrison (eds) (Gollancz, London, and Taplinger, New York, 1972)

The Animals Report, Richard North (Penguin, London, 1983)

A Bibliography on Animal Rights and Related Matters, Charles Magel (University Press of America, Washington, DC, 1981)

The Civilised Alternative, Jon Wynne-Tyson (Centaur Press, 1972)

McCance and Widdowson's The Composition of Foods, A. A. Paul and D. A. T. Southgate, fourth revised ed (HMSO, London, 1978)

Diabetes, Coronary Thrombosis and The Saccharine Disease, Cleave, Campbell and Painter (John Wright & Sons Ltd, Bristol)

The Extended Circle, Jon Wynne-Tyson (ed.) (Centaur Press, 1986)

Food Fit for Humans, Frank Wilson (Daniel, 1975)

Food for a Future, Jon Wynne-Tyson (Centaur Press, 1979)

Food Science – A Chemical Approach, Brian A. Fox and Allan G. Cameron third ed (Hodder & Stoughton, London, 1977)

History of the Humane Movement, Charles D. Niven (Johnson, 1967)

In Defence of Living Things, Christine Townend (Wentworth, Sydney, 1980)

Medical Nemesis, Ivan Illich (Calder & Boyars, London, 1975)

The Moral Status of Animals, Stephen R. L. Clark (OUP, 1977)

The Philosophy of Compassion, Esmé Wynne-Tyson (Centaur Press, 1970)

The Question of Animal Awareness, Donald Griffin (Rockefeller University Press, New York, 1976)

The Rights of Animals, Brigid Brophy (*Sunday Times*/Vegetarian Society, 1965)

The Scientific Conscience, Catherine Roberts (Centaur Press, 1974)

Vegan Nutrition, T.A.B. Sanders and Frey R. Ellis (The Vegan Society, 1985)

Veganism – Scientific Aspects, T. A. B. Sanders (The Vegan Society, 1983)

A Vegetarian Sourcebook, Keith Akers (G. P. Putnam & Sons, New York, 1983)

Victims of Science, Richard D. Ryder (Davis-Poynter, 1975)

Appendix 5
Abbreviations and Measures

Imperial	Metric	Nutritional Analysis
oz = ounce(s)	g = gram(s)	kcal = kilocalorie(s)
lb = pound(s)	kg = kilogram(s)	
fl oz = fluid ounce(s)	ml = millilitre(s)	
F = Fahrenheit	C = Celsius	

Table of Approximate Conversions Used in the Recipes

Imperial	Metric	American
½ oz	15 g	NB:
1 oz	30 g	the number of
2 oz	60 g	tablespoonfuls
3 oz	90 g	or cups varies
¼ lb	125 g	according to
5 oz	150 g	the ingredients
6 oz	180 g	
7 oz	225 g	
½ lb	¼ kg	
10 oz	300 g	
¾ lb	350 g	
1 lb	½ kg	
1¼ lb	575 g	
1½ lb	¾ kg	
2 lb	1 kg	
1 tsp	5 ml	1 tsp
1 tbs	15 ml	1 tbs
¼ pint	125 ml	½ cup
8 fl oz	200 ml	1 cup
½ pint	¼ litre	1¼ cups
¾ pint	400 ml	2 cups
1 pint	½ litre	2½ cups
1¼ pints	650 ml	3 cups
1½ pints	¾ litre	3½ cups
2 pints	1 litre	5 cups

Note: The standard measure for a tablespoon is 15 ml and we recommend that you use measuring spoons, as ordinary spoons vary in size from 15 ml to 25 ml

Exact Conversions

1 oz = 28.35 g   1 lb = 453.6 g   1 pint = 568 ml
100 g = 3.53 oz   1 kg = 2 lb 3 oz   1 litre = 1.76 pints

Oven Settings and Temperatures

Description	Fahrenheit	Celsius	Gas Mark
very cool to cool	225–300	107–149	¼, ½, 1, 2
warm	325	163	3
moderate	350	177	4
fairly hot	375–400	190–204	5,6
hot	425	218	7
very hot	450–475	232–246	8, 9

Appendix 6
Glossary of Unusual Ingredients

Including US equivalents of common English terms

(*Note:* all the items listed are readily available in wholefood shops, some in Chinese or Asian shops and a few in the larger supermarkets, delicatessens and good grocery stores.)

Agar Flakes   A setting and thickening agent derived from seaweed. It is rich in iron and other minerals and has no taste, making it suitable for sweet and savoury dishes. It is also found in more concentrated powder form.

Apple Concentrate   Concentrated apple juice. Used instead of sugar as a sweetener and for its flavouring qualities.

Arrowroot Powder   Used to make thin or transparent sauces and glazes. In Victorian times it was commonly given as a bland food to convalescents because it is so easy to digest. It is derived from the root of a plant of the same name and sometimes sold in wholefood shops labelled with its Japanese name 'kuzu'.

Aubergine   = Eggplant (US).

Bean Sprouts   The sprouted shoots of seeds and pulses. Used in salads and in Chinese stir-fried dishes. (See *Sprouting Seeds and Pulses*, page 262.)

Buckwheat   A variety of wheat with an unusual, triangular-shaped seed. It originated in Russia and was once called beechwheat. It is nearly always sold ready roasted.

Bulgur   Kernels of wheat that have been cooked, dried and cracked. Fine grades require no cooking if soaked. Coarser grades cook much like rice but need less water. It has a pleasant, nutty taste.

Carob Powder (or flour)   Flour made from the roasted, ground seedpods of the locust tree. It is nutritious, naturally sweet and has a similar taste to chocolate.

Chick Peas   A pulse in the form of rock-hard, cream-coloured peas that are ubiquitous in the Middle East. They can be sprouted for use in salads, ground to make gram flour, or cooked and mashed to make hummus.

Chick Pea Flour   = Gram Flour.

Cornmeal (fine)   = Cornstarch (US). Finely-milled, wholegrain cornmeal can be found in most wholefood shops. Used as a thickening agent in preference to the chemically-adulterated cornflour to be found in most grocery stores.

Courgettes = Zucchini (US).

Creamed Coconut Solidified extract of coconut. It can be used as a thickening in stews, melted and blended to produce an alternative thick cream, or thinned right down and poured over cakes to set into an alternative, sugar-free icing.

Demerara Sugar = Dark brown sugar (US). See also Raw Sugar.

Fennel Similar in texture and crispness to celery, this delightful, fresh vegetable has a pleasant liquorice flavour. The variety most often found in street markets in the UK and USA originates in Italy and is called 'Florence'.

Fennel Seeds Similar to anise seeds, but milder in flavour. Said to be an antidote to flatulence.

Garam Masala Basic ground curry spice mixture (page 257). Ten times better than commercial ready-made curry powder!

Ginger We recommend you to use the fresh root if you can get it because it loses a lot of its delicate, pungent aroma when dried. Fresh ginger root can be bought in Chinese and other ethnic stores, many street markets and in some wholefood shops and large supermarkets. To prepare the root, cut off a single branch, peel it (potato peelers are fine) and grate it for immediate use. The ginger plant originates in the West Indies and looks a little like lily-of-the-valley. It has been used for centuries for its medicinal qualities as it is said to be good for the digestion, soothing to sore throats and settling for upset stomachs and diarrhoea.

Gram Flour Made from ground chick peas and used for its nutritional value and as a binding agent. Also sold as chick pea flour.

Grilled = Broiled (US).

Healthfood Many shops with this name over their door sell cakes, biscuits and sweets that are crammed with sugar, eggs, butter and cream. Such food cannot by any stretch of the imagination be described as 'healthy'. We have preferred to avoid such misconceptions by using the term 'wholefood' throughout.

Juniper Berries The dark, bluish-black fruits of the juniper tree. Pungent and sweet if eaten raw, they are used for seasoning and to impart aroma (particularly in gin). They have been used as a herbal remedy for centuries and are considered to be beneficial for a range of medical conditions.

Marrow = Squash (US).

Miso A paste traditionally made in Japan from fermented soya beans. It is extremely rich in vitamins and minerals and is used to flavour soups and stews. The bacteria which made it are still alive when you buy it and are said to be good for you, so it's best to add it to a dish just before serving and thereby avoid cooking and killing them.

Poppy Seeds Used since ancient times as a condiment and medicine. Extremely nutritious and a valuable source of protein.

Raw Sugar Generally speaking we have avoided using sugar, or used it sparingly and have always specified 'raw' sugar because in this less-refined state it still contains much of its original fibre, vitamins and minerals.

Sugar is a plant's way of storing energy and is a component of all vegetation. But the white, granulated form commonly found in most grocery stores is so chemically pure that it is no longer possible to tell which was its plant of origin.

Although it is now generally acknowledged by the medical profession that the large-scale consumption of refined white sugar is responsible for many of the illnesses that are symptomatic of our civilized society, it is worth reminding ourselves that we may eat as much as we want of the original, unrefined plants. Your jaws will ache and your stomach be full long before you can eat the equivalent, in raw sugar-cane or sugar-beet, of even 2 or 3 spoonfuls of the white granulated stuff!

Soya Flour Made from ground soya beans. It has a high protein content and makes a useful contribution to the protein balance of wholewheat bread. We've also used it as a thickening and binding agent.

Soya Milk Milk made from soya beans by a process of grinding, soaking and filtering. See introductory notes in *The Alternative Dairy* (page 233).

Soya Sauce Made from fermented soya beans and used to season and flavour soups, stews, stir-fries and so on. Every part of the Far East has its own variation. We always buy Japanese soya sauce – called 'shoyu' or 'tamari' – from wholefood shops because it is made by a painstaking, traditional process that does not involve the use of any chemical additives or sugar. The brands available in large stores and Chinese shops contain preservatives, dyes, sugar and the ubiquitous monosodium glutamate.

Spring Onions = Scallions (US).

Tahini Ground sesame seed paste. Available in pale and dark forms. We always buy the dark type because it is made from the whole, unhulled seeds and has more flavour as well as a high fibre content. Used as a spread and to thicken sauces and dressings.

Tofu Soya bean curd. See introductory notes in *The Alternative Dairy* (page 235).

Wholefood Grains, pulses, seeds etc. which have not been chemically adulterated or refined.

Wholewheat Berries Live, unhulled kernels of wheat containing the bran, germ and gluten as well as the starch which is all that is left after refining into white flour. They can be sprouted and eaten as a salad, or cooked like rice.

Wholewheat Semolina Ground particles of durum wheat. We've used it in biscuit recipes to make them crispy. Don't buy the refined varieties found in large supermarkets.

Index

291